PRAISE

Just Another

"I loved this charming, funny homage to small towns and first loves and what happens when we leave them behind. (Or don't.) Kerry Winfrey's writing is as warm as a hug, and Hank Tillman is my new book boyfriend."

—Virginia Kantra,
New York Times bestselling author of *Beth and Amy*

"*Just Another Love Song* is such a warm, funny, cozy read. It's as sweet and nostalgic as a great country song."

—Beth O'Leary,
international bestselling author of *The No-Show*

"Witty, warm, and compulsively readable, *Just Another Love Song* has all the makings of your next favorite romance. From the Stars Hollow–esque town to the hunky country singer Hank and second chance at love, I alternated between swooning and laughing out loud. If you love Emily Henry, you'll adore Kerry Winfrey."

—Colleen Oakley,
USA Today bestselling author
of *The Mostly True Story of Tanner & Louise*

"With the quirky, small-town charm of Frank Capra, the quick wit of Amy Sherman-Palladino, and a heroine with Nora Ephron heart, Kerry Winfrey's *Just Another Love Song* is a hilarious, hopeful romantic comedy about one woman's journey from living a life that's good to the one she's always yearned for. . . . You will never want this novel to end."

—Louise Miller, author of *The Late Bloomers' Club*

"A small town, first love, and the one who got away. What more could you want than this sweet, funny romance by Kerry Winfrey? Her dialogue is sparkling; the town is filled with believable, wonderful people; and the kid is ridiculously adorable. . . . Every page of the story leads to that wonderful conclusion. Lighthearted but with emotional depth, this book is a real treat."

—Kristan Higgins,
New York Times bestselling author of *A Little Ray of Sunshine*

"A warm, heartfelt novel that'll get stuck in your head like your favorite love song." —*Kirkus Reviews* (starred review)

"Winfrey's sweet, low-heat read, with endearing and humorous characters and small-town setting, will appeal to fans of Candis Terry and Victoria James." —*Library Journal*

"Winfrey's trademark snappy dialogue and well-paced character development provide much to enjoy along the way." —BookPage

"*Just Another Love Song* is not only a story about long-lost romances and second chances, it's a novel about accepting the truths about past decisions and coming to terms with them. It's a true coming-of-age story." —*The Free Lance-Star*

Titles by Kerry Winfrey

Waiting for Tom Hanks

Not Like the Movies

Very Sincerely Yours

Just Another Love Song

Faking Christmas

KERRY WINFREY

BERKLEY ROMANCE
NEW YORK

BERKLEY ROMANCE
Published by Berkley
An imprint of Penguin Random House LLC
penguinrandomhouse.com

Library of Congress Cataloging-in-Publication Data

Names: Winfrey, Kerry, author.
Title: Faking Christmas / Kerry Winfrey.
Description: First edition. | New York: Berkley Romance, 2023.
Identifiers: LCCN 2023019638 (print) | LCCN 2023019639 (ebook) |
ISBN 9780593638361 (trade paperback) | ISBN 9780593638378 (ebook)
Subjects: LCGFT: Romance fiction. | Christmas fiction. | Novels.
Classification: LCC PS3623.I6444 F35 2023 (print) |
LCC PS3623.I6444 (ebook) | DDC 813/.6—dc23/eng/20230508
LC record available at https://lccn.loc.gov/2023019638
LC ebook record available at https://lccn.loc.gov/2023019639

First Edition: September 2023

Printed in the United States of America
1st Printing

Book design by Katy Riegel

For Harry, who makes Christmas fun

Faking
Christmas

Chapter One

Michael Bublé croons about Santa Claus coming to town as I cruise down I-70, my eyes ping-ponging between the road and the clock. It's not that I'm late . . . in fact, a mere seven months ago, I would've considered this early. But that was back when I was Old Laurel, the one who was the conductor of her own personal Hot Mess Express, the one who never met a situation she couldn't screw up, the one who, as my best friend, Jamilah, put it, ran on "Laurel Time" (which is to say, always at least fifteen minutes late).

But that's not who I am anymore, I remind myself. Now I'm New Laurel, the one who arrives on time and doesn't implode her life with her own poor decisions.

My downfall this morning was stopping at Starbucks. I intended to grab peppermint mochas for my boss and myself, but *then* I got wrapped up in a conversation with the Starbucks drive-through employee when she complimented my

Christmas tree earrings and *I* said I loved *her* Santa earrings, and then we talked about our Christmas plans and . . .

Well, long story short, now I'm going to get to the office for my pre-holiday meeting right on time.

I get off the highway as Michael Bublé fades out and the radio DJ tells everyone that a white Christmas is in the forecast. Personally, I'll believe it when I see it. As someone who came out of the womb loving Christmas—my twin sister and I were born on December 25—I literally dream of a white Christmas, but I'm used to gray ones. I don't know if we really had more snow in Ohio when I was a kid or if my memories are fudged by the blurry lens of nostalgia, but I've been burned too many times to put much stock in the meteorologist's promise of snow.

It's three days before Christmas, and although I typically work remotely, my boss scheduled a meeting before my official holiday vacation starts. I started working at *Buckeye State of Mind*, a magazine and website whose slogan is "Everything great in the Buckeye State," a little over six months ago. Our main purpose is to highlight restaurants, tourist attractions, parks, businesses, and anything that's special in Ohio. I run our social media, write a monthly online column, and soon I'll be writing other stories, too (well, fingers crossed, anyway).

I pull into our strangely empty parking lot—only Gilbert's Subaru is here—and turn off the car. I close my eyes, picturing myself in my Mind Oasis, as outlined in the book *Creating Your Mind Oasis and Finding Inner Peace*. New Laurel has a Mind Oasis that's a calm, clean, all-white room. The Mind Oasis even has a white sofa, because in my mind I can't get red wine or brownies or Cheeto dust on it. The Mind Oasis is a place of perfect peace, and it's where I go when I need to center myself. No longer am I sitting in my Toyota Camry, surrounded by empty Starbucks cups littering the floor, reminding me of peppermint mochas long since gone. Now I'm on my pristine Mind Sofa, listening to the sound of the ocean waves on the shore (the Mind Oasis is on a beach, naturally), simply *being*.

Old Laurel didn't even have a Mind Oasis. She had a Mind Junkyard. But now, with the guidance of every self-help book the Columbus Metropolitan Library system had on the shelf, New Laurel is ready to conquer this meeting, this day, and my entire life.

I check my hair in the rearview mirror. My shaggy, long bob hangs in blond waves. I brush them out of my face, then use a finger to flick away an errant mascara flake and dab at my Starbucks-smudged seasonally appropriate cranberry red lipstick. I give New Laurel a wink. She's got this.

I use my hip to slam the door of the Camry, since I'm currently double-fisting peppermint mochas, and walk into the building. It would be great if magazine life were glamorous, like in *The Devil Wears Prada*, and I could run through city streets as I hurried to make it to my downtown high-rise office before my stylish but cold boss realized I was late. I'd spill coffee on myself, and she'd look down her nose at me, and I'd spend the next hour and forty-five minutes of screen time attempting to win her approval before finally realizing that there's more to life than work.

Jamilah also says I have a tendency to turn everything into a story. That's why she encouraged me to apply to this job at the magazine, actually—she thought I'd love writing other people's stories. And I would, but that's only *sort of* what my job entails.

Of course, my real life is nothing like that fantasy sequence, mostly because our office is out in the Columbus suburbs where the rent is cheaper, and Gilbert isn't a stylish older woman with a severe bob and a tendency to judge people. He's a middle-aged man with a kindly orange mustache, and I've never heard him yell at anyone. The most upset I've ever seen him was when he got mildly annoyed that Jimmy John's left the turkey off the turkey sub he ordered for an office lunch meeting, and even then he pretty much immediately pivoted to positivity and ate his bread, lettuce, and cheese sandwich without complaining. ("You know, I've been trying to eat less meat, anyway.") He doesn't critique my fashion choices, probably because his button-down shirts have seemingly permanent mustard stains on them from dropping his lunchtime hot dogs on himself.

But that doesn't mean I'm not a little uneasy as I step into the office to find it empty and dark, aside from the light coming from Gilbert's office in the back corner. It's a typically gloomy Ohio December day, so even with the window blinds open, it's almost pitch black. The tinsel on the office Christmas tree dances silently in the warm air pumping from the heating vent. It's like *Die Hard* in here, but without Bruce Willis around to rescue me (unless he's crawling through the air ducts, as he's wont to do).

I tiptoe toward Gilbert's office and the golden light peeking out from his partially open door. Should I turn around and run? Am I an idiot for walking in here? This certainly feels like a situation in which I'm either going to get murdered or propositioned, and I can't think of which one of those is less likely coming from Gilbert.

"I am capable," I whisper to myself, repeating a mantra I learned from *Manifesting the Badass Within: How to Use Mantras to Supersize Your Life*. "I am strong. I can defeat any intruders with my brute strength."

Okay, so that last one wasn't in the book, but it seemed like a good one to add right now.

I hold my two coffees up like a shield and shout, "I have a black belt in karate!" as I kick open Gilbert's door. This isn't strictly true, given that I took one karate class in fifth grade before giving up, but I need to project a strong image.

Gilbert, slumped over his desk, looks up at me. "That's really great, Laurel." He sniffles. "That must've taken a lot of work, but I'm not surprised. You're one of my most dedicated employees."

That's when I realize that Gilbert is crying, and not the kind of eye-leaking you can disguise as allergies. This is full-on sobbing, the kind I never expected to see from my boss, a man who unironically listens to "Never Gonna Give You Up" as his morning pump-up jam.

"Gilbert," I say, putting his coffee down in front of him. "Is everything okay?"

He shakes his head, and I hand him a tissue.

"Some things are okay," he says. "I'm alive. That's good."

I nod slowly. "So we're starting with the basics here."

He sighs. "Just trying to have an attitude of gratitude."

"I know that's important to you." I point to the poster behind his desk: a waterfall with the words "The best attitude is gratitude" written on it. Honestly, it's a wonder that Gilbert became a regional magazine/website editor instead of a middle school guidance counselor.

He blows his nose with a honk, then lets his head fall to his desk. "Charlene left."

I pause, then sit down across from him on the maroon office chair. "Left to go . . . where?"

He rolls his head to the side, peering up at me. "My wife left *me*, Laurel."

"She left you?" I gasp, which sets Gilbert off again.

"It sounds even worse when you say it," he sobs.

I exhale and look around the room, as if the posters on these office-neutral beige walls might guide me on what to say. "It's her loss," I say.

He sits up and shakes his head. "She left me for our accountant. I'm the one who's the loser. She's gone and her new man knows all my financial details. It's humiliating."

I have nothing else to say—I've only spoken to Charlene once when she stopped by to pick Gilbert up for lunch after one of our in-office meetings, and we mainly talked about their kitchen renovation. Not enough detail for me to decide whether she's a good person, but leaving Gilbert for their accountant might slot her firmly into the "bad" category.

"I brought you a peppermint mocha," I finally say.

Gilbert sits up and sniffs the red cup appreciatively. "You remembered."

I give him a sad smile. "Yeah. It's your favorite."

He shrugs and takes a sip. "What can I say, I'm a basic bitch."

In any other circumstance, I would immediately text

Jamilah and tell her that my boss unironically referred to himself as a basic bitch. But we've got bigger problems here.

"So." I clear my throat, wondering if a subject change might be good for Gilbert's mental health. "Where is everyone? I thought we had a meeting."

He puts down his cup and waves a hand dismissively. "I sent them all home and canceled the meeting. It's the day before holiday break starts, I'm a mess, and they might as well go enjoy their lives while they can. Before everything goes to hell. Sorry I forgot to tell you it was canceled, but I was busy surveying the wreckage of my marriage."

"Well . . ." I trail off. "That's okay."

Gilbert seems to use all his strength to give me a watery, pasted-on smile. "So what's going on with you?" The visible tears on his cheeks make him look more "sad clown" than "interested boss."

"Just getting ready for Christmas with my family. I'm heading to my sister's . . . I mean, my sister's heading to *my* farm tomorrow," I stammer quickly.

Good save, Grant.

"That's so nice," Gilbert says with unnerving cheer. "How wonderful that you have a big family to spend Christmas with."

"Not so big." I try to downplay it. "My parents retired last year, and they're spending the holiday in Hawaii. Maybe I should be offended, since Christmas is also my birthday so they're kind of missing two big days, but Christmas in Hawaii has been their lifelong dream, and I guess they've earned it. And my brother, Doug, is on a ski trip and he won't be getting in until, like, Christmas Eve at midnight because he's terrible at planning anything."

Gilbert stares at me.

"So . . . no big deal," I say.

Gilbert bursts into tears again.

"Oh, no," I say. I have no idea what to do in this situation. It's not like I haven't been around tears before . . . I have one of those faces that people tend to talk to, so I've consoled my fair share of drunk girls in bar bathrooms. I've learned a lot about the cheating boyfriends of Columbus and ended up with mascara stains on many of my best shirts. But nothing prepared me for a sobbing boss in the midst of a dissolving marriage.

I hand him another tissue, and he takes it with a grateful nod.

"I wish . . . oh, I wish she'd planned this all a little better. It's not like Charlene to mess up the holidays. We love Christmas. Bundling up and going to Wildlights at the zoo, driving around and looking at the Christmas lights, decorating our tree together, watching *The Holiday* . . ." His face droops. "She should've left me at Easter. We don't really do anything for Easter."

Unsure of how I'm supposed to respond to this, I nod.

He meets my eye, looking so despondent that *I* want to cry. "I wish I had a big family Christmas to go to like you."

I give him a closed-lip smile. "I wish that, too, Gilbert. I really do."

"Your family sounds so wonderful," he says. "So close. I'd love to meet them someday."

"Yeah," I say. "I'd love that, too."

He puts a hand on his heart. "Laurel. That is so generous of you."

I open my mouth, but no words come out because I'm not exactly sure what Gilbert's talking about. I feel like I temporarily blacked out and missed a few lines of our conversation.

"What's that?" I ask carefully.

"Of course I'd love to come over," he says, tears welling in his eyes yet again.

Oh, no. Oh, no, no, no. This cannot be happening.

"Oh, you don't want to come over," I stammer. "It's crowded. Lots of tiny rooms. Too many people. The kids . . . they're loud."

"I love kids," Gilbert says, standing up. "And tiny rooms. I watch those home renovation shows on HGTV, and I think, who needs an open concept? Keep those rooms separate."

Think, Laurel. Think.

"But I . . . I don't have a gift for you!" I say loudly. "Or matching pajamas. We all wear matching pajamas on Christmas morning."

"Oh, don't worry, Laurel," Gilbert says. "I would never think of intruding on Christmas."

I exhale, relieved. I underestimated Gilbert. Of course he wouldn't invite himself to his employee's house for Christmas—I must have misunderstood him.

"I'll only be there tomorrow, for Christmas Eve Eve," he says. "I know all about the traditional dinner you serve on the farm."

"Traditional dinner?" I ask slowly, dread filling my body.

"You know," he says. "You wrote about it in this month's column."

"Right," I say, nodding. What he's saying is true. We always have a big dinner with our immediate family on Christmas Eve Eve, left over from the days when we'd head to my grandma Pat's house on Christmas Eve and stay the night. My mom liked to have a fancy holiday meal early, with just us, as a quiet moment before the travel and gifts. Even after Grandma Pat passed away, we Grants kept up the Christmas Eve Eve tradition, and it's still our biggest meal of the season. I wrote all about it in the monthly column where I detail my simple, hardworking, sometimes chaotic life on the farm.

"Well," Gilbert says, grabbing his briefcase. "I think it's pretty clear we're not getting any work done around here until after the holidays, so I'm heading out now. Gotta get ready for tomorrow, after all!"

I smile weakly and mentally repeat one of my mantras. *In the midst of disorder, I find order. In the midst of chaos, I find calm. In the midst of turmoil, I find peace.*

I am not finding order, or calm, or peace. I can't even *access* my Mind Oasis right now—in fact, I have a sinking suspicion that the Mind Oasis might have burned down.

"I can't wait to see the farmhouse and taste those delicious sugar cookies," Gilbert says.

"Well, it wouldn't be Christmas without them," I say through a tight smile.

Because here's the thing: Gilbert thinks I live in a farmhouse an hour away from Columbus with my husband and our two children. He thinks I know how to care for goats and how to make beef Wellington. He thinks I can my own tomato sauce and make my own soap. He thinks these things because I may have let him believe them, back when I interviewed for this job six months ago.

But I don't live in a farmhouse at all. I live in a two-bedroom apartment in Columbus with Jamilah, and I've never canned anything in my life. I don't 100 percent know what beef Wellington is, I can't make soap, and I don't have kids.

That's all my twin sister, and Gilbert thinks her life is *my* life.

But he's about to find out that I've been telling him a huge, monumental, colossal lie.

Chapter Two

SO, BEFORE YOU hate me, let me say . . . I really needed this job.

I'd just been dumped, fired, and evicted in spectacular fashion because I was dating and living with the lawyer I assisted. I know, not my finest decision, but in my defense, Old Laurel wasn't known for her good choices. I'd found out that morning that my boyfriend/boss/roommate, John, actually had a whole other girlfriend named Alaina. She'd been in the Peace Corps and conveniently out of the country for the entire time I'd been dating John, thus making me an unwitting other woman. Trust me, I've never wanted to be the other woman—I'm simply not deceptive, sexy, or discreet enough.

I only found out about Alaina when she showed up at my then apartment door holding a duffel bag and surrounded by an air of general charity and goodwill, which evaporated as soon as she realized that I was sleeping with her boyfriend. I tried to pitch her the idea of the two of us teaming up, becoming best friends, and getting revenge on John through a series of uproarious but ultimately harmless schemes.

She wasn't into it, though, which she made clear by pushing me out of the apartment and closing the door in my face, leaving me in the hallway with only a toothbrush and a Garfield sleep shirt that barely covered my ass. If it hadn't been for the charity of one of our neighbors, who let me in to call John and convince him to come home and let me get all my stuff, I would've been forced to wander the streets in a sleep shirt that said *I need less week, more weekend*. Things could've gotten ugly.

And, well, they did get pretty ugly when John decided to get back together (or, I guess, *stay* back together, since they'd never officially broken up) with his Peace Corps girlfriend, leaving me homeless, jobless, and filled with shame at being, however accidentally, the other woman. It didn't feel great, but I resolved to let this experience be a positive one. Maybe I could learn something from this—and, sure, I'd wanted to learn that through befriending Alaina and humorously torturing John until we figured out that the true friendship between us was more important than ruining his life.

But maybe this was meant to teach me that there was something better out there for me. Something more than being an inadvertent side piece and an assistant to a lawyer, a job I didn't even like and wasn't particularly good at.

When I saw a job opening at *Buckeye State of Mind*, Jamilah pushed me to apply. I'd moved into her place when I got kicked out of John's.

"You've always loved talking to people and hearing their

stories and even making up your own stories," Jamilah told me as we stared at my laptop screen.

"Yeah, but this isn't actually writing for the magazine," I pointed out. "It's social media."

"Which you have experience with!" Jamilah said. "I've seen the Meadow Rise Farm Instagram. Remember that pie picture you posted last week with the caption 'Rise and Pies'?"

I nodded. "Some of my best work."

My twin sister, Holly, is the one who runs Meadow Rise Farm, because she's one of those infuriatingly self-sufficient people who would probably get along fine if the apocalypse happened. (I, meanwhile, would cease functioning when the Wi-Fi went out.) While she may be great at every aspect of owning and operating a small farm alongside her husband, Darius, she's terrible when it comes to social media. (She thinks TikTok is called "Tic-Tac.") So I offered up my services as the more tech-savvy Grant twin and have been running her Instagram page and updating her website ever since. Not to brag, but I've increased her sales 110 percent by making her farm life (and products) look dreamy and aspirational, as if by buying her custom-made furniture, baked goods, and soap you can pretend you're waking up on the prairie with milkmaid braids, about to make breakfast out of herbs you foraged or whatever. It's all about showing people a vibe, not the reality of running a farm—which is that it's extremely difficult physical work that doesn't offer any time off.

Jamilah closed the laptop and put a hand on my arm. "I know you, Laurel, and I know that hanging around this apartment all day is driving you up the wall. You've been trying to find a project, but you're an awful knitter and an even worse baker."

"Some of the cookies I made were edible," I reminded her, thinking of how the week before I'd attempted my mom's classic ginger shortbread recipe, one of the things Holly sells to a local coffee shop, but had burned them so badly that the cookie sheet had been ruined.

"No, babe," Jamilah said gently. "I pretended to eat one to make you feel better, but I actually threw it away. I don't have a death wish."

I gasped in shock.

"You need to get a job, and not only because you're eating all the Pop-Tarts," Jamilah continued. She was a social worker, her passion, and it didn't exactly pay great. She was right; I was a freeloader who needed to start contributing to the Pop-Tart budget. "You need something to do. You're bouncing off the walls."

"I'm doing a thirty-day cardio challenge," I corrected her. "Every morning at six thirty on YouTube."

"I know," Jamilah said. "Shawn downstairs complained about the noise, remember? He said you're keeping his elderly chihuahua awake."

"Maybe his elderly chihuahua needs some aerobic exercise," I suggested, but then I sighed. "Okay, you're right. This job looks . . . good, actually. Are you sure I'm qualified?"

"Come on," Jamilah said. "You're Laurel Grant."

And that's how, two days later, I found myself in Gilbert's office, wearing a suit that I'd last worn when I interviewed for a position with John and then immediately started dating him. *That won't be happening this time*, I reminded myself firmly.

This wouldn't be like the time I got fired from my high school job at Wendy's for making out with the fry cook by the dumpster instead of taking drive-through orders. It also wouldn't be like the time I had to quit waiting tables at Chili's because all the other servers accused me of getting the "good" tables just because I was dating the manager. (Strangely enough, said manager kept his job.) This time, I wasn't screwing up my whole life by making a terrible decision just because it sounded fun or made things easier or helped me avoid working the drive-through. This time, I was doing things the right way. This time, I'd maxed out my library card (after paying off the fines that Old Laurel racked up when she checked out and then immediately lost about fifteen Christmas movies on DVD) by checking out every self-help book I could get my inner-truth-seeking little paws on.

I'd passed the point where being unable to hold down a steady job was simply an adorable quirk. In your twenties, it's fun to be kind of a mess—that's why there are so many sitcoms about it. But once you hit your thirties, it starts looking a lot less cute and a lot more "we're worried about you, Laurel." People are more forceful about setting you up with their last single cousin or using their connections to get you a nice, respectable office job. Your continued existence as a flailing woman who doesn't quite know what she wants makes them uncomfortable, and knowing that you're a disappointment to the world at large makes *you* uncomfortable. It's one big burrito filled with layers of regret and frustration and subpar guacamole.

But I had a chance to change things, a chance to show myself that I could do this.

I was getting this job.

When I walked into Gilbert's office and he offered me an enthusiastic handshake, I knew that an office romance wouldn't be an issue. He was about twenty-five years my senior with a wedding ring, a bushy orange mustache that screamed "high school principal," and ketchup on his striped button-down. (The food stains on his clothing would prove to be a persistent theme.)

I sat up straight in the chair across from him, smiling politely and answering all of his questions about my work history. Yes, I'd read the magazine (well, one issue right before this interview). Yes, I was a self-starter. (After all, I'd started that YouTube cardio challenge.)

No, I wasn't a hot mess. No, I hadn't torpedoed my last job, relationship, and living situation. No, I wasn't desperate for employment that would make me feel more like a real adult and less like a bumbling toddler in the body of a thirty-three-year-old.

I was New Laurel, someone with no (current) library fines, a stable(ish) living situation, and a whole lot of positivity.

"I probably don't have to ask this, since everyone's on it these days—heck, even I have an Instagram account so I can follow Ina Garten—but do you have experience with social media?" Gilbert asked, looking at me expectantly.

I didn't ask him about the Ina Garten obsession, which was oddly specific but certainly not unwarranted. "Actually, yes, I have professional social media experience." I pulled out my phone and toggled away from my personal profile and over to the Meadow Rise Farm account. I slid the phone across his desk.

"As you can see, I run the social media for Meadow Rise Farm, a small farm in Baileyville, about an hour outside of Columbus—"

Gilbert cut me off, scrolling through the posts with his eyes wide. "Oh, yes, your farm! I saw this on your resume, and I've gotta say, Laurel, I'm impressed."

I tried to correct him. "Oh, no, it's not—"

"But it *is* impressive," Gilbert continued. "I love our staff members, but they're all city folks, and our magazine is meant to serve the entire state. After all, Ohioans aren't only urban dwellers—a good portion of them live in rural areas, and many of them are farmers like you."

"Yes, but—"

"So I really think you'd be a great asset to our team, Laurel," he said, looking up. "We need someone like you. Someone who understands social media engagement *and* how to milk a goat."

We need someone like you. Those words went in my ear and straight to my heart. When was the last time I'd felt needed, like I actually had something to offer in a work environment? Gilbert looked at me like I could be a valued employee, and God, that felt good. I could get used to that feeling . . . but could I do it if it meant I had to lie about owning a small farm?

Yes, I decided on the spot. I could.

"I sure do know how to milk a goat," I said slowly as I nodded. "And then I make soap out of that goat milk. That's a thing I do!"

Gilbert laughed. "Amazing! I bet no one else here even knows soap comes from goats. I sure didn't!"

I didn't bother telling him that not all soap comes from goats. I just smiled and kept on nodding.

"Well, Laurel," Gilbert said, sliding my phone back across the desk. "I had two other applicants interview this morning, and they were great, but I'm gonna tell you right now: this job is yours if you want it. You clearly have the experience using social media, and we can use your viewpoint on the team here at *Buckeye State*. If you're interested, we'd love to have you."

My jaw dropped. "I mean . . . I . . ."

Gilbert held up a hand. "I was going to ask you if you're okay with working remotely. As you can see, this office is pretty small, and we simply don't have enough room for desks for everyone. But I think this might work out for the best, since it's a real hike for you to get here every day."

"It certainly is . . . a hike," I said.

"So if it's okay with you, you can come in for major meetings but otherwise do your work at home."

"That's perfect," I said quickly. My address—my real address—was listed on my resume, but Gilbert must not have looked too closely, and I certainly wasn't going to correct him now.

Gilbert slid a piece of paper across his desk. "Here's what I can offer in terms of salary and benefits . . . I know it's not much, but we're a small publication and—"

"Whoa," I said before I could stop myself. He was right—it wasn't a ton of money, but it was a little more than I made as an assistant, and I was dazzled by the words *health insurance*, including vision and dental. A symphony played in my head as I daydreamed of getting a complete dental examination and filling the cavities I surely had from all the candy I'd been stress eating.

But Gilbert mistook my thrilled silence for hesitation, and he let out a conspiratorial laugh. "Okay, okay, so I wasn't going to do this unless you tried to negotiate, but I like you, so I know we can actually offer you five thousand more a year. Does that work for you?"

"Y-yes," I stammered, blinking. "That works. Thank you."

"No, thank you," Gilbert said, reaching into a desk drawer and grabbing a folder, which he handed to me. "I'm so glad you came in, Laurel, because I think you're going to be the perfect fit for our team. Fill out these forms as soon as you can, and we'll get everything set up, okay?"

"Okay," I said as I stood up, still stunned. I forced myself to shake Gilbert's hand instead of hugging him—although, given his warm and friendly demeanor, I didn't even think he'd see an interview hug as inappropriate. Still, though, I was trying to keep things professional this time, even if Gilbert had more "supportive dad vibes" than "hot lawyer boyfriend vibes."

Gilbert walked me to the door, and I couldn't stop a smile from overtaking my whole face. I did it. I got a job.

"Thanks so much for coming in today," Gilbert said as he held open the door. "I can't wait to hear more about life on the farm."

My smile, so natural only seconds ago, suddenly felt frozen and forced. Right. My life on the farm . . . the farm I didn't own or live on or know anything about, really, other than the pictures I posted and the fluffy captions I wrote for Holly.

Tell him, New Laurel insisted, her persistent whisper in my head. *Tell him the truth right now, before it's too late.*

"In fact," Gilbert said, tapping his chin, as if he was a cartoon titled "Man Looking Thoughtful," "I'm having a great idea. You know I said I want to put more of a spotlight on rural Ohio . . . what if you write us a monthly column about life on the farm?"

"What if I . . . Are you . . ." I stammered. Apparently New Laurel was incapable of finishing a sentence.

Gilbert held up his hands. "Okay, okay, I get it. Slow your roll, Gilbert! It's too much, too soon! Maybe we'll do a sample column, online only, and see where it goes from there, okay?"

This was it. I would finally have the chance to do my own writing, in my own column. All I had to do was . . . pretend I owned and operated Meadow Rise Farm.

New Laurel disappeared. It turned out that Old Laurel was still alive and well, rattling around and livening up the joint. *Don't you dare say a single word*, she instructed me. And I listened, the way I always did, because her way was easier.

"I can't wait to get to work," I said to Gilbert, and although I meant it, the sick feeling in my stomach reminded me that I might be making another one of my classic Laurel mistakes. And even if Old Laurel wasn't listening, New Laurel reminded me that those mistakes had a way of coming back to bite me right in the ass.

Chapter Three

"OKAY, FIRST OF all, you need to breathe," Holly says. "We can fix this."

We can fix this: the magic words I love to hear from my twin. She was born three minutes before me, and while those 180 seconds may seem like a measly difference, the truth is that I think of her as my big sister. Ever since we were kids, she's been the one fixing my mistakes. When I hit a baseball through our living room window, shattering the glass, she helped me clean up the mess and draft a passioned apology to my parents. When I failed a math test in fourth grade, she sat up all night going over times tables with me. When gross Rodney Swartz grabbed my boob at prom, she poured punch on his tux, and then the two of us laughed as we ran to the parking lot.

If anyone can turn my mess of a life into something workable, it's Holly. Holly is the anti-me: She has her life *completely* together. She's the practical one, the reliable one, the one who knows how to do things, like mend a sweater and chop firewood. The one who has a family and a home. I'm the one who's *really* good at movie trivia. And our brother, Doug, is the one who can bench-press both of us.

I'm well aware she's my parents' favorite kid, and I'd be offended if she weren't my favorite person on earth.

But *this* problem? The worst one I've ever created? The one I lied (well, lied by omission, but still) my way into? I don't think even she can fix this one.

I mean, I've been writing a column for the past six months where I pretend I run Holly's farm. Once a month, we have an hour-long phone conversation that's entirely dedicated to her explaining a chore or a hilarious farm mishap, and then I write my column, pretending I'm some sort of expert on country life. But I didn't need a conversation with Holly to write this month's column about our Christmas Eve Eve traditions—they're some of my most vivid, cherished memories.

As if to drive home the point that Holly is the talented twin while I'm the . . . *other* twin, she's currently talking to me from the shed she and Darius built in the backyard that houses her woodshop. Because, in addition to farming, Holly and Darius also build custom furniture. This is where they get the bulk of their income, because the people of Baileyville love nothing more than a quality, custom-built dining room table.

Meanwhile, I'm eating a cold Pop-Tart because I burned the last one I toasted and the smell lingered in the apartment for days. Jamilah and I both decided that it might be time for the toaster and I to take a break. If I used power tools like Holly does, chances are good that I'd be down at least one finger.

"Holly," I say, groaning as I rub my hand over my forehead. "What am I going to do, bring Gilbert to my apartment and hope that if he squints, I might be able to convince him that it's a rural farmhouse? This is hopeless. I might as well quit now."

"Well, with that attitude, sure," Holly says. "But there has to be a solution. There always is."

Maybe in Holly's world there's always a good solution, but in my world, the solution often involves getting fired. At this point, my best idea involves telling Gilbert the truth and hoping he takes pity on me and lets me keep my job.

"Let's think," Holly continues. "How much does Gilbert know about the farm?"

"Um, whatever I post on Instagram," I say. "And then my monthly column."

And then it hits me. Holly never lets me post about her on the farm's Instagram, because she's one of those women they write pop songs about: she really doesn't know she's beautiful. And if it sounds strange to say that my twin is beautiful, just know that somehow, she actually is better looking than me. (Also, she's a full cup size bigger, which seems unfair.) When she *is* pictured, it's always in service of the product, or showing a behind-the-scenes look at how the farm runs. I know this because whenever I try to take more pictures of her, she screeches, "Laurel! This is supposed to be about the farm, not about me!" I've told her a million times that sex sells and that maybe she should show off the goats while wearing a bikini, but she always demurs on account of how that's "impractical" and "weird." I mean, I'm the social media expert here, but whatever.

Basically, she has no idea what makes for good social media. She won't even let me exploit her children or Darius by posting pictures of them. So it's basically all farm, all the time. Unless Gilbert looked very closely at the website (and given that he didn't even notice my address on my resume, that's unlikely), he wouldn't find her name.

I'm already faking being a farm owner in a column. Why not fake it in real life, too?

"I'll pretend for the day," I say. "Like I do in my column but . . . in person."

Holly's silent for a moment, and I assume that she's thinking of a way to tell me that this is the worst idea she's ever heard. But then she says, "That's brilliant."

"Really?" I squeal.

"I don't see why not!" she says, getting excited. "This will be fun!"

"So Gilbert will show up, I'll greet him at the door, and for one evening, I'll be the owner of Meadow Rise Farms," I say, thinking it through out loud. "But wait. I mention the kids a lot in the captions."

I frequently talk about Holly's kids in a relatable, "aw, shucks" kind of way: "My kiddos love helping me harvest our bounty of vegetables every day. When you buy from Meadow Rise Farm, you're supporting a true family business and helping us raise the next generation of farmers." The kind of stuff that's supposed to make people feel like it's their moral imperative to buy from Meadow Rise Farm, otherwise they hate children and families and the entire concept of farming in general.

"So pretend they're your kids," Holly says, then sneezes. "Sorry. Got some sawdust in my nose."

"What? I love Noah and Lexie, but I'm not ready to be a parent!"

"It's *one* dinner," Holly reminds me. "You can absolutely pretend to be the mother of my children for one dinner—you're basically their second mother, anyway."

My phone vibrates against my ear, and I pull it back to see a text from my mom in our family group text.

> Just boarded plane to Maui!! Your father is wearing his Tommy Bahama shirt and flip-flops!

"Did you see that text from Mom?" I ask Holly.

"Yes," she says, and even over the phone I can hear her smile. "I cannot believe Dad wore flip-flops. It's twenty-five degrees here."

"I can believe it," I say.

My phone buzzes again, and I see a text from our brother, Doug:

> Hell yeah! Enjoy vacation life see the rest of you on Christmas Eve!!! As long as the snow holds off for another day looks like a monster storm is rolling in!!!

My mom responds with a paragraph of emojis, most of which seem to hold no relevance to this conversation.

"What is wrong with this family?" I ask when I put the phone back to my ear. "Why does Doug use punctuation randomly, and why do they love nonsensical emoji usage so much?"

"Well, the mermaid emoji says more than words ever could. Hold on, I'm responding to the group."

A text from Holly buzzes on my phone: Please make it here in one piece—no skiing accidents!

No promises lol!!!! Doug responds, adding an emoji of a hot dog.

"What does it mean?" I muse. "Is he going to eat a hot dog while skiing? Is that how the presumed accident might occur?"

"I wouldn't put it past Doug," Holly says. "The last time he twisted his ankle while skiing, it was because he was trying to get a bag of gummy worms out of his pocket and he fell over."

"Yeah," I say. "Classic Doug."

I pause, thinking about how this holiday will be a lot different without my parents around. And Doug won't even be here for Christmas Eve Eve. That's great when it comes to keeping Gilbert in the dark, because Doug absolutely cannot and will not keep any kind of secret, as all of his emotions play out across his face and then spill out of his mouth. But it's kind of a bummer when it comes to the whole "beloved family Christmas traditions" thing.

And not only am I missing out on our typical Grant family holiday, but now I have to be the one who runs the show.

Pretending Holly's kids are mine is one thing. But can I pretend to know the first thing about running a farm? Can I pretend to be married to Darius (who's great, but I've never been interested in stealing my sister's husband)? Can I . . . cook?

"There's a giant flaw in this plan. I can't possibly make dinner," I say. "Gilbert's expecting the full Grant Christmas Eve Eve experience. Beef Wellington. Hasselback potatoes. A Caesar salad. I barely even know how to make Easy Mac, Holly!"

"But you only need a microwave for Easy Mac."

"I know!" I wail. "But you can still mess it up. Ask me how I know."

"I trust that you—"

"I know because I started a fire in the microwave! Because I set the timer for twenty minutes instead of two, and it turns out it's very possible for that Easy Mac container to go up in flames if you aren't careful."

"Well, there you go. All you have to do is avoid the microwave while you're here," she says cheerfully. "I'll cook. We'll tell Gilbert you want to spend time with him so I'll handle it and he'll be none the wiser."

I nod uncertainly. "I just . . . I don't think this is gonna work."

"Laurel," Holly says with force. "It's going to work because we're going to make it work. You love this job and you're not going to lose it. You're going to pretend to own Meadow Rise Farm for one evening, and you're going to fool your boss and keep your job. We're making this happen. Got it?"

"You're right," I say, determined. It's me and Holly against the world.

"I know," she says lightly. "Listen, I've gotta go brief my children on how you're coming over tomorrow and pretending to be their mother, okay? At least we don't have to worry about Mom and Dad being there."

"True," I say. I guess that's the one upside to my parents being gone for this holiday—that's two fewer people who have to keep up my ridiculous story.

"And if anything goes wrong," Holly says, "just remember: we're twins. I can always bail you out."

"You're right," I say. "We can *Parent Trap* it, switch back and forth. Just call me Lindsay Lohan."

"Exactly! He'll never know the difference, like how Granny Doris could never tell us apart."

"Yeah, but sometimes she couldn't even tell us from Doug because she wouldn't wear her glasses," I remind her. "I think Gilbert is a little bit more observant."

"We're gonna be fine," Holly says firmly. "Take a deep breath and go to your Mind Oasis."

I love that Holly says *Mind Oasis* as casually and seriously as if she were asking me to pick up some snacks at Target (not that she would ever do such a thing—she would make the snacks from ingredients she grew, then serve them on a wooden serving platter she made).

"The Mind Oasis is under construction right now, unfortunately," I tell her.

I can practically hear her rolling her eyes—but in a fun, loving way where she knows I'm her adorable but wacky twin.

(I think.) "Go pack your stuff and I'll see you tomorrow, okay?"

We hang up, and although I'm dreading tomorrow and the monumental feat of acting it's gonna require, for just a moment I let myself believe what Holly says. If she says it will be fine, it will be fine.

Chapter Four

WHEN I TOLD Jamilah what I was doing, she didn't think it was as ridiculous as I would've suspected. In fact, she said, "This sounds like another classic Laurel Grant caper," as if I'm in the habit of creating entire fake holiday scenarios to keep my job.

While I may not be in the habit of it, I'm definitely doing it. But as I step out of my car and onto Holly's driveway, I don't feel nervous. I feel the same way I always do when I'm at her place: at home.

I got here early because I wanted some time to settle in and get prepared before Gilbert arrives later for dinner. Although, of course, my idea of "early" is much different from Holly's—no doubt she's lived an entire day by midmorning.

Even with the cloudy Ohio lack of sunshine, the big white farmhouse shines brightly. I know that it only looks this warm and inviting because Holly works hard to make it that way. There's the wraparound porch and the porch swing covered in red and green pillows. There's even a wooden snowman greeting me with a sign that says, "There's Snow Place Like Home," which Holly made herself using a band saw, because she's both a Pinterest mom *and* a woman who knows how to use power tools.

This is the life that Holly and Darius built, and it's beautiful. Some people, like Holly, just *know* what they want to do with their lives. And some people, like me, bounce around and try thing after thing, never really finding the perfect one and burning plenty of food in the process. It takes all kinds . . . or at least that's what I tell myself.

The tiny footprints and snow angels all over the yard are proof that the twins have been here. I glance up to see if they're waving from the front window, but all I see is the huge Christmas tree (chopped down from right here on Meadow Rise Farm, of course) all lit up with colorful lights. A few snowflakes twirl down around me, and it feels pretty perfect. It's not the exact Christmas of my childhood—my parents are singing "Mele Kalikimaka" thousands of miles away and my grandparents haven't been around for years—but it's pretty damn close. In some ways, even better.

Lexie and Noah come bounding out the door, running up to me and wrapping their little arms around my hips the way they always do. Even if we saw each other last week, they greet me as if it's been years.

"Mom says you're pretending to be our mom today!" Lexie shouts.

"Basically, yeah. You guys cool with that?"

Noah laughs. "It's funny, because our *real* mom knows how to make us lunch."

"Hey!" I say. "I can make you lunch! Did I or did I not give you guys pizza Lunchables last time I babysat?"

Holly comes to the door. "Get in here!" she shouts. "It's freezing outside!"

Noah runs toward her and Lexie gives me another hug. "You're more fun than Mom, though," she whispers.

"Thanks," I whisper back. And she's right. I may not know how to cook, but I *am* fun. We all have our strengths.

Holly gives me a big hug and shuts the door behind me as the twins immediately run back to their basement playroom—I can't compete with Magna-Tiles. I kick off my boots and sigh. "I can't believe we're doing this," I say as I walk across the room to stand in front of the fire. My favorite thing about Holly's house is that every inch of it is cozy. It's a new build, because Holly and Darius built on land that belonged to my grandparents, but somehow Holly kept it from feeling too modern. It has a lot of things that actual old farmhouses don't have—a finished basement, walk-in closets, and a lot more space—but it has a homey charm, too. Holly wasn't interested in the open-concept trend, preferring to keep her rooms separate, which means that the kitchen is actually through a swinging door. "The kitchen is like a bedroom or bathroom," she insisted. "You need privacy in there."

Holly's living room is already the coziest room in the house, but at Christmas, that coziness is ratcheted up to almost dangerously festive levels. The fire warms my cold fingers as I look around at the sparkling Christmas tree, full of ornaments made by the twins. A quilt Granny Doris made is draped over the back of the sofa, and cheerful seasonal pillows are propped on any surface where a butt could land.

Holly and Darius's elderly basset hound, Frank, who as far as I know spends at least 75 percent of his time asleep, snoozes on the armchair in the corner. My eye catches the framed family photos on the mantel, and I smile, forgetting for a moment that I'm engaged in an act of subterfuge.

I'm so happy to be here, with my favorite people at my absolute favorite time of year. As soon as the clock strikes midnight on Halloween, I pull out my Christmas decorations and crank up the Mariah Carey. I know people think we "Christmas isn't a day, it's a lifestyle" folks are annoying, but I can't turn my back on something that fills me with so much joy.

"Oh, no." Holly runs toward me when she sees me eyeing the family pictures. "I didn't even think of these photos! It would kind of give this whole elaborate ruse away if your boss saw pictures of me and Darius posing with *your* kids."

I snort. "*Elaborate ruse*? You're loving this, aren't you?"

She nods. "Well, yeah. It's the same thing every day around here. It's exciting to have something new going on."

But then something she said snags in my brain. "Wait. You said it would give things away if Gilbert saw you and Darius posing with the kids. But . . . Darius is pretending to be my husband today, and we look alike, so I don't see the problem there. Unless Gilbert really looks closely at these photos, he'll assume that's me."

Holly looks at me, eyebrows raised. "Oh, no. Darius isn't going to be your husband. I'll let you pretend to own my farm and mother my children, but pretending to be married to my husband is a bridge too far."

I freeze. "But Gilbert thinks I'm married."

"Uh-huh," Holly says, holding the framed photos against her chest.

I frown. "Well, unless you plan on pretending I'm married to one of the goats, then I'm not sure where you're going with this."

The sound of tires crunching over gravel distracts me from whatever Holly's saying.

"Oh, crap. Gilbert isn't supposed to be here for hours!" I say, panicking.

"That's not Gilbert," Holly says without even looking outside. "Actually, we're having another guest for dinner tonight."

"Who?" I ask. My parents are on an island, Doug's out of town, and we've never been in the habit of inviting nonfamily members to Christmas Eve Eve (aside from me accidentally inviting Gilbert, that is).

"Laurel! You're here!" Darius says as he jogs down the stairs. Darius is possibly the most positive person I've ever met, and I'm certain that even if he were alerting me to an imminent apocalypse, he'd do it in an upbeat way.

I'm about to greet him when he opens the front door, and the words dry up in my throat. Because standing right here in Darius and Holly's living room is a man I hoped to never see again. My nemesis. A nightmare in thick-rimmed black glasses.

Max Beckett.

Chapter Five

DOES *NEMESIS* SOUND a little dramatic? Well, the way I feel about Max is dramatically negative. He's Darius's best friend, and he was the best man at their wedding. Given that I was, naturally, the maid of honor, we had to spend a lot of time together—time that he made *very* sure I knew was torture for him.

He didn't want to help me plan the joint bachelor/bachelorette party because he wasn't "really a party person." And when I did plan a full-on extravaganza, he didn't want to participate in any of the games or do karaoke. Do you know what it feels like to pour your heart into Vanessa Carlton's "A Thousand Miles" when there's a tall, bespectacled man in the front row, arms crossed and black hair rumpled, staring at you with a smirk on his face? Nothing can ruin the transcendent experience of singing that song, but it really puts a damper on things.

And when it came to the wedding, he refused to use the photo booth, even though I ordered props and everyone else was doing it. He didn't shed a tear during the ceremony, while I cried enough to ruin my makeup. He was as stiff as the stick that was surely shoved up his ass when we walked back up the aisle after Holly and Darius said their vows, his stupid tall body not yielding in any way as I held his arm and smiled beatifically at my relatives in the crowd.

I nicknamed him Can't Relax Max because he was infuriatingly unable to chill out, but also because I felt like *I* couldn't relax around him. His judgmental presence, his narrowed eyes behind his glasses, and his crossed arms at the edge of every crowd were a constant bummer on what should've been the happiest day of my life (assuming I never get married myself).

But all of that would've been forgivable. What I can't forgive *or* forget is what Max said to Darius before the wedding started, when he apparently didn't think I could hear him. Because of that, I know all too well what Max thinks of Holly and our family, and honestly, I'd be more than happy to let him spend Christmas Eve Eve dinner in the goat barn. I've only seen him briefly in the years since the wedding—at the twins' birthday parties, when I could easily avoid him since neither of us wanted to talk to each other. I had no reason to think I'd ever have to interact with him again.

I shake my head. There's no time to focus on that now, because Max Beckett is right in front of me in my sister's home, and I need to figure out how to fix this.

"What are you doing here?" I ask.

He gives me a wave, his black hair bouncing the slightest bit. There's the one thing in his "pro" category: the man has quite voluminous hair. "It's great to see you, too."

I snort. "Right. Because you were *so* broken up when we last parted. I'm sure you've been waiting anxiously for the day we could see each other again."

"Been counting down the days in my diary," he mutters, refusing to even meet my eyes.

"Writing some pretty sad poetry, I assume."

"I'm basically Edgar Allan Poe," he says with no trace of a smile.

"Oh, because you murdered someone and stuffed their dismembered body under your floorboards?" I ask with wide eyes. "Was it someone who *really* pissed you off by having too much fun at karaoke?"

Max opens his mouth to offer up his retort, but Holly cuts him off forcefully. "Max is spending the holiday with us this year, and we're so glad to have him."

Darius looks between us with trepidation etched all over his face. He has, I'm sure, never met two people who clash as severely as Max and I do.

"So glad," I say through my teeth.

Max tilts his head, a lock of his hair falling over his forehead in what might seem charmingly boyish on another man. However, I'm certain Max was never boyish, not even when he was really a boy. He probably popped out of the womb and immediately complained about his mother's breast milk and the air conditioning in the hospital.

"I hear I'll be your hubby tonight," he says in his infuriatingly deep monotone voice.

"No." I shake my head, looking at Holly with pleading eyes. "Absolutely not. I take back what I said about the goats. I'd be happy to be a goat wife. At least they presumably don't use the word *hubby*, because they don't have the power of speech."

"Actually, if we're choosing new spouses, I think I might prefer a goat, too," Max says, looking out the window, as if he wishes he could drive back home.

"Laurel," Holly says with the exaggerated patience she sometimes uses when the twins won't go to sleep. "This was your idea."

"Not exactly," I correct her. "Actually, we came up with this plan together, and I thought I'd be married to your husband."

I flash a smile at Darius, and he gives me an uncomfortable one back.

"Right, but it was your idea to keep your job, wasn't it?" she asks, a slight edge creeping into her normally unflappable attitude.

I feel my shoulders slumping. The absolute last thing I ever want to do is make Holly mad or inconvenience her in any way, and yet here I am, making her entire family play pretend for Christmas Eve Eve dinner, the most sacred of Grant family meals.

"You know," Darius says, forced joviality in his voice, "I think this is actually going to be a great time for us. It'll be such a fun memory to look back on, and it's a chance for two of my favorite people to get to know each other a little better."

I look at Max. He narrows his eyes slightly in what I can

only interpret as a challenge. He's not going to be the one to disappoint Holly and Darius. He's game for this; am I?

I think about a line I highlighted in *Step Into Your Power, Babe: A Guide to Finding Your Cosmic Tiara and Owning Your Kingdom*. "Face your challenges with the confidence that you are the woman for the job. You can handle whatever life throws at you with your head held high and your tiara in place."

Honestly, it's getting kind of stressful to imagine so much empowering imagery. First a Mind Oasis, now a tiara? When will I find a self-help book that's like, "Bitch, take a nap"?

But I imagine it. I'm wearing a pretend tiara, I own my metaphorical kingdom, and I can handle this challenge.

"You know what, Darius? You're right," I say. "I, for one, would love the chance to get to know Max better. In fact, I can't wait to spend every single second of the next few hours together."

"I couldn't agree more," Max says, his mouth in a straight line that contradicts his words.

"Wait," I say, considering something. Darius is Black, and the twins have a skin tone that falls in-between his brown skin and Holly's and my "so pale we're practically translucent" skin. "Isn't Gilbert going to wonder why two white people have biracial children? I mean, probably no one would ask such a rude question, right?"

Holly barks out a laugh. "Oh, you have no idea the kinds of questions people ask me, their actual mother. A lot of 'are they really yours?' But given that he's your boss and a guest in my—I mean *your*—home, he might understand that asking questions about your children's background isn't really appropriate. And if he does . . . well, you're the writer. Come up with something!"

I frown. I don't love the idea, but then again, Gilbert has never been the most observant person (see: constantly being unaware he has food on his shirt, not noticing my real address on my application).

"Anyway!" Holly claps. "I need to go check on the goats, and Darius . . . don't you have a thing?"

"Oh, yeah. The thing!" Darius nods quickly, then walks upstairs, mumbling, "Gotta go do the thing."

"Don't leave me," I whisper, grabbing onto Holly's arm.

"This seems like a great chance for you two to chat!" She yanks her arm free and heads to the kitchen. "How are you supposed to be fake married if you barely know each other?"

The door swings shut behind her, leaving the two of us standing awkwardly in the middle of the living room. The twins' screeches drift up from the basement, Frank snores on the armchair, and the antique clock on the mantel ticks away the longest seconds of my life. But those are the only sounds in the room as the silence between Max and me stretches to unbearable lengths.

"Well, here we are," I say, unable to stand another second of standing around without saying anything. "Married."

"Indeed." Max sits beside Frank on the armchair, and Frank stands up and plops his body across Max's lap. Max scratches Frank's ears, looking for all intents and purposes like the man of the house.

I sit down on the sofa. This is going to be like pulling teeth—actually, I'd rather perform amateur dentistry right now than try to get to know Max, the man who wanted to ruin my sister's wedding. I think back to how he seemed so offended that he had to slow dance with me during the bridal party dance, and I scowl.

"If we want to project a happy marriage, you might not want to look at me like that," Max says, rubbing Frank's exposed belly.

"Like what?" I ask, erasing the look from my face.

"Like you wish I were dead," he says matter-of-factly.

"I don't wish you were dead," I say honestly. "I just wish you weren't in my house."

"Holly's house," he corrects. "And ouch."

I roll my eyes. "Oh, don't act like you're offended. I'm well aware of how you feel about me. You wish I was dead, too."

Max's eyes move from Frank's belly to my face. "I'm glad you're not dead, Laurel."

"A low bar in a marriage, but we've cleared it. Okay, let's stop with the small talk. What are your hopes? Dreams? Most traumatic childhood memories?"

Max stops rubbing Frank's belly, and Frank looks up at him with confusion. "Um, what?"

"We're supposed to be getting to know each other, and how are we supposed to pretend to be married if I don't know your innermost thoughts?"

"I've never faked a relationship before, but that seems like jumping into the deep end," Max says. "And I don't really know about this whole situation, anyway. Holly briefed me on it, but why are you lying to your boss about owning the farm?"

"Because I'm in over my head," I say, crossing my arms.

"And this is my only hope . . . but it's not too late for you to back out."

I wait a moment, silently hoping he doesn't agree. As much as I don't want to be fake-married to Max, this whole plan falls apart without him.

"No, I'm in," Max says, and I breathe a sigh of relief. "But I'm a little . . . unsure. I've never been a husband."

"Well, I've certainly never been a wife."

"Could we start with the basics?" Max asks, and I can't help but notice that he looks a little uneasy—maybe like he's actually taking this seriously. "What's your favorite color?"

This feels like building the world's strangest in-person dating profile, but whatever. I'll go with it.

"Favorite color on three," I say. "One, two, three—"

"Green," the two of us say at the same time.

"Weird," I mutter. "Okay, favorite restaurant."

I'm sure we won't have the same answer this time, but as soon as I say *three*, the two of us say "Harvest Pizzeria" in unison.

I gasp. "No! Quick, favorite ice-cream flavor."

"Pistachio," we both say, and I scream and throw a pillow at him.

"That's not even a normal favorite! What's going on? Are you stalking me?"

"Do you think I've been standing outside your window, watching you eat ice cream?" Max asks with a scoff.

"I'm starting to suspect that, yes," I say firmly. "Next question: What's your favorite childhood Christmas memory?"

"You know, the usual. Walking in a winter wonderland, building a snowman, calling him Parson Brown, etc."

"That's a line from a song, not a memory."

"How do you know it's not both? Parson Brown is a great name for a snowman."

I sigh. "Just throw me a bone. You already know everything about my family. Give me the basics on yours."

"Why?" Max asks warily, like he thinks I'm asking him personal questions to gain the answers to his security questions and steal his identity.

"Because that's what we're doing here, right?" I widen my eyes. "How am I going to complain to Gilbert about my mother-in-law if I don't even have the specifics?"

"I have a mother and a father," Max says, his eyes on Frank. "Let's move on."

"Fine." I roll my eyes—I don't have the time or energy to draw more details out of him. "What's our favorite thing to do together? In case Gilbert asks us what we like to do?"

"Ask each other invasive questions about our pasts," Max says, and I almost laugh before I hear the thump of little feet coming up the basement steps. With a beleaguered sigh, Frank hops off Max's lap and goes to lie in front of the fireplace.

"Max!" Noah shouts with the enthusiasm of a child who walked into an all-you-can-eat ice-cream buffet.

"We missed you!" Lexie yells, and the two of them jump into the spot on his lap that Frank just vacated.

"I missed you guys, too," Max says, his voice sounding remarkably lighter than it did when I was peppering him with questions.

"Tell us a joke," Lexie says seriously, her eyes big.

"Okay," Max says. "I've been saving this one since last week. Knock knock."

"Who's there?" the twins ask.

"Interrupting cow."

"Interrupting cow wh—" they start.

"Moo!" Max shouts, putting more emotion into a cow noise than I've ever seen from him.

The twins dissolve into peals of laughter as Noah falls off of Max's lap.

"Oh! I have one!" Noah shouts as he climbs back up. "What did the cow say to the other cow?"

"Sticking with a cow theme, I see," I say.

Everyone turns to look at me. "Aunt Laurel, you're interrupting," Lexie says.

"Sorry." I sink down into the sofa, chastised. Max raises his eyebrows at me.

"What did the cow say?" Max asks.

"Potato!" Noah yells, and the twins laugh so hard that they both fall off Max's lap.

"Oh, I was not expecting that," Max says with a wide smile. I swear, that smile takes up half of his face, and this is the first time I've ever seen it at full wattage. "That's how you know it's a really good joke. It goes in an unpredictable direction."

Noah nods. "I came up with it myself."

"Hey, I can tell jokes, too," I say. "Knock knock!"

"Is this going to be the 'orange you glad I didn't say banana' joke?" Lexie asks flatly. "Because you've told us that one."

"No," I say. I wrack my brain for another joke, but I can't think of anything that tops the sheer absurdity of Noah's potato joke. "Fine. It was."

"That's okay," Lexie says, taking pity on me and coming over to sit in my lap. "Not everyone is good at jokes."

"I'm good at jokes!" I defend myself. "Really. Everyone thinks I'm very funny."

Lexie looks at me skeptically. "Max is *great* at jokes, though. He knows them all."

"Hey!" Holly says, walking into the room. "I see everyone's bonding. Look at you two, pretending to be parents!"

"Am I bad at jokes?" I ask.

"Oh, sweetie, not everyone can be good at everything," Holly says.

Before I can tell her she's not being very reassuring, we hear the sound of tires on gravel for the second time today.

"Who is it now?" I ask, walking over to peer out the window. "Because it's still way too early for Gilbert to be here . . ."

I trail off as I realize that Gilbert is, in fact, here, but he's not driving his typical Subaru Outback.

No, he's driving a tiny yellow sports car I've never seen before, one that I can only assume is part of some midlife/"my wife dumped me" crisis, and he's absolutely blasting music as he cries, staring through his window at the barn.

"Is he listening to . . . Adele?" Holly asks as the British singer plaintively wails loudly enough for her voice to be heard through our windows.

"Oh, God," I mutter, running outside.

Chapter Six

I TAP ON GILBERT'S window, shivering as the snow falls harder.

He waves and gives me an apologetic frown, then presses the button to roll the window down. Adele's "Someone Like You" assaults me at full volume.

"Are you okay?" I ask.

"Well, I'm here," he says. "And I'm happy about that. But I looked at your barn and I thought about how Charlene and I got married at the zoo, and then I got sad again."

I wait to see where this is going.

"There's a barn at the zoo," he explains. "Where they have the goats you can pet."

"Did you get married in the animal barn?" I ask.

"No," he says, shaking his head. "That's not where they hold the weddings. Way too unsanitary, not to mention confusing for the goats."

"Okay." I rub my hands on my arms, deciding to let this topic drop. "How about coming inside?"

"Probably a good idea," he says, resigned. As he's about to turn off the car, "Rumor Has It" starts playing.

"Also maybe try listening to something that isn't Adele," I say gently.

He turns off the car. "This is my all-purpose Adele mix," he says as he steps out. "I listen to it all the time, but it just so happens most of her songs are about being sad or getting cheated on."

"Well, at least that one was upbeat." I pat him on the arm.

"That's the thing about Adele." Gilbert wipes his eyes with a tissue. "She has range."

The topic of global superstar Adele is certainly a safer one than Gilbert's relationship with Charlene, so I'm prepared to keep talking, but then the front door swings open and Max walks stiffly down the stairs, that exasperating hair falling in his face.

"Do you two need any help . . . sweetie?" he asks, and I can't tell if he's uncomfortable or taking glee in my discomfort. Perhaps Max is willing to put aside his own disgust toward me in the service of making me miserable. He must think it's what I deserve for being a member of the Grant family.

"No thanks, *sweetie*," I force myself to say through a grit-teeth smile.

"Well!" Gilbert says. "This strapping young gentleman must be your husband."

"That's me," Max says with a small smile as he holds out his hand. "I'm Max."

Gilbert shakes his hand, his mouth half open in marvel as he looks between us. "I'm Gilbert, and I must say, it is *so* nice to meet you. As Laurel may have told you, I'm going through a bit of a rough patch right now."

Max turns to look at me, eyebrows raised, and I shake my head quickly.

"She certainly told me. About the rough patch," Max says, nodding with what he must imagine sympathy looks like. Not that he would know, given that it's a human emotion.

"I'm incredibly grateful that you two opened up your home to me." He turns to take it in. "And what a home! Laurel, it's even more beautiful than it looks online."

"Well, that's very kind of you." I stifle a laugh when a snowflake lands on a lens of Max's glasses, and he reacts as if he received an electric shock. At least I can still feel joy at how uncomfortable Max is right now. "What do you say we take this party inside, boys? We can introduce you to the rest of the fam."

Gilbert walks up the stairs ahead of us as Max turns to me, mouthing, *Fam*?

I scowl. I don't know why I'm talking like this. *Let's take this party inside?* I'm so nervous about pulling off this dinner that I'm turning into an entirely different, significantly cornier person.

Max puts an arm around me, and while his body heat actually feels quite nice in the bitter cold, I elbow him. "If you don't get that arm off me, I'm going to knee you in the balls," I say with a growl.

"I'm trying to sell this," Max hisses in my ear, his breath sending goose bumps down my body.

But when I was threatening to harm Max's most sensitive parts, I forgot that Gilbert was right in front of us. He turns around in shock right before he opens the door, and Max lets out a loud, obviously fake laugh. "Oh, now don't threaten me with a good time, honey."

Gilbert tilts his head and gives us a conspiratorial smile, pointing at us. "You two. This banter! It's so fun. So witty. So . . ." He trails off, his gaze growing distant. And then he bursts into tears again.

I'm starting to think this is going to be a long day.

Chapter Seven

INTRODUCING A CRYING middle-aged man to my family isn't what I envisioned doing this holiday season, but I have to work with what I've got. Holly is her usual calming presence and immediately gets Gilbert set up on the couch with a steaming mug of Christmas tea. (Yes, she dried the leaves and spices and blended it herself.)

"I'm Laurel's brother-in-law," Darius says, shaking Gilbert's hand and smiling broadly. "We're so glad you could be here with us today."

Holly elbows him.

"In Laurel's house. Not my house," he adds.

"And these are Noah and Lexie, my kiddos," I say, despite never using the word *kiddos* in my life.

"Honey, I think you mean *our* kiddos," Max says, putting an arm around me and squeezing. "After all, I'd like to think I had some part in their conception."

I make a horrified face that Gilbert doesn't notice because

he's looking at Noah and Lexie, who seem too confused to say much.

"That's how babies happen, right?" Max whispers helplessly, raking a hand through his hair. Apparently, he's as panicked about faking this relationship as I am.

"Twins must run in the family!" Gilbert exclaims with delight, and Holly tells him about how we have sets on both sides of our family.

"Just . . . stop talking," I hiss at Max while Gilbert is distracted. "Stop being weird. Stop making references to impregnating me or using the word *conception*."

Gilbert looks at us again. "I'm so happy Laurel invited me over."

I offer him a tight smile. *Invite* might be a generous way of describing what happened. He sips his tea, humming "Someone Like You" to himself.

"Gilbert," I say, a warning in my voice.

He shakes his head quickly. "You're right, you're right. I promised no more Adele!"

Holly claps her hands. "How about some Christmas music?"

The kids cheer—they've clearly inherited the Grant family passion for Christmas—as I shrug out of Max's embrace and head over to the stereo system in the corner. Sure, it's easy to play music on your phone, but we spent our childhood amassing quite the collection of Christmas CDs, from good (the Phil Spector Christmas album) to bad (an inexplicable Lynyrd Skynyrd holiday album) to baffling (who convinced Jessica and Ashlee Simpson to cover "Little Drummer Boy"?).

I flip quickly through the CDs but stop when I feel a looming, judging presence beside me. "Are you here to approve my music choices?"

"I am, and that one gets an *absolutely not*," Max says about the *NSYNC album my hand currently rests on.

"How am I supposed to wish everyone 'Merry Christmas, Happy Holidays' without them?" I ask. I glance over to see that Gilbert is sharing the couch with and talking to Darius (although only Gilbert has a blanket that says *The Holiday Snuggle Is Real* wrapped around his shoulders).

"I guess you'll have to find a way to express your love of the holidays without Justin Timberlake."

I keep flipping through CDs. "I was more of a JC girl, but okay." I hold up the Beach Boys. "Is this acceptable?"

"No." Max shakes his head.

"You don't like 'Little Saint Nick'?" I ask flatly. "Seriously?"

"I would prefer to never hear 'Little Saint Nick' again in my life." Frank waddles over, and Max leans down to scratch him behind his floppy ears. It strikes me that Max is being much more friendly toward Frank than he has ever been toward me . . . not that I want him to scratch behind *my* ears.

I slide the CD case back where I found it and shake my head as Frank wanders off in search of another hand to scratch him. "Does the sound of children's laughter also bother you? What about birdsong? A babbling brook?"

A half smile breaks through Max's typically serious face.

"What about the sound of a kitchen timer that means the cookies are ready?" I continue. "Or the *Golden Girls* theme song? Or that really funky hold music the doctor's office plays where you're mad you have to wait so long but it still *kind* of makes you want to dance?"

He shakes his head, looking completely confused. His eyes, I notice for the first time, are smooth milk-chocolate brown. It's a shame those eyes are wasted on such a complete and utter pill.

"What are you doing?" he asks.

"Naming sounds that bring me joy," I say. "Do you hate them all?"

"You guys, uh, pick anything out yet?" Holly asks. She raises her eyebrows at me from across the room.

"Yeah, okay," I say, popping *A Charlie Brown Christmas* into the CD player. "You can't complain about this one. Everyone likes this smooth jazz."

This has actually been pretty fun, I think with surprise. Yes, Max is being annoying, but in a way that feels more playful and less antagonistic. Maybe he's even reconsidered his stance about my family being unworthy of Darius.

"It's not about any particular album," he says with a groan. "It's Christmas music in general. I don't like it."

I pause with my finger over the Play button. "Not any of it?"

"No."

"Okay, but you *have* to like Mariah Carey."

"Absolutely not," he says, disdain dripping from his voice.

As if his feelings about my family aren't bad enough, now he has to insult the Queen of Christmas Mariah Carey? This is too much. This cannot stand.

"Max," I say, my voice heavy with patience. "I'm sorry, but you're going to have to grin and bear it."

He shrugs. "I'm used to grinning and bearing it."

"Never seen you grin," I mutter as the music starts playing.

"Oh, I grin plenty," he says. "At home, alone, while reading a book. But Christmas doesn't make me happy. All this commercial, glittery décor."

He holds up a pillow that says *Don't Get Your Tinsel in a Tangle*. "This. I hate this."

I grab the pillow out of his hand and throw it at his head. "I love that pillow. That pillow is my favorite thing about the entire season."

I've actually never noticed that pillow before—I think Holly must've picked it up this year at TJ Maxx (she's a real Maxxinista). But it's the principle of the thing.

"Traditions matter." I pick the pillow up off the floor and hold it to my chest.

"What tradition does that pillow represent, exactly?" Max crosses his arms. "Buying cheaply produced garbage that no one needs so it can end up in a landfill in ten years?"

I gasp. "This pillow is a treasured family heirloom. It's been in our family for generations."

Max squints at it. "You're telling me your great-grandmother hand stitched a pillow that says *Don't Get Your Tinsel in a Tangle*?"

"Yes," I hiss. "My great-grandmother loved making pillows with hilarious seasonal sayings. It was kind of her thing."

"Sorry," Max says with a smug smile, holding his hands up. "I had no idea that tacky holiday decorations were your family tradition."

I fume. Max obviously knows I'm lying, but he seems to be enjoying this conversation. Me? Not so much.

"Why are you even here then, Max, if you hate Christmas

so much?" I say in a low voice, glancing at the rest of the family out of the corner of my eye. The twins are telling Gilbert something (knowing them, they're exhaustively recounting the plot of an episode of *SpongeBob SquarePants*), and he looks appropriately interested.

"Because, Laurel," Max says, "I have nowhere else to go."

And then he walks away, leaving me openmouthed by the stereo system as a choir of angelic children sing about Christmas time being here.

"Well, that was odd," I mutter to myself, giving the pillow a fluff and putting it back on the wooden chair by the window.

I cross my arms and frown as I watch Max chat happily with everyone. At one point, he puts his arm around Darius. Noah even hugs him, and he doesn't recoil—he seems to *enjoy the hug.* I thought he hated our family. Clearly he's gotten over that, and it's just me and the general concept of Christmas that he hates.

"Laurel!" Holly calls with cheer in her voice that sounds faker than a department store Santa's beard. "Get over here, girlie!"

My frown deepens. Holly and I have never been the kind of sisters who call each other *girl* or *sis* or *chica*—we pretty much stick to each other's names, and the nickname combined with her scary-wide eyes make my stomach sink.

"I was telling Gilbert that I'd be happy to cook dinner so you guys can catch up," she says once I join them, putting an arm around me.

"And *I* said," Gilbert says from the couch, where he's still sitting wrapped in a blanket and holding his mug with two hands, "no way. I came here for the full Christmas Eve Eve dinner, and that means I need Laurel's cooking. I've read such great things about that beef Wellington. My mouth is watering just thinking about it."

My mouth, however, goes as dry as the beef Wellington surely will be when I'm done with it. I lean into Holly and whisper, *"Execute plan Parent Trap!"*

"You know something else funny?" she asks, giving my shoulder a squeeze that's a smidge too hard. "Gilbert also said he can tell us apart quite easily."

He nods. "It's true. Holly has that tiny beauty mark on her cheek, and your left eye is slightly bigger, Laurel."

Max lets out a laugh that he disguises as a cough, but Gilbert doesn't notice.

"It's my party trick, I guess. I've always been able to tell the Olsen twins apart, too. They have very different smiles. Anyway!" He lifts his mug to his lips and takes a sip. "Need any help in the kitchen, Laurel?"

"Nope!" I say too loudly and too quickly. "No offense, but I'm very focused in the kitchen. I'm a lone wolf when I get a knife in my hand."

"Oh, well, I feel bad enforcing gender stereotypes," Gilbert says, looking genuinely concerned. "It doesn't seem right to have a woman cooking for me while I put my feet up and relax. I love . . . well, I used to love being in the kitchen with Charlene."

He gazes forlornly into his mug, the wiggle of his mustache warning me that the tears are coming again.

"I'm totally good in there, I promise," I say. Nothing could be further from the truth, of course, but the only thing worse than trying to make an entire meal by myself is trying to make an entire meal while Gilbert watches over my shoulder.

"And anyway, she won't be alone," Holly says with a smile. "Max will be helping."

"What?" I croak, and Holly subtly kicks me.

"Woo, gender parity!" Darius shouts with way too much enthusiasm.

"There is nothing more romantic than equal distribution of household labor," Gilbert says, his eyes welling with tears again.

"If I remember correctly, that was part of our wedding vows," Max says, meeting my eye.

I stare back at him. "Was it? I got stuck on the 'until death do us part' line. Hey, Holly? Can I speak to you for a sec in the kitchen?" I give Gilbert a conspiratorial smile. "Girl talk."

He waves me off, taking another sip of hot chocolate. "Oh, I know how it is."

I speed walk into the kitchen, pulling Holly by the arm.

"Ow!" she says as the door swings shut behind us. "When did you become so strong?"

"Probably around the time I learned to cook a Christmas Eve Eve meal!" I whisper-shout. "What am I supposed to do?"

She crosses her arms and frowns at me. "Well, first of all, I can tell you're not in your Mind Oasis right now."

"I'm not even in the same country as my Mind Oasis," I tell her. "Why did you do this to me?"

She raises her eyebrows. "Um, did I miss something? Because last time I checked, we're all doing this because of you."

I take a deep breath, trying my best to push down the shame and guilt that creep up from the pit of my stomach. I am New Laurel, I remind myself. Yes, I'm in a messy situation, but it's only because I wanted a job and now I'm simply in too deep. But New Laurel can fix this.

"You're right," I say slowly. "But why did you volunteer Max for kitchen duty? It's bad enough that I have to do this, but now I have to do this with Judgy McJudgerson standing beside me, scoffing at every mistake!"

"I've never heard Max scoff," Holly says.

"That's funny, because he's scoffed at every single thing he's ever seen me do."

"I scoff at you sometimes, too."

"But those are love scoffs," I point out. "Max doesn't love me. He doesn't even know me."

"Exactly," Holly says. "And you don't know him. You need to get over this vendetta you have against him—I swear, Laurel, he's a good guy. So what if he didn't want to do all the wedding activities? Who cares if he doesn't like karaoke? Those aren't valid reasons to hate someone, and I don't know why you're holding on to this."

I press my lips together, as if they can form an impenetrable wall to keep the barrage of antiMax words from spilling out. Holly still has no idea what I overheard Max say at her wedding. If she did, she'd understand why I hate him so much . . . but then again, if she knew what he said, she'd also be incredibly hurt, and I would never do that to my sister.

So I keep my mouth shut, and Holly keeps extolling Max's apparently endless virtues.

"He's always there for Darius. He's an amazing babysitter

for the twins. He's really smart, he's well read, he's so funny—"

"Okay, hold up." I put up a hand like I'm a school crossing guard. Smart? Sure. Well read? I'd believe that. But . . . "Funny?"

Holly nods, eyes wide. "Yes."

"Max Beckett. That guy." I point toward the living room. "That guy is funny? As in, he makes jokes that aren't solely at other people's expense?"

"Yes!" Holly nods vigorously. "I swear, he tells the best stories and he has great timing. He's always cracking Darius and me up when he comes over for dinner."

"You have him over for dinner?" I rear back with a gasp, processing this shocking betrayal.

Holly rolls her eyes. "Yes. Get ahold of yourself. But the main relevant quality that Max possesses is that he's a great cook, which is why I thought you could use his help."

Holly's not wrong . . . I could use his help. In fact, I could use *any* help. I'm starting to think we might be better off letting the twins put together dinner.

"Everything's going to be great." Holly leans forward and gives me a quick squeeze. "I promise. Now if you'll excuse me, I'm off to find your hubby!"

"You know I hate that word!" I shout, but the kitchen door is already swinging shut behind her. I'm alone in the kitchen.

Until Max Beckett walks in, looking just as uncomfortable as I feel.

SILENCE HANGS HEAVY over the kitchen as the door shuts behind Max. I watch him warily, like he's a bobcat and I'm a hapless squirrel who's about to be devoured.

But he isn't a bobcat, I remind myself. He's simply some dude who made the mistake of insulting my favorite person in the world, and although I'm now honor bound to hate him for the rest of my life, I'm perfectly capable of preparing beef Wellington with him.

"Well, let's do this," he says as he walks to the counter, not looking at me.

I cross my arms, my eyes on his back, as my resolve to play nice instantly dissolves. It's one thing to invade my family's home, but now he can't even look at me? It's as if he sees me as nothing but an impediment on the road to a perfectly cooked meal.

I stride purposefully, like the badass bitch the self-help books say I am, to the fridge. There the beef tenderloin sits, wrapped in butcher paper on the bottom shelf. I pull it out and heave it onto the counter, where it falls with a satisfying slap.

"Wow," I breathe. "It's huge."

Max lets out a sound that's either a startled cough or a laugh, and I turn toward him, narrowing my eyes. Is that "sense of humor" Holly mentioned showing up *now*? "You can't possibly be making a 'that's what she said' joke. Grow up."

He holds up his hands. "No, of course not. You keep waxing poetic about the length of beef you're staring at."

"I'm gonna wax poetic about what I'd like to do to you," I mutter. I intend violence, but staring at the girth of the tenderloin, it comes out oddly sexual. Max, to his credit, ignores my comment.

Max sits down at the small round table and pulls out his phone. I thought he was supposed to be the chef in this fake marriage, but it's just as well—I can miserably overcook this tenderloin plenty fine on my own. Unsure of what to do, I turn on the oven. 450 degrees. Wait, 250 degrees. "Low and slow," I say quietly, which sounds like something I've heard on a cooking show once.

To distract myself from my current misery, I text Jamilah. Do you remember Can't Relax Max from Holly's wedding?

The guy who sent smoldering looks your way the entire night? she texts back.

They weren't smoldering, they were aggravated, I correct her. But yes. Well, he's here and he's pretending to be my husband.

This entire situation is getting weirder and weirder. Is he still hot? she asks.

He was never hot, I lie. Anyway I have to go make an entire Christmas Eve Eve dinner because Gilbert can tell Holly and me apart and I'm supposed to be the cook in the family.

Okay, have fun! she texts with the carefree spirit of someone who doesn't have to spend their holiday pretending to be someone they're not.

I open the fridge, inspect all of Holly's meticulously organized condiments as if I know what to do with even one of them, and close it again. I groan, then google "what is beef Wellington?"

"I thought you had beef Wellington every year."

Max's voice is hot in my ear, and I whip around, hiding my phone behind my back as if he caught me looking up porn. He's so close to me that I can feel his breath on my neck, a sensation that wouldn't be unpleasant if he were anyone else.

"We—we do," I stammer. "But I don't really know what it . . . is?"

"You eat beef Wellington every Christmas."

"Correct."

"And you never thought to notice what was in it?"

I throw my hands in the air. "I'm sorry I wasn't inspecting every bite of my Christmas Eve Eve dinner, meticulously cataloging the ingredients, and quizzing my mom and Holly to find out what they put in it. I never anticipated a future in which I'd have to"—I lower my voice to a hiss—"convince my boss that I know how to run a farm and cook literally anything that isn't a frozen pizza."

"So you were going to attempt making this complex dinner with absolutely no cooking knowledge?"

I press my lips together. "I wouldn't say I have no cooking knowledge. I once worked the funnel cake stand at a Renaissance fair."

Max doesn't say anything.

"My boyfriend at the time was a knife thrower and he got me the job," I say haughtily. "And, yes, I was let go when I started a grease fire, but that wasn't my fault and I don't wish to discuss it further."

"So you don't know how to cook anything at all?" he clarifies.

"I know how to order food, which I feel is an important skill."

Max crosses his arms, a satisfied smile on his face. "So you might say . . . you need me."

"I absolutely do not." I shake my head. "I think, with the power of the Internet and the spirit of Mariah Carey cheering me on, I can do this by myself."

Max simply raises his eyebrows and sits back down at the round kitchen table. I feel a slight tinge of regret—he *is* attempting to help me, and I *do* need that help. Desperately. Should I tone down my avowed hatred of him for one night, or at least one meal?

But then I think of Holly's face on her wedding day, her excitement, her nerves. Holly, my best friend and favorite person. As far as I'm concerned, Max can keep looking at his phone for as long as he likes.

With a sigh, I turn back to the counter and my phone. I scroll through the ingredients in the first recipe I click on. Beef, obviously. Puff pastry. And . . . mushrooms? I'm supposed to make something called a duxelles, and tingles of sweat break out all over my body. That sounds very French, and my knowledge of French food is basically limited to the French delicacies known as "fries" and "toast." Also, have I been eating mushrooms on Christmas Eve Eve this entire time? "I don't even like mushrooms," I mutter.

"Okay, first step." Max's chair scrapes across the floor as he stands. "Thaw the puff pastry."

"Excuse me," I say as he opens the freezer door and pulls out a box. "At what point in the last few minutes did you become Mr. Wellington?"

Max tilts his head, still holding the freezer door open. "Mr. Wellington?"

I shrug, suddenly feeling less sure of myself under his steady observation. For all his faults, this man has a piercing gaze, and I feel like he's not looking at me but *through* me, right down to my bones and heart and my deceptive "lying to my boss" soul.

I give myself a shake. "I figured it must be named after someone, right? Mr. Wellington. Sir Beef."

For one tiny, brilliant flash, Max's face glows with a real smile. "Sir Beef." He says it as a statement, not a question, like he's trying the words out for the first time.

"I can only assume that's what his subjects called him. You know, because he was known all over town for this mushroom, beef, puff pastry"—I gesture toward the box in his hands—"concoction."

Max closes the freezer. "Scoot over," he says, tossing the box of puff pastry on the counter and cracking his knuckles. "Sir Beef is here."

I snort. "Under no circumstances am I going to call you that."

Max rubs his neck. "Say what you want, but by the end of the night, you're going to be calling me Sir Beef."

My jaw drops. "I'm sorry?"

Max's face blooms as red as the poinsettia on the table. "That came out wrong."

A laugh jumps out of my throat. "How could you possibly intend that to come out? You told me I'll be calling you Sir Beef by the end of the night, like you're trying out a bizarre beef-themed pickup line at a bar."

Max's sigh is heavy with frustration as he looks at the ceiling. "I was trying to make a joke. Not sexually harass you with the tenderloin."

"Okay," I say slowly. "But I've gotta say, this one wasn't as successful as the interrupting cow joke."

"Maybe it's because I have a less receptive audience. Can we please drop it?" he asks, an expression of pure embarrassment on his face.

"Yes," I say, stifling a laugh. "Consider it forgotten. Sir Beef who?"

"Thank you," he mutters.

I frown, studying him as he opens the box of puff pastry. "Okay, seriously. How do you suddenly know how to make beef Wellington? Are you a chef?"

It strikes me that I don't even know what his job is—I don't know anything about Max, really, other than that he suffers from a life-threatening allergy to anything remotely fun.

He looks at me with a half smile. "Definitely not a chef."

"Let me guess. You're a psychologist who runs experiments on people that will later be deemed cruel and unethical."

Max squints at me. "No. I'm an engineer."

"An engineer?" I repeat, like I'm a career-obsessed parrot. "Hmm. That makes sense."

Max frowns. "How does it make sense?"

"It's obvious. You get to sit at a desk all day. Look at blueprints. Avoid human contact and wacky photo booth opportunities. All your favorite things."

The sides of his mouth quirk up. "Wacky photo booth opportunities?"

"I know you hate them because you refused to wear a fake mustache in the photo booth at Holly's wedding. In fact, you refused *all* the props," I remind him.

"Sure, but I don't think my antipathy for photo booths is a defining part of my personality. And I actually don't sit at a desk that much," Max says.

"What?"

"In my job. As an engineer. I visit a lot of jobsites. Even wear a hard hat, which might be considered a prop."

I frown. "In a very boring and labor-focused photo booth, sure."

I want to ask Max more questions about his job—like, what does he do all day? And why does the idea of him wearing a hard hat kind of turn me on? And why am I imagining a romance novel cover with Max wearing a flannel shirt and a hard hat and staring off into the distance while holding an axe (which I don't think is a typical engineer implement, but it's important to the fantasy I have going on)?

But then real Max—the one who's currently holding a kitchen knife instead of an axe—interrupts my rugged train of thought. "Anyway. I'm not a beef Wellington expert. I looked up a video on America's Test Kitchen."

So he wasn't idly scrolling through his phone . . . he was looking up ways to help me. Hot shame hits me, and I feel myself turning as red as Max did when he made that accidental beef-themed double entendre.

He props his phone up on a cookbook stand, and a video of two women preparing a beef tenderloin plays. "I have no idea how this compares to your traditional family recipe—" he starts.

"That's the problem," I interrupt. "We don't even have a traditional family recipe. My mom and Holly cook with some internal hard drive full of knowledge that has been passed down from generation to generation. They know how to make a piecrust or thicken a gravy or spatchcock a chicken, but somehow my internal hard drive didn't come with any of that information. Mine is, like, random celebrity gossip and a thorough analysis of every Jimmy Stewart movie. I don't even know what a duxelles is."

I exhale as the familiar embarrassment that comes when I overshare floods through me. *You don't need to tell Max everything about your life*, I remind myself. I wonder why the words spilled out of my mouth so easily, despite Max being Grant Family Enemy Number One. I guess it's because I don't have to impress him. I already know he thinks Holly isn't good enough for his best friend, and if he doesn't think she's great, then he definitely isn't going to like me, the generic, "not quite as good" version of Holly. If Holly is Meghan Markle, I'm the Lifetime movie version starring an actress who kind of looks like Meghan, if you squint and have a few drinks.

"Well," Max says, pointing at the video playing on his phone, where two people are chopping herbs. "We didn't really do traditional family recipes in my family, either, but that's what the video is for. Once I discovered these America's Test Kitchen videos, I realized I could learn to make just about anything."

Holly's words come back to me. *Max is funny. The twins love Max. Max can cook.* So far, all of those things are proving to be true. But that doesn't change the fact that Max seems to dislike me just as much as I dislike him.

"Funny that you bring up spatchcocking," Max continues, chopping mushrooms that seemingly appeared out of nowhere. His knife is almost in perfect sync with the women in the video. "Because I actually used one of these videos to teach me how to make chicken one night for Darius and Holly."

"Interesting."

"I just told you I spatchcocked a chicken," Max says, chopping thyme and not looking at me. "And you didn't make any sort of inappropriate joke about it."

"I'm above all that," I say airily. "These infantile jokes are more your thing. You can make all the meat-based innuendo you want and you'll hear nary a peep from me."

Max lets out a little snort-laugh. "Nary a peep?"

"Nary a peep," I confirm, hopping up to sit on the counter on the other side of the sink, a safe distance away from the man with a sharp knife.

Not that I would tell Max this, but in times of trouble I sometimes like to pretend I'm an actress in a movie from the 1940s, the kind of movie where the leads are suave and debonair and impossibly well dressed. In those movies, the women always know what to say. They deliver a cutting remark just so, and everyone thinks they're so smart and witty instead of mean. They also, especially when it comes to Katharine Hepburn in any given movie, say some truly bonkers things in extremely weird accents. I find it all very comforting. In an ideal world, I'd swan around glamorously, offering pithy bon mots, and everyone would laugh.

The fact that I have a tendency to make a mess of my own life, and in fact, might be doing so again right now if I can't pull this off, would be simply hilarious if I were one of those women. Perhaps in 1940s movie world, I wouldn't be making a mess of my life at all. Perhaps there, everything would be black-and-white and warm-and-fuzzy and I'd be with a man who clearly thought I was the bee's knees (and he'd probably say that, too), one who loved arguing with me but adored me, one who—

"Hello? Laurel?"

I'm jolted out of my silver screen fantasy by the most unpleasant of sounds: Max's voice. Okay, so the voice itself isn't unpleasant—it's actually quite lovely, deep and resonant, the kind of voice you might like whispering in your ear about beef tenderloin. You know, if it were attached to any other person.

"What?" I ask, hopping off the counter.

"I asked if you know where Holly keeps the skillets," Max says. "But you were staring off into space, moving your lips like you were talking to yourself."

"You must be mistaken," I say quickly, opening a cabinet and getting out a skillet. "Because I wasn't doing that."

"Okay." Max draws out the word and returns to his chopping. "Well, while you were being totally normal and not talking to yourself, I tied the tenderloin, so now we need to sear it."

I take a look at the beef tenderloin, tied with kitchen twine in four places. “Damn, you went full *Fifty Shades* on the innocent tenderloin.”

Max shakes his head. “I wouldn’t assume this tenderloin is so innocent. You should hear the places it’s been.”

“Please don’t slut shame the tenderloin.” I give Max a stern look.

“My apologies to the tenderloin,” Max says, leaning toward me to turn on the gas burner under the skillet. His arm, bare where his shirtsleeves are rolled up, brushes against mine, and I jump back, as if I touched the skillet instead of his arm.

“You should apologize to tenderloins the world over,” I say quickly, trying to avoid thinking about the way I felt when Max’s arm touched mine. Because what the hell is the point of that? So he has nice arms. Maybe Elizabeth Bennet would also have admired Mr. Darcy’s forearms if people were allowed to show any skin back then. The dude still hated her family. This is basically exactly like that, other than the part where it ends with Elizabeth and Mr. Darcy together, because Max will always be preredemption Darcy. “For the way society treats them.”

“Does society treat tenderloins poorly?” Max asks distractedly, heading to the fridge. “This is one of the more expensive cuts of meat.”

“What’s the next step?” I ask, eager to end my Mr. Darcy train of thought. *Fifty Shades*, *Pride and Prejudice* . . . Why is my brain a tangle of classic and modern romances right now? Think horror, I tell my brain. *Hostel*. *Scream*. The shower scene in *Psycho*.

"I promise it's not as challenging as whatever you're thinking," Max says, casting a wary glance at me. My horror-related feelings must be showing on my face. "We need to shingle the prosciutto—"

"I have literally never heard that combination of words in my life."

"—spread the duxelles over the prosciutto, coat the seared tenderloin in Dijon mustard, roll the tenderloin in the duxelles-covered prosciutto, and then put the whole thing in the fridge for thirty minutes to make sure it stays together."

I pause a beat. "Oh, is that it?"

"And then we cover the tenderloin in puff pastry, make an egg wash, bake until it reaches a hundred twenty-five degrees—speaking of which, where's the meat thermometer?—and then let it rest before we slice it. So this would be a good time to start on the potatoes. Can you grab them?"

I blink a few times before locating the potatoes on the counter behind me. What is happening? Why are phrases like "spread the duxelles" and "make an egg wash" getting me positively turned on? Especially when Max is saying them? Is this a Stockholm syndrome situation? Because I don't even care how much he dislikes my family, I would have a hate-fueled make-out session with him right here on this counter, this very second, if he looked at me the right way.

After he washed his hands, of course. He's been touching raw meat.

He looks at me impatiently. "If we don't get started on the potatoes, they won't be done at the same time as the beef."

I roll my eyes. Can't Relax Max is back in action, reminding me why we're fundamentally incompatible. I prefer to take a "no recipes, only vibes" approach to food preparation. This might be why I burn every meal I attempt, but the point remains: I simply cannot be beholden to instructions.

"In chaos, I find calm," I mutter to myself as I pull out a cutting board, attempting to be quiet enough so that Max doesn't hear me, but he seems to have supersonic hearing because he asks, "What?"

"Nothing," I say. "It was a mantra."

"A . . . mantra?" he asks slowly.

"Yes. A thing I say to calm myself down," I murmur as serenely as possible as I grab a potato. Something about Max's presence—combined with the act of attempting to cook—makes it almost impossible for me to take up residence in my Mind Oasis. The couch in the Mind Oasis is currently covered with a huge red wine stain, the trash cans are overflowing, there's dirty laundry on the floor, and this is all Max's fault. Whenever I try to picture my all-white couch, I just see him sitting on it, showing off those ridiculous forearms and bossing me around in the kitchen. I feel myself flush, and honestly? I can't tell if this feeling is coming from being annoyed by this man or being annoyed that the whole "kitchen boss" thing is kind of working for me.

"I can see that it's really helping," he says, going back to whatever he's doing to the tenderloin.

"It's not working at this moment, because I have to work with *you*," I grunt as I slip the knife through the potato way too quickly and almost chop a finger.

"I'm helping you," he says, grabbing the knife out of my

hand . . . which, to be fair, might be a good idea given that I almost lost a digit.

"Well, I didn't ask for your help, in case you forgot," I remind him. "Holly did. You know, my wonderful, perfect sister?"

"Do you always use so many adjectives when talking about her?"

"Yes," I say. "Because I think the world needs to know how great she is."

Max slowly hands the knife back to me, his fingers briefly closing around mine as he makes sure I have a grip on the handle. "I get it. Holly's great. You don't have to tell me."

"Oh?" I ask. "Are you sure about that?"

Max is quiet for a moment, his face unsure. "Why do I feel like this is a test?"

I shake my head. I can't believe he's going to stand here and pretend like he has no idea why we are never going to be friends. I don't know why he's here (he said he had nowhere else to go, but what did that mean?), but it can't be for anything good. Yes, he's been helping me, and the man clearly knows his way around a beef tenderloin, but that doesn't mean I'm going to ignore what happened at Holly's wedding.

"Forget it," I mutter, focusing on the potatoes again.

Max sighs, sounding truly angry for the first time. "I don't know what it is that you have against me, but—"

"You don't know?" I spin around and point at him, then realize I'm still holding the knife and lower my hand. "Are you really pretending that you don't know why I don't like you?"

"I'm not *pretending*," he says, pronouncing the word like it's something I made up. "I don't *know*. I've been perfectly nice to you, but I don't have to help you, Laurel. This wasn't my idea, either, but I'm trying to be a good sport about it—"

I ignore the way my name sounds coming out of his mouth and cross my arms. "Oh, that's a first for you."

"But maybe I'm sick of being a good sport! I don't have to be part of this ridiculous charade you're performing. It actually doesn't matter to me at all whether or not you keep your job. I could go out there right now and tell Gilbert the truth, he'd leave, and I could stay in here and finish dinner by myself. It would be a hell of a lot easier."

My eyes widen as my face grows hot. What would I do if Max did go out there right now and tell Gilbert what was happening? I may hate Max, but I'm counting on him. Yes, he's possibly a special agent sent here to destroy my family, but I need him on my side. And he's right—he has been helping me. While I'll never get over what he said about Holly, I can at least be grateful that he's here now. He's here and he's dealing with a sous-chef who can't even chop a potato—who could blame him for getting frustrated. The Hot Mess Express cannot, *will* not, ruin this meal or this opportunity to save my job.

He sighs, focusing on the tenderloin to avoid looking at me. "I'm sorry, I—"

"No, uh . . ." I swallow and turn toward the counter. "You're right. We need to work together on this, so let's get it done."

"Laurel, I—"

I shake my head quickly, staring at the floor. "You're absolutely correct. I'm asking you to do something ridiculous to help me, and you're doing me a favor. As silly as it sounds, I need Gilbert to believe that I run this farm, and that you're my husband. I know this isn't your idea of a good time, but can you . . . can you really try to sell it for the rest of the day?"

I meet his eyes and try my best to be Professional Laurel—not Starting a Petty Fight Laurel. New Laurel. "I need you," I say quietly.

He nods, and I see him swallow. "Okay," he says, his voice barely audible.

As we finish the meal, we don't say much other than Max giving me instructions and me apologizing every time I bump into him or make a mistake. And despite the fact that we got into an argument, I feel a strange sort of comfort working here with him. I chalk it up to the fact that I haven't felt a man's touch since I got kicked out of John's apartment. I'm lonely, and Max is here, and suddenly I understand why people (myself included) make so many bad decisions when it comes to relationships and sex.

But I don't do that anymore, I remind myself. Now I'm Smart Laurel. Mature Laurel. Doesn't Have Impure Thoughts About Can't Relax Max Laurel. So what if he's being temporarily nice and I temporarily need him and we're temporarily pretending to be a happily married couple? People can fake a lot of things for one day.

Chapter Nine

LAUREL, I CAN'T believe you made all this," Gilbert says in wonder, staring at the spread in front of him. We're all in our seats at the dining room table, a veritable feast laid out on the table on the serving dishes passed down from Grandma Pat. It's just like the Christmas Eve Eves of my youth.

"I had help," I say, giving what I hope is a humble smile.

"From her hubby," Max says.

"From my . . . hubby," I say, flashing Gilbert my widest grin.

"Cooking is one of our favorite things to do together, wouldn't you say so, babe?" Max looks at me and smiles. He places his hand over mine. He raises his eyebrows, and I realize that I'm staring at him with my mouth open. I *did* tell him to sell it, but I didn't expect that Max would play the role of "doting husband" quite so easily.

"Absolutely," I say, looking back at him with what I hope

is a loving expression. "Any time we can make duxelles together, we're happy."

Gilbert smiles fondly. "Oh, you two. I thought I'd never get my appetite back, but this meal is amazing."

"Then please, eat as much as you want," I say. Gilbert may be a bit odd, but he certainly didn't deserve to get dumped right before Christmas. If I can pull off this sham and help him have a happy Christmas Eve Eve, then I'll consider today a success.

"Where's my sandwich?" Noah asks, staring at the slice of beef Wellington on his plate.

"We're not having sandwiches today, sweetie," I say. "Eat your potatoes."

Lexie's mouth falls open. "Potatoes?"

I shrug, unsure what's happening. "Or your salad. Or the beef."

"We don't. Eat. Beef," Noah says slowly. "We eat peanut butter sandwiches."

"No crust." Lexie crosses her arms.

I shoot a panicked look to Holly, and she says, with false joviality, "It's great that you're trying to get them to eat something new. But maybe tonight they can have their old standby, peanut butter sandwiches. You know, like you've told me they do every night."

"Every night?" I ask slowly.

Holly tilts her head to the side. "Well, it's like you always tell me, *sis*. Parenting is full of tiny battles, and you're not willing to make dinnertime one of them. One of your children demands a peanut butter and jelly sandwich every night, and the other one demands a peanut butter but *no* jelly sandwich every night, and that's something that you've learned to accept about your life."

"Mom," Noah says to Holly in what he must think is a quiet voice, "I don't want to eat this."

"Oh, that's funny," Gilbert says as he chews. "Even the kids get you two confused?"

"They sure do," I say with a resolute nod.

"Peanut butter!" Lexie says in a hoarse whine.

Holly stands up. "How about I help you out and go make sandwiches for these two?"

"That would be great," I say, but the kitchen door is already swinging shut behind her.

"So," Gilbert says, swallowing a bite, "tell me how you two met."

I almost choke on my potatoes when I realize that I don't have a story for this. "He was my brother-in-law's best man and it was hate at first sight" wouldn't exactly help my cause.

But then Max reaches over and squeezes my hand. "Do you want to tell it or should I?"

"Go ahead, sweetie," I say slowly, curious and a bit nervous to see where this is going.

Max gives my hand one more squeeze before letting go. He leans forward, tenting his hands on the table. "You want the short version or the long version?" he asks Gilbert.

"Oh, the long version, please," Gilbert says, eyes wide. "I have nothing but time. Nowhere to go, no one who loves me. Really, this meal is the only thing I have going on."

"Okay." Max takes a deep breath, shooting me one more look before turning to Gilbert. "So it was the day of Darius's bachelor party, which was actually a bachelor-and-bachelorette party with Holly and her bridesmaids. I walked in, expecting to have a terrible time because I hate bachelor parties."

I nod. So far, this is all true. "*All* parties, actually. You hate all parties."

"Thank you for the clarification, honey," Max says without looking at me. "And I expected to hate Laurel, too, because she'd sent me several very pushy emails about planning the party."

I gasp, forgetting to stay in character as a lovestruck wife reminiscing about the day she met her soulmate. "They were not pushy. And your responses were very rude."

Max finally turns to me. "I wasn't rude. I was concise. I simply told you that I couldn't be any help because I didn't know the first thing about party planning."

I hold up a finger. "No, you *rudely* told me that you wouldn't help me and then refused to weigh in on whether we should do cosmic bowling or a game day."

"Actually what you called it was 'an elaborate, no-holds-barred game day the likes of which the world has never seen,' and I don't see how my response was rude."

I frown. I'm pretty sure Max is quoting me exactly. Did he do *research* to prepare for the possibility that Gilbert would ask how we met?

"Because you only used periods. Not a single exclamation point." I take a bite of the beef—it *is* really good. I'm surprised I had even a small part in making it.

"Oh, Max." Gilbert shakes his head. "You've gotta add in a few exclamation points. They're the peppermint mocha of emails, is what I always say."

"Thank you." I nod at Gilbert.

Max sighs. "Anyway. For reasons that should now be very clear, I was dreading this party. I already didn't like Laurel. I already didn't like parties. And now I had to do a game day and then go to, of all things, a karaoke bar. It was like Laurel designed this day by analyzing my worst nightmares."

"You decided against cosmic bowling?" Gilbert asks with so much shock that I feel the need to justify myself.

"Holly nixed the black lights," I say, my voice full of regret.

"They scare me. Too many visible stains and people's eyes look creepy," she says as she comes back into the room and deposits a sandwich in front of each twin. "What are we talking about?"

"Max is telling everyone the story of how the two of us met," I say sweetly.

"I'm listening." She raises her eyebrows as she sits down.

"I'm captivated," Darius says, shoveling a bite into his mouth. "And this salad is to die for."

"Thank you," Max and I say at the same time.

"So the obstacle course is a bust," Max says. "I got paired up with Laurel and Holly's brother, Doug, for the three-legged race, and he tried to get me to shotgun a beer before we started. When I said no, he shotgunned his *and* mine."

He stops to look at me. "We did not do well in that three-legged race."

"I remember," I say. "Doug puked."

"He puked a *lot*," Max says. "On me."

"Not to brag, but we won," Holly says, leaning toward Gilbert. "Me and Darius."

"Because we're such a good team!" Darius says brightly.

"I'm not surprised," Gilbert says. "Just looking at you, I

can tell you'd be great at a three-legged race. And a wheelbarrow race?"

Darius nods. "Absolutely, my man. We dominated every event."

Max and I shoot a quick look at each other, and for the first time, it feels like we're on the same team, like we have an inside joke. "Right," Max says. "So game day doesn't go well, I'm covered in puke, and I'm in a terrible mood."

"How could you tell?" I ask, but he ignores me.

"But then we head to the karaoke bar. I have to borrow a shirt from Darius that doesn't fit me because mine was, as previously established, covered in puke."

"You get puked on *one* time, and you dine out on that story for years," I mutter. "Do you even know how many times I've been puked on?"

Noah takes a bite of his sandwich. "I hate puking up," he says, shaking his head.

"Let's move this conversation along," I say. "So what happened next?"

Max raises his eyebrows at me. "You should know. You were there."

"I was," I say thoughtfully. "But I *do* love to hear you tell the story, babe."

"So." Max turns back to Gilbert, who has now finished all his food and is leaning forward, chin in his hands. "I wasn't looking for love. Actually, I was at one of the lowest points of my life. I was changing jobs and I'd just broken up with someone. And now here I was, at a karaoke bar listening to 'Margaritaville.'"

"Hey!" Holly says. "I do a great Jimmy Buffett!"

"She really does," I agree. "It's one of her best songs."

"This isn't about the quality of your singing, Holly," he says, and I narrow my eyes quickly, wondering how he can talk to her so calmly, with such friendliness, when I know he didn't want Darius to marry her. "This is about me. I was about to get up and leave when Laurel took the stage."

"The stage being the corner of the room across from the bar," I clarify to Gilbert.

"She was wearing a T-shirt that was covered in Life Savers," Max continues.

"You mean the candy?" Gilbert asks, looking confused.

I sigh, because I can't believe I have to explain this. "So I made a traditional bachelorette party T-shirt for Holly that had Life Savers stuck to it. The whole point is that people you run into while you're out partying are supposed to suck the Life Savers off of it, but—"

"But *I* thought that was a disgusting hotbed of germs," Holly says, taking a bite of her beef.

"I did offer to suck them all off myself," Darius says.

"Aw." Holly pats his hand. "That was very chivalrous of you."

"I ended up wearing it myself because I didn't want it to go to waste. The funny part is that the shirt said . . ." I trail off, remembering that I'm talking to a crowd that includes my boss and two small children. Maybe I shouldn't tell them how the shirt said *Suck for a Buck.*

"What did it say, sweetheart?" Max asks innocently, taking a sip of his water.

"It didn't say anything," I finish. "Just a shirt with Life Savers."

"So she's up there in her Life Saver shirt, singing 'A Thousand Miles'—" Max continues.

"Doing air piano," I add.

"Doing air piano. And when I saw her, all I could think was . . . this is a woman who knows how to enjoy life. She doesn't care that she's being silly in front of a crowd, or that she's wearing a shirt covered in candy that several adults have tried to pull off of her with their mouths, or that she's extremely off-key—"

"Hey." I smack him on the arm.

"She's . . . herself. She's not crushed by the weight of self-loathing or awkwardness or social anxiety. She's living her life, and she's the most beautiful woman I've ever seen."

My irritation shifts into confusion tinged with flattery. Is Max saying I'm *beautiful*?

Max shrugs. "And, I guess, that's the moment I fell in love with her. I knew right then that my life depended on marrying Laurel Grant someday."

Gilbert shakes his head like he can't believe what he's heard. "That's the most romantic story I've ever heard, Max."

Darius sniffles. I give him a shocked look—after all, he knows this isn't real—but he looks at me helplessly and says, "What? It's a great story!"

"It really is," Holly murmurs.

My heart beats heavy in my chest. Apparently my heart, along with other vital parts of my body, is as traitorous as my family. I'm trying to remember who Max is and what he's like, but it's hard when he's looking at me like this. I know this is a game he's playing, one that I *asked* him to play, but what am I supposed to think when he's saying these words?

That I'm the most beautiful woman he's ever seen? What the hell?

Gilbert smiles. "You two make me believe in love again."

And then he takes another helping of potatoes. "You also make me believe in the power of a good meal with good people. Thank you so much for inviting me here tonight. This would've been a lonely holiday, so it means a lot to spend the evening with people I care about."

"Aw, Gilbert," I say. I mean, I do care about Gilbert, in a boss-employee way, but he literally just met the rest of my family, so perhaps he's laying it on a little thick. But I think that's his way, and I appreciate that he's comfortable here. "We're happy to have you, too."

"Seriously," Holly says. "I loved hearing about the entire first season of *FBI* while Laurel and Max were cooking."

"It's a good show," Gilbert says. "The cases are interesting, but it's the interpersonal drama that really gets you. You should watch it."

"Oh, I don't think I need to now," Holly says lightly. "You pretty much summarized every episode."

We eat dessert (apple pie that Holly, mercifully, baked before I got here), and Gilbert gets all bundled up to leave, which takes a while because he starts talking about an *FBI* spinoff called *FBI: Most Wanted*, and eventually I have to actually put his scarf on him myself and open the door.

"Thank you so much for coming, Gilbert," I say, smiling at him as I hold open the front door. "It was really fun having you here."

And, honestly . . . it *was* fun. I feel empowered after making a fancy dinner, even if I was under the guidance of two competent women from America's Test Kitchen. And even though Max got on my nerves, he was trying to help me. He made up that elaborate story about the terrible day we met, and while I wish he had left out a few of the real-life details (ahem, *Suck for a Buck* shirt), I'm grateful. He did exactly what I asked him to do: he sold it. He sold *us*.

But then I notice that Gilbert is looking out the door in horror, and so is everyone else. I turn slowly, like this is a scary movie and I'm about to come face-to-face with a serial killer.

What I find is much worse. I would rather see Michael Myers or Freddy Krueger or even the scary doll from *Child's Play*. This is a *blizzard*, snow falling hard and fast in snowflakes so big that they look like cotton balls. And through it all, I can barely make out the shape of what was once Gilbert's yellow sports car, now covered in thick, heavy snow.

"I guess we were having such a good time hearing your beautiful love story that we didn't notice how bad it had gotten," Gilbert says, peering past the porch. "Is my car even out there?"

"Can we play in the snow?" Noah asks, running outside without waiting for an answer.

"You don't have your snowsuit on!" Holly calls after him, but Lexie follows her twin outside. The two of them slide down the stairs, disappearing into what must be at least a foot of snow.

"I'm makin' a snow angel!" one of their little voices calls before dissolving into giggles.

"Bud," Darius says, clapping Gilbert on the back. "I don't think you're going anywhere tonight."

Chapter Ten

"THIS IS NOTHING we can't solve with a little elbow grease." I grab my coat off the hook by the door. "Come on, Gilbert. You get in and the rest of us will push."

"Laurel!" Holly says. The twins pelt each other with snowballs, laughing as they dive into the snow. "There's no way that car is getting out of the driveway."

"It can if we all work together," I say, my voice rising to a frantic pitch. "Once he gets to the highway, it will be smooth sailing."

"The highway is five miles away," Holly reminds me, shaking her head.

"Gilbert needs to get home, *sis*," I say, giving her wide eyes that will hopefully remind her of our mission. Gilbert cannot be here tonight. How am I supposed to keep this facade up? I did okay at dinner, but barely, and I know that if he's here overnight, that will only give me more chances to blow my cover, lose my job, and ruin my entire life.

That's what I try to communicate with one panicked glance, but Holly shakes her head again as if she's disappointed in me. "*Sis,* even if Gilbert could get out of our driveway—which, again, he can't—it would be incredibly dangerous to be on the road right now. Gilbert, that little toy doesn't have four-wheel drive, does it?"

Despite my panicked state, I almost laugh at Holly's derisive way of speaking about a sports car. For her, if it can't go off-road, it isn't even a vehicle.

Gilbert puts his hands on his hips and sighs. "Unfortunately, Holly, I can't say that it does. When I bought it yesterday, I was only thinking of my waning youth, not inclement weather."

I'm pretty sure Gilbert's youth waned a good twenty years ago. I crack my knuckles and grab Max by the elbow, pulling him down the steps. "Come on, lover. Help me out."

Max and I sink into the snow as we trudge to Gilbert's car. "*Lover* is taking it a little bit far. You sound like a mid-nineties SNL sketch."

"You're the one who made up a story about how you fell in love with me! Maybe you're the one who should be doing sketch comedy!" I snap as the wind whips snow into my face. I brush my hair out of my eyes.

"You told me to sell it!" Max shouts above the howl of the wind. "I thought I was doing what you wanted!"

"I did, and thank you. But I wasn't expecting you to be quite so creative," I say. "We both know that it was hate at first sight."

Max presses his lips together, and I remind myself to stop staring at his lips. "Right. We know that."

"Come on!" I shout at him. "Help me push this car."

I reach to open the door, but Max grabs my shoulders, pulling me close to him. "Laurel. Give it up."

Give *what* up? I can barely understand language when our faces are this close—even in this cold, I feel his breath in warm puffs on my cheeks. I really do need to take Jamilah up on her offer to set me up with one of her hot, single, civic-minded social worker friends when I get back to Columbus, because this is ridiculous. I can't be filled with lust when some random man grabs me by the shoulders in a snowstorm like he's the lead in a romance-action thriller or something. Snow falls in his ridiculously perfect black locks, and I fight the urge to reach up and brush it off. I imagine how his hair would feel on my fingertips—soft and smooth.

"What?" I ask in an exhale, the word barely audible.

"Gilbert isn't leaving tonight. It's too dangerous. Even if we could get his car out of the driveway, I looked at the weather on my phone, and we're in a level-three snow emergency. No one's allowed on the road, especially not a yellow sports car that would end up in a ditch the second it hit pavement."

He reaches out, seemingly without thinking, and brushes a finger across the tip of my nose. I rear back, shocked. "What are you doing?"

"A snowflake was right on the tip of your nose," he says. "I thought I'd . . . Never mind. I should've left it there."

"Maybe you should have. Maybe I wanted a snowflake on

my nose," I say, ignoring the way my cheeks blaze, even out here in the howling wind. I shake my head, letting some of the snow fly out of my hair, even as more of it falls every second.

"Someone could plow," I say hopefully.

Max directs me back toward the house as I sadly trudge through the snow. He puts an arm around me, which I appreciate because everyone's watching us, and we, apparently, need to sell this relationship for another night.

"Marge Jamison down the road has a plow, but this snow's gonna keep coming down, so she won't bother until it's over," he says.

I turn to face him. "How do you know about Marge Jamison and her snowplow?"

"I spend a lot of time here, Laurel," Max says without looking at me.

Holly herds the twins inside, and everyone else follows, so I lean closer to Max and whisper a warning. "Listen, I appreciate that you're helping me out, but I don't get what you're doing here. I know what you think about us, and Holly will find out eventually. You can't keep up a charade forever."

An expression of hurt flickers across his face, and I feel a quick twinge of regret from being too mean. But I know what I heard Max say, and I know that he doesn't even like Holly. I'm not sure what he's doing hanging around here so much, but he's clearly up to something.

We reach the front door, and Max holds it open for me, ever the gallant fake husband. I'm kicking the snow off my boots before going in when he leans in close to me. Too close.

"Laurel," he says, "there are a lot of things about me that would surprise you."

I freeze, unsure how to react. His mouth is mere inches from mine, and I can feel the heat radiating off his body. But before I can figure out what I'm supposed to do, he heads inside and shuts the door in my face, leaving me alone and confused on the porch.

Chapter Eleven

We had big plans to spend the rest of our evening doing what we call Christmas Cookie Dance Party. It's exactly what it sounds like. Holly rolls and cuts out the sugar cookies, made from Grandma Pat's special recipe (the sour cream and lemon zest make all the difference), and the twins and I frost them while scream-singing to my amazing playlist called, naturally, "Christmas Cookie Dance Party 4ever." Darius's job is to wander in after we're done, eat a few, and give out the award for best-decorated cookie. This tradition has only been going on for a few years, and in the beginning, the twins' efforts were amateurish at best, yet they consistently tie for first place. There's something suspicious about that.

Of course, there's a wrench named Gilbert thrown into our plan, which means that now I have to somehow roll and shape these cookies myself. Accuracy has never been my strong suit—I prefer the loosey-goosey creativity of decorating, where I can express myself through the medium of icing.

But with the Jackson 5 cranked up high enough and the enthusiasm coming from two kids who want nothing more than to eat entire bowls of frosting while my back is turned, I'm ready to do my best and help these kids sugar crash right before bedtime.

With me, Holly, the twins, Max, and Gilbert crammed into the kitchen (Darius stayed out so as to keep his anonymous judging fair), it's a bit crowded. It doesn't help that I'm feeling especially weird about being so close to Max, given the strange moment we shared outside just now. Is he mad at me? Did I hurt his feelings?

And most importantly, why do I care?

But this is nothing a little Christmas music can't fix. I press play on my phone and the opening of "Last Christmas," one of my favorite songs (Christmastime or not) starts playing. I sigh in relief. Something about this song, whether I hear it in my car or the grocery store or the aisles of TJ Maxx as I'm shopping for more discount holiday décor to give Holly, makes me feel like I'm home. And right now, I am. Okay, so it's not my home, and yes, there are a few extra people here, but it could be worse.

"A classic," Gilbert says as Max asks, "This song? Seriously?"

I whip around, looking at Max as if he injured a kitten instead of insulted George Michael. "Are you kidding me right now?"

Gilbert flinches in shock, and Holly gives me an almost imperceptible head twitch that translates to "check yourself, lady."

I give myself a quick shake. "Sorry, this is an argument we have every year."

"A lover's quarrel, would you call it?" Max looks at me, eyebrows raised.

Okay, so he's not too mad to keep playing along. "Exactly. You see, Max has terrible taste in music—"

"I have flawless taste," Max interrupts. "But I don't like the cheesy, overly commercialized schmaltz that makes my ears bleed—"

"Then don't go to Target in December, dude!" I shout. I can't help it; when people insult festive music from the 1980s, my claws come out. "These songs are a joy. No one's *making* you listen to Christmas music."

Max points to my phone, his mouth a flat line. "My own wife is forcing me."

Right. His wife. I smile at him. "Well, the kids love it, so we'll keep it on."

"I want 'Feliz Navidad'!" Lexie shouts. "On repeat!"

"No, 'Grandma Got Run Over by a Reindeer'!" Noah yells. "On repeat!"

I forgot about the twins' obsession with listening to songs on repeat. At best, it's harmless, and at worst, it means you spend two hours listening to the *Wild Kratts* theme song until you slowly lose your sanity and then come full circle and decide it's actually the greatest song ever written and recorded. But this sounds like the perfect thing to truly drive Max to the brink. Maybe it will even convince him to leave. Sure, it's basically impassable outdoors, but Marge Jamison might welcome his bad attitude with open arms.

"Okay, I'll add both those songs to a playlist and put them on repeat," I say, and I can feel Max's shoulders slump.

"I love Christmas music," Gilbert says, holding the steaming mug of hot chocolate that Holly made him. "Charlene and I always listen to the Carpenters while we open gifts." He pauses. "Well, we did."

His lip begins a telltale tremble, and I ask, "Gilbert, do you want to roll out the dough?"

He brightens. "Are you sure you trust me with such an important task?"

Max chuckles. "Oh, I'm sure you'll be even better at baking than Laurel."

I'm rising above this. "Feliz Navidad" is playing, and I'm feeling *tons* of felicidad. "I have complete confidence in your dough-rolling abilities. Here, I'll get you set up on the counter."

Holly has already floured the countertop and put out the rolling pin, so we're good to go. I let Gilbert go to town with the rolling pin and turn around to find that Holly has put bowls of colorful icing on the table.

"You're a miracle worker," I whisper over the sound of festive guitar music. Gilbert's very focused on the rolling pin as he sings along to "Feliz Navidad," so he doesn't notice our conversation.

"I'm stealthy," she whispers back, wiggling her eyebrows.

We cycle through our two-song playlist as the kids use the cookie cutters we've had since I was a kid—a candy cane, a Santa, a bell, a tree, a snowman. When the first tray is out of the oven, it's my time to shine.

"Try to keep them, you know, *normal* this year." Holly eyes me skeptically.

"You're jealous because my Sexy Santa was so evocative last year," I say, focusing on my current masterpiece.

"That's one way to put it," Holly mutters, working on a Christmas tree that will no doubt look like it belongs in the pages of *Martha Stewart Living* when it's done.

"Sexy Santa?" Max asks.

"She made Santa a tiny red bikini," Holly says wearily.

"I think maybe the guy gets tired of wearing that big, heavy red suit all the time. Surely he wants to relax on a beach sometimes, right?" I ask.

"Are there beaches in the North Pole?" Lexie asks, eyes wide.

"Cold ones," Max answers.

"You're telling me Santa can't take a week off after the rush of a busy holiday season? Whatever. Santa's going to Maui like Grandma and Papa." I frown and brush extra frosting off my snowman's face.

And then it's quiet as we all work, the only sound coming from the song's lyrics about grandma and her unfortunate run-in with the reindeer. The twins dump sprinkles on many cookies that are covered in uneven lumps of frosting. I watch skeptically as Max finds them another container of sprinkles after they empty the first one. I don't know what's happening with Gilbert's cookie, but he inspects it, adds more frosting, then inspects it again, as if he's Bob Ross and it's his canvas.

When I look at Max, he's looking back at me, his mouth quirked up in an uncharacteristic smile.

I shrug and widen my eyes, the universal gesture for: *Why are you staring at me, you weirdo?*

"You were really concentrating," he murmurs.

The kitchen is toasty warm, but a shiver still runs up my

spine when his voice lowers. A man this exasperating shouldn't be allowed to sound this good.

"You were even sticking out your tongue a little," he adds, and I frown.

"Quit making fun of me," I say, finishing my cookie and starting on another one. "You won't be laughing when my cookie wins."

"Remind me what the prize is again?" Max asks, dipping his knife into more frosting as the twins squabble over who gets to frost the last star.

"Respect. Dignity. Pride."

"So . . . nothing. You're getting this worked up about nothing."

I place my knife on the table and inhale deeply, turning to look at him.

He rubs his neck, that infuriating gesture again. "I'm just saying, it seems kind of silly."

"One could say the same thing about most Christmas traditions, and yet we still do them," I say, forcing myself to remain calm.

"One does say that." He points to his chest. "And not everyone does them."

"This must be why you're such a good match," Gilbert says, and I sit up straight, vowing to turn down the argumentative side that rears its head whenever Max insults my favorite holiday. "Max, you have Laurel around to make sure you don't live in a bleak, joyless bachelor den."

"Thank you, Gilbert," I say, brushing my hair out of my face. "I think that's exactly what I bring to our relationship.

A vivacity to liven up Max's otherwise sad existence. A joie de vivre that counteracts his naturally surly tendencies. A—"

"You have frosting in your hair," Max says, leaning over and tugging on a blond lock.

"Thanks," I say with more sugary sweetness than the frosting.

"And what do you think I bring to the table, sweetheart?" Max asks.

"The ability to notice when I have frosting in my hair, of course."

"Wait," Max says, lifting my hand to get a better view of my cookie. "What is this?"

"Evil snowman. Duh." I hold my cookie up for everyone at the table to see. "Red Hots for glowing evil eyes. Sprinkle fangs and angry eyebrows. A general air of maliciousness."

Max's fingers brush mine as he takes the cookie from my hand and holds it up beside his face. I can't deny that I did give the cookie glasses and voluminous dark hair.

"It's a Max cookie!" Lexie says.

"It sure is," Max says.

"The resemblance is purely coincidental." I ignore Holly's laugh.

"I couldn't decide how I wanted my star to look," Gilbert says, holding up a star cookie that has a little bit of each frosting color, all smushed together and then covered in every kind of sprinkle we have. "So I did what I'm calling a Christmas medley."

"I made a Christmas tree," Holly says, holding up a tree-shaped cookie on which she somehow made picture-perfect ornaments and even a shiny, glittering star at the top.

"We worked together on a candy cane," Lexie says, holding up a blue-and-green candy cane that one of them already took a bite out of.

"I love it!" I say. "The bite mark adds some excitement. What about you, Max?"

Max holds up a snowflake that he's frosting entirely in gray. "This snowflake. Black like my cold, dead heart."

I squint. "I'd say that's more of a gray."

He sighs. "Surprisingly hard to make black out of the colors we already have here."

I can't help myself—I laugh. Sure, he subverted the spirit of Christmas Cookie Dance Party by making what might be the most depressing cookie I've ever seen, but he *did* put in an effort. And as someone who made an evil snowman, I can't really judge him.

My phone buzzes: a text from Doug.

We've got HELLA SNOW you guys!!! Will try to make it tomorrow night as planned but might be stuck here.

Followed by the poop emoji. At least that one makes sense . . . it *is* crappy to think my brother might not be here to help us have a traditional-ish Grant family Christmas.

Holly looks at her phone and murmurs, "There's no way he's making it here."

The ski lodge is only a couple of hours away from here—it may surprise people from out of state, but you can ski in Ohio. We may not have any major mountains, but we have large hills, and if you don't want to get on a plane, they'll do.

In fact, that would be a great slogan for Ohio: It Might Not Be Ideal, but We'll Make It Work.

"I think he'll get here," I say with determined optimism. Holly glances out the window into the darkness and shakes her head.

Now that we've all chosen the cookie we want to enter in the contest, we lay them out in a row on the table, *Great British Bake Off* style. Darius is our Paul Hollywood, but without the piercing blue eyes or the constant comments about soggy bottoms.

Darius comes in, rubbing his hands together. "Oh, we've got 'Feliz Navidad' going? I love this song."

Max narrows his eyes. "Come on, man."

Darius shrugs, unbothered. "It's a classic for a reason."

"Thank you," I say. "This song brings joy to all our hearts and minds."

"All right," Darius says, focusing himself on the task at hand. He walks back and forth, inspecting the cookies. He smiles at Max's depression snowflake and pauses at my evil snowman. He picks up Holly's Christmas tree and says, "While this cookie does not win first place, it does win the coveted award for Decorated by the Most Beautiful, Talented Wife."

Holly does a dramatic fancy bow, and I frown. "Um, how do you know that one wasn't mine?"

Darius gives me a skeptical look. "Did you make this artistic Christmas tree?"

I shake a finger at him. "This is supposed to be anonymous judging. Please follow protocol."

He rolls his eyes good-naturedly. "Okay, the winner is . . . drumroll please . . ."

All of us except Max lean over the table and do a drumroll with our hands. "Oh, I love this anticipation!" Gilbert whispers, a look of glee on his face as he drums.

"This star!" Darius says, holding up Gilbert's cookie.

Gilbert gasps. "My Christmas medley!"

Darius's mouth drops open. "Oh, dude . . . this is yours? I thought . . . I thought this was from one of the twins."

Gilbert takes the cookie out of Darius's hand and faces all of us. "I just want to say . . . thank you for believing in me and my cookie-decorating abilities."

"I didn't know this was a speech situation," Max says in a low voice so that only I can hear.

"It isn't usually, but I want to let this play out," I whisper, shushing him.

"Thank you to Laurel for including me, and to Holly for creating a beautiful cookie that inspired us all."

Holly gives him a salute.

"And thank you to everyone else who was nominated for pushing me to do my best work," Gilbert says, looking each of us in the eye. The twins, who seemed confused at first that they didn't win, have turned their attention to scooping out the leftover frosting with their hands.

"This tastes so good," Noah moans.

"Congratulations, Gilbert," Max says, leading us in a round of applause. Gilbert bows and wipes a tear from his eyes, and I'm glad he's crying about something other than Charlene right now.

I clear my throat. "Now that the decorating and judging are done, it's time for the best part of the Christmas Cookie Dance Party . . ."

I grab my phone, pausing "Grandma Got Run Over by a Reindeer."

"Thank God," Max mutters.

"Oh, babe, now you won't know how it ends," I say, feigning sympathy. "Do you want me to put it back on?"

"I've heard it at least ten times since we started the cookies," Max assures me. "I get the gist."

"Their grandma gets smushed by the reindeers," Noah says matter-of-factly.

Max points at Noah. "See? We all know the story."

I ignore him and press Play, and then the first beautiful notes of "All I Want for Christmas Is You" fill the room. From across the table, Holly reaches out a hand, and I reach mine back. As we lace our fingers together, we both do our best low-voiced Mariah (still an effort, but much easier than a high-voiced Mariah) as we sing "I-i-i-i-i . . ."

"What's happening?" Max looks at us uneasily.

"Please don't interrupt us," I say in between breaths. And then the fast, staccato piano starts, and all of us dance, the twins high on pure sugar and the promise of a late bedtime.

Well, all of us except for Max, who simply raises his eyebrows and walks out of the kitchen.

"What's wrong with him?" Gilbert asks, doing some very interesting footwork.

"He doesn't like Mariah," I say, and when Gilbert responds with openmouthed shock, I say, "I *know*. What's this dance move?"

"The mashed potato," Gilbert says. "I've gotta be careful because I once broke my big toe mashed potato-ing too enthusiastically at a tiki bar in rural Kentucky, but I can't help myself! I hear music, and my legs start mashing!"

"There's so much to unpack in that sentence!" I shout back as Mariah hits some truly impressive high notes.

"A story for another time, I guess!" Gilbert says, already out of breath.

The twins try to copy his dance move, giggling so hard they almost fall over, but I look toward the swinging door. Where did Max go? And why is he physically unable to remain in the room when anyone's having the slightest amount of fun? Would it really be so hard to stay in here with the rest of us and belt out the lyrics we all know by heart? Even Darius is bobbing his head as he chows down on a cookie.

Sure, Max may have majorly helped me out tonight, and he may have somehow ingratiated himself into my family despite his open dislike of Mariah Carey. But that doesn't change the fact that he's one big gray, depressing snowflake, and I can't believe I have to spend another evening with him.

Chapter Twelve

ONE THING I didn't consider when I found out Gilbert would be staying overnight here: we'd *all* be staying overnight, which meant we'd all be keeping up this ridiculous ruse. Which means, you guessed it—Max and I are sharing a room because we're a normal, crazy-about-each-other married couple.

However, I push that thought out of my mind and focus on what we're doing now: giving Gilbert a tour of his room. Since the guest room is occupied by Max and me, Gilbert is setting up camp on an inflatable mattress in Darius's LEGO room. "Some men have a man cave," Holly once told me. "Darius has a LEGO lair."

Holly stays downstairs with the twins—after all, she's seen it all before—as Darius, Max, and I show Gilbert around. I'm hoping Darius can handle most of the questions, given that I have no idea what anything in here is.

It's not that Darius doesn't care about farming—he does

as much work as Holly, and on at least one occasion I've heard him refer to the goats as his *fur babies.* But running a working farm is Holly's passion. Darius's passion is creating elaborate buildings, animals, and occasionally sitcom sets (he loves his *Friends* LEGO) out of bricks.

The walls of the LEGO lair are lined with floor-to-ceiling shelving, most of it open but some of it behind glass—you know, for the really intricate sets that he doesn't want the twins to get their grubby little hands on.

I haven't spent much time in the LEGO lair, mostly because my brain is incapable of understanding LEGO instructions, and because the one time I attempted to work with Darius as his sous-builder on the Great Pyramid of Giza, I screwed things up so royally that even unflappable Darius sent me away. But now, as I walk around and inspect the sets in his glass cases, I'm impressed.

"Whoa," I say, pointing to the Death Star from *Star Wars* that sits by itself on a stand. "I didn't know you finished this."

"You don't remember?" Max asks, shooting me a reminder with his eyes.

"Oh, right." I smack myself on the forehead. "How could I forget all those late nights and weekends? The Death Star became your life."

Max scoffs. "Well, yeah. Do you have any idea how much that set costs?"

I blink a few times. I thought Max was pretending to be a LEGO fanatic to maintain my lie, but he sounds like he knows what he's talking about. Is he a brick bro, too?

"No," I say slowly. "How much of our savings did you spend on this set?"

"Oh," Gilbert says, shaking his head. "Money problems. Charlene and I had a few, too. I wanted to spend our tax refund on a bearded dragon habitat. She wanted to spend it on a new dining room table. We could *not* meet in the middle."

"So . . . what happened?" Max asks, looking genuinely interested.

Gilbert sighs. "We went for the table. Honestly, she was probably right, but I would've been happy eating dinner on our laps while watching our bearded dragon enjoy his home."

Darius nods as if he understands. "Who wouldn't?"

"I guess that's the only upside to this whole situation," Gilbert says, a thread of hope in his voice. "No one can stop me from getting a bearded dragon now. Anyway, what's this one?"

He points to an enormous castle, protected in the case. It has a drawbridge, a moat, and a very ornate dragon that's breathing fire toward a group of knights.

"Oh, we designed that one ourselves," Max says, his tone unfamiliar. I think it's pride—something I've never heard from him before. Condescension, yes. Unflattering words about seasonal décor, of course. But pride? Not so much.

"You and Laurel?" Gilbert asks, his finger toggling between us.

Max and Darius laugh. "No, Laurel couldn't be less interested in LEGO," Max says, shaking his head.

"Not true," I butt in. "I could actually be a lot less interested."

"Darius and me," Max clarifies. "LEGO has been our thing since we were kids. We took a brief break when we went through our dark ages, but then we got back into it."

"Wait," I interrupt. "Did you say . . . dark ages?"

Max pauses and looks away for a moment, as if realizing he's said too much. "Yes. Dark ages."

"And what does that mean?" Gilbert asks, a hand propped under his chin.

Max sighs and looks as if he's weighing whether he should continue. But he doesn't need to because, as usual, Darius is all too happy to discuss LEGO with anyone at any time.

"A lot of LEGO users quit building when they hit their teenage years. There are other things to capture their interests—sports, school—"

"Girls." I wiggle my eyebrows.

Darius nods sagely, but Max shakes his head. "Not a big issue for some of us. Darius maybe, but I didn't date much in high school. Or college."

I smack him on the arm. "No need to recount how pathetic your romantic life was before you met me. I know all this."

"Anyway," Darius continues. "A lot of people find their way back to LEGO as adults, and those in-between years when they didn't build are called their dark ages."

"Wow," I say slowly.

"Wow is right!" Gilbert says brightly. "I am fascinated by all this. So, do grown-up LEGO enthusiasts have a name?"

I look at Max expectantly, and he scowls as he realizes how much joy this is bringing me.

"Oh, of course!" Darius says. "On the forums, we're referred to as AFOLs. Adult fans of LEGO."

"On the forums," I repeat.

"The BrickLink forums," Darius clarifies.

"This is a whole world I knew nothing about!" Gilbert says. "Honestly, this might be better than a bearded dragon habitat."

"Certainly not as smelly," I add.

Darius points to the castle behind the glass. "There are a lot of LEGO castles out there, but Max and I wanted to make our own because they were always our favorite when we were kids. So we made this one with all of our favorite things—a library for Max, and a goat pen for me because I love goats."

"Aw, cute," I say, leaning forward. I hadn't even noticed the little LEGO goats grazing behind the castle.

"The goats are very rare, you know," Max leans over and tells me, as if he can't help himself from pointing this out.

"Do you help Max and Laurel out with the goats a lot?" Gilbert asks, inspecting the tiny animals.

Darius shoots me a panicked look.

"He sure does! In fact, you might say he knows even more about goats than I do," I say.

"I'm a goat aficionado," Darius says, "not a professional."

I gesture at him to change the subject.

"And," he says, his voice changing from panic to excitement, "we made these guys to represent us."

He points to the top of the castle, where two knights stand on a tower, facing down the dragon. A Black LEGO man smiles as he raises his sword, while a white LEGO man with glasses sports a grimace and holds up a bow and arrow.

"I'm the Black one with the sweet sword," Darius helpfully points out.

"And I'm the one who looks like he's about to run back to the library," Max says flatly.

"I think we would've figured it out without the clarification," I say, leaning in to get a closer look. "Why does Darius have a sword and you have a bow and arrow?"

"Uh, because bow and arrows are cool?" Max says.

"This is amazing," Gilbert says. "Maybe instead of the bearded dragon I'll get into LEGO."

"Come on, sweetie," Max says, grabbing my arm firmly. (His grip is stronger than I imagined . . . not that I spent much time imagining his warm hands on me.) "Let's let Gilbert get situated and get the kids ready for bed."

"Why would we get the kids ready—" I start saying as Max pulls me out the door and Darius tells Gilbert all about how he can create his own custom LEGO minifigure.

"Because we do bedtime stories every night with them," Max says.

"Wow," I say now that we're out of Gilbert's earshot. "Deception is very difficult for me. I can't keep this lie straight."

Max chuckles wryly. "Yeah, I can tell."

"I had no idea you were an AFOL," I say as Max lets out a groan.

"You're never going to let this go, are you?" he asks.

I think about it for a second, pausing outside the guest bedroom door. "No. I'm not. On my deathbed, I'm gonna be like, 'And then I found out the nonLEGO years were called the dark ages.'"

"Okay," Max says, but while he might be slightly irritated, there's a hint of a smile on that infuriating face. "I get it. I'm a nerd. I have a hobby that you clearly think is ridiculous."

I stop pretending I'm on my deathbed and frown. "I don't think it's ridiculous."

"Don't start taking my feelings into account now."

"Oh, please. I would never care about your feelings. You know that." I grab his arm. "But I don't want you to think I'm some sort of hobby snob. I mean, yes, the acronyms are hilariously specific, but I think it's really nice that you and Darius have something you can bond over that isn't, like, going to a strip club or gambling."

Max raises his eyebrows. "What kind of men do you normally hang out with?"

"Bad ones!" I say forcefully. "I thought we'd established this!"

Max takes me in for a moment, and I can feel his eyes sweeping over my face as we stand in the hallway next to a framed photo of the twins at Halloween. Even though I can hear Gilbert and Darius down the hall, still discussing LEGO ("Do they make a bearded dragon LEGO?" Gilbert asks), my stomach does a little flip-flop as I register that Max is close, and he's warm, and my hand is still on his arm.

And then Max clears his throat, and I pull my hand back as if I touched a hot cookie sheet.

But things go from awkward to worse when I yank open the bedroom door and the two of us see the full-size bed. Somehow, even though I logically knew we'd be sharing a room and pretending to be a married couple, my brain blanked on the fact that we'd have to share a bed. I think it may have been protecting me from the trauma.

"I'll sleep on the floor," I volunteer immediately.

Max groans. "You're not sleeping on the floor. Don't be dramatic."

"Oh, sorry," I say, unzipping the duffel bag I threw in the

corner earlier, when I was young and full of hope that by this evening I'd be done with my elaborate ruse. "I forgot you were the only one who's allowed to be dramatic."

"When am I dramatic?" Max asks, arms crossed.

"Um, making up a story about how we met? Making a gray Christmas cookie like you're a disaffected teen wandering the aisles of Hot Topic in 2005? Leaving the room in a huff during the all-important Mariah Carey portion of Christmas Cookie Dance Party?"

Max frowns. "Okay, well, first of all, the story of how we met wasn't even made up."

"You know what I mean. You embellished the story a bit."

Max reaches up again to rub the back of his neck. He's probably quite tense from a long day of being himself. "Right. Well, I thought you'd find the gray Christmas cookie funny."

"Sure, because you're known for your warm sense of humor," I say, but pause when I see the look on his face. "Wait, you were *trying* to be funny?"

"Yes, Laurel," he says, shaking his head. "I thought it would make you laugh because you're always complaining about how grumpy I am."

I'm strangely touched by this, even though the idea confuses me. After this holiday from hell is over, we're hopefully going to go back to rarely seeing each other, so I don't know why he cares about making me laugh.

"That doesn't explain leaving the room for Mariah Carey."

"There was dancing," Max says.

"Yes. It's not called Christmas Cookie Stand Around and Mope Party."

"I don't dance."

I crinkle my nose. "You mean . . . ever?"

He shakes his head slowly. "Not if I can help it."

"How often are you in situations where you can't help it?" I ask. "Do you often get forced to do the hustle at gunpoint?"

"Holly and Darius's wedding," Max says. "I had to dance with you."

And then, I remember. With everything else he did that day, I'd forgotten that, after Holly and Darius's dance to "Let's Stay Together," the entire bridal party joined the floor to dance to "At Last." I blocked out most of my memory of that dance so I could avoid tainting a perfectly romantic song, but as I think about it now, I do remember Max's stiff posture. The way he wouldn't look at me. The way it seemed like he was in another room, even though he was right in front of me, his hands on my hips, mine on his shoulder, slowly shuffling in a circle like this was a high school dance but even more awkward.

"Oh, yeah," I say. "You hated that."

"I hated that," he confirms.

"Well, I'm sorry you had to dance with me. You may not remember because you hightailed it off the dance floor as soon as Etta sang her last note, but right after that, the DJ played 'Everybody (Backstreet's Back),' and Holly and I performed a dance we choreographed in elementary school. I had fun, anyway."

Max focuses on my face now. "Laurel, I'm telling you the truth. It's not you, it's the dancing. I don't like it."

"At all?"

"Nope."

"Not even by yourself?"

He looks at me as if I've suggested dancing naked in the snow. "Why would I dance by myself?"

My mouth drops open. "Uh, because Carly Rae Jepsen released a new single and you want to express your joy through movement?"

A small smile plays across his lips. "Does that happen a lot?"

"Not often enough, if you ask me."

"I don't have any sort of rhythm. And I don't like people looking at me. It feels like they're judging me."

"There's a whole clichéd saying about this. *Dance like no one's watching.* Because no one is!"

"Yeah, I think I've seen that on a refrigerator magnet somewhere. Possibly in this home."

"Just dance! That's what Lady Gaga says."

"I get it," Max says. "Popular music will not rest until I've danced. But no matter what Lady Gaga says, I don't like it."

We watch each other from across the room, me in the corner with my duffel bag and him on the other side of the bed. There might be more to Max than I suspected back when we walked down the aisle together. He may be uptight and no fun, but he's struggling with that, too. I'm not the only one who's bothered by his inability to let loose.

"I'm gonna go find Darius and get some pajamas," Max says. But before he leaves the room, he stops in the doorway. "This wasn't my idea, you know."

"What wasn't your idea?" I ask.

"Sharing a room. I was supposed to sleep in the LEGO lair."

I frown. "You were planning on spending the night here? On Christmas Eve Eve?"

He lets out a sharp exhale that sounds almost like a laugh. "Why do you keep saying Christmas Eve Eve like it's a real holiday? It's not federally recognized. It's, like, your family and Phoebe from *Friends*."

"I'm surprised you're familiar with *Friends*, given its joke-based format," I say, folding my pajama pants in my hands.

"I'm in my thirties. I absorbed *Friends* into my bloodstream without even trying. There are memes, Laurel."

I nod. "Okay, fair. But don't worry. I didn't assume you were trying to share a room with me. I know you don't want to spend any time with me at all, whether sleeping or waking."

"Why do you keep—" Max starts, but I cut him off.

"Wait, why do you need to borrow pajamas from Darius if you planned on spending the night here?" I ask, the gears slowly cranking in my head.

"I don't think we need to talk about this," Max says.

"Shouldn't you already have pajamas?" I ask.

"Because normally I sleep in boxers," Max says quickly, his face red. "But I'm sharing a bed with you, so . . . that's not going to work tonight."

I wish this was a fact I didn't know, because now the mental image of Max sleeping next to me wearing only a pair of boxers is in my head, and I fear I'm not going to forget it for a long time. In fact, it may torture me for all of my days. Why does Max have to be so hot?

"Are you happy now?" he asks, talking to the quilt on the bed instead of looking at me.

"No! Of course not!" I shout. "Go get your pajamas! I

want to go to bed and end this day before any other unforeseen disasters or weather events happen."

Max stares at me for a long time before stepping into the hallway, and I make my way to the en suite guest bath. I change into my very cute pajamas that include tiny shorts covered in unicorns (I didn't anticipate sharing a bed with my nemesis when I packed these), brush my teeth, pull my hair into the world's spikiest ponytail, and take off my makeup. If this was a real sleepover with a real guy, I'd keep the makeup on, clogged pores be damned. I love to make men think my eyelashes are naturally dark, long, and curled, for no real reason other than that it's fun to fool them. But this is Max. Who cares if he sees the naturally ghostly pallor of my skin or my short, almost invisible eyelashes? What's he going to do, like me *less*?

But when I come out of the bathroom, Noah and Lexie are sitting on the bed, nestled under the blankets. Holly pops her head in.

"Hey," she whispers, pointing to the kids. "They need a bedtime story, and it would look strange if I was reading them one."

"Okay," I agree. "I love reading to them. But is Gilbert really going to know?"

Holly widens her eyes. "He's already come out of his room twice. Once to ask if the house is haunted, and a second time to ask Darius to remove the *Stranger Things* LEGO because it was scaring him."

I stifle a laugh. "So what's on the docket?"

"Uncle Max said he bought us a new book," Lexie says.

My face involuntarily screws up into a "what the hell" expression. "*Uncle* Max? He's not your uncle."

"Thanks so much," Max says gruffly from behind me, shuffling into the room.

It takes me a moment to realize that he's shuffling because he's wearing pajama pants that are much too large. I wouldn't describe Max as small—he's tall and he has those infuriatingly broad shoulders—but he and Darius have very different builds. Darius is more "a dad who has a home gym in his basement and also spends all day hauling heavy items around a farm."

Also, apparently, Darius sleeps in a T-shirt that says "Best Wife Ever" with an arrow pointing to the left. At this point, I'm not sure that Holly and Darius own anything that isn't covered in a quote. Maybe they should hang out more with Gilbert; they all share a love of quote-based merchandise.

"I'm going to sleep on this side," Max says, pointing to the right side of the bed. "That way this arrow will not be pointing toward you."

"It will if you sleep on your stomach," I point out.

"I'm going to sleep on my back, hands folded on my chest like a vampire, like always," Max says, and I can't help myself—I laugh.

The twins laugh, too, even though they once got scared by a Halloween episode of *Sesame Street*, so I seriously doubt Holly and Darius are keeping them informed about vampire lore.

"What story did you bring this time?" Noah asks, climbing onto Max's lap as he sits down on the bed.

This time? Does Max have a habit of reading stories to my niece and nephew? I kind of thought that was my thing.

Max reaches into his bag. "*Katy and the Big Snow.* Have you guys read this one?"

They shake their heads, but I say, "Yes. Holly and I used to love this story." I'd forgotten all about it, but seeing that blue-and-red cover shoots a sharp arrow of memory straight through my heart. I remember snuggling with Grandma Pat, Holly on one side of her and me on the other, the three of us on the mauve couch that always had at least one crocheted blanket tossed over the back. (Even back then, Doug couldn't sit still long enough to listen to a story.) I see her wrinkled fingers flipping the pages, and a visceral feeling of comfort washes over me. I am five and I am safe and my grandma is reading a story.

I lie down on the left side of the bed, my head propped up on a Santa Claus pillow (seriously, is Holly keeping the entire decorative holiday pillow business afloat?), and listen as Max reads to the twins. He has, as I've been forced to admit to myself many times already, a very nice reading voice. Sometimes I listen to celebrities reading me bedtime stories on the Calm app to fall asleep, but right now I'm thinking I'd really prefer to hear Max read *Katy and the Big Snow*. Honestly, the man should get into the audiobook business. People would drop some serious coin to listen to that voice read a steamy romance novel.

The twins are enthralled, the way they always are by books and anything that delays bedtime, so the room is silent other than Max's words. I feel so comfortable, so warm, so at home, and the next thing I know, I'm jostled awake by the bed moving.

I open my eyes and see Max sliding into bed beside me in the dark. "What's going on?" I ask, sitting up.

Max stops moving, one leg under the quilt. "Sorry. I tried not to wake you up."

I shake my head, confused. I'm still on top of the blankets, and I think I drooled on the pillow a little bit. "Where are the kids?"

"I put them to bed," Max says, sliding under the blankets.

"What—Why . . ." I stammer. I've never been someone who wakes up in the morning prepared to have a lucid conversation about breakfast. I tend to wake up confused, still half dreaming. My family often tells a story about a time that a fire alarm went off in our hotel when we were on vacation, and while they were all panicking and throwing on clothes and shoes so they could rush out the door, I sleepily got up, went into the bathroom, and turned on the shower.

And right now, Max beside me in bed seems like one big confusing hallucination. A fire alarm *in my soul.*

"Here." Max stands up again and leans over the bed, yanking the blankets down. "Get under the covers."

I'm too tired to argue, so I do what I'm told. "Do you wish I was this compliant during the day?" I ask.

The moonlight coming through the window illuminates Max's smile. I can't help feeling like that smile is there against his will, like there's something about me that makes him smile even when he doesn't want to. "No. I like you the way you are."

Now I know I must be dreaming, because there's no way Can't Relax Max likes anything about me. He tucks the blankets up around my chin. "Snug as a bug in a rug," I mutter, and he laughs. As he slides into bed beside me, I wonder if maybe this bedroom, this bed, has taken us into an alternate universe. One where Max and I can coexist peacefully, one where his presence beside me is warm and welcoming and helpful, not judgmental and rude.

But, of course, I know what Max thinks about Holly and, by extension, the entire Grant family, including me. I can't let this moment go on, can't keep feeling that Max might be *fond* of me and that he might be starting to grow on me, too. So I ruin our unspoken truce by opening my big mouth.

"I know how you feel about Holly."

Max lifts his head off the pillow. "What?"

"I know what you said," I tell him. "At the wedding."

"At the . . ." He trails off, and even in the darkness, I can see it when the realization hits his face. The lit-up snow globe plug-in from Bath & Body Works that's pumping Winter Candy Apple scent through the air illuminates enough of his face that I can see the emotions flicker past—shock, acceptance, irritation—before landing on regret.

"Can I please tell you what happened?" he asks, but I don't need him to, because I was there.

Chapter Thirteen

IT WAS ALMOST time for the ceremony to start, and I was performing all the typical maid-of-honor duties—touching up Holly's makeup, making sure she ate a few mini bagels, placing a napkin under her chin every time she sipped juice so it wouldn't spill on her dress, and providing tissues whenever she got teary-eyed thinking about her beautiful future with Darius. Everything was going according to plan.

The wedding planner asked me to find Darius and tell him we were ready for the guys to take their places. I've wished a million times since then that I'd simply sent him a quick text, but I decided to go tell him in person. I loved Darius, and I wanted to congratulate him in person for getting to marry the best person in the world—my sister.

And so I ran down the back stairs of the church to the guys' prep room, which was shoved way down in the basement where he'd have no chance of accidentally running into Holly. But as I rounded the corner, I saw him and Max standing in the hallway, Darius leaning up against an old drinking fountain. They didn't hear me because I was wearing the pink fluffy slippers I bought for all the bridesmaids. Something about the way they were standing made me hesitate—I leaned back into the stairwell before they saw me.

"Trust me," Darius said as I peeked my head around the wall. "I know what I'm doing here. I'm marrying Holly because I love her and I want to spend the rest of my life with her. You'll understand someday."

Max let out a short laugh, one so bitter that I reared back. Up until now, my experience with Max had been decidedly unfavorable, but I thought that meant he was merely another man on the long list of people I'm not compatible with. But this was the laugh of someone cruel, the laugh of someone about to say something expressly designed to hurt feelings.

"Give me a break," he said, shaking his head as if Darius were simply a misguided child. "Love has nothing to do with it. It's not too late to change your mind . . . If you want to get out of here, say the word. I'll drive."

I couldn't believe it. Max—Can't Relax Max—was saying this about someone as perfect, as beautiful, as lovely and talented and funny as Holly? I watched the two of them there in their white button-downs and vests, their arms crossed as they kept talking—I couldn't hear what they said because the sound of my own pumping blood rushed through my ears. My eyes filled with angry tears, but I blinked them away, then tiptoed back up the stairs and ran down as loudly as I could. "Hey, groom! We're ready for you guys to take your places!" I called out cheerily, not even focusing on their faces before I ran back upstairs, my fluffy slippers tripping me as I made my way back to Holly. I had to tell her what had happened. I had to tell her there was a traitor in our midst, someone who might object in the middle of the ceremony, someone she couldn't trust.

I didn't need to hear Darius respond to Max's suggestion that he leave my sister at the altar, because I knew he'd never do such a thing. He loved Holly more than anything in the whole world, and I could see it in every interaction they had, in the way he looked at her every time they were together. As for Max . . . well, if he wanted to be an asshole so cartoonish that he'd attempt to ruin a happy relationship, then I was all too glad to do whatever I could to make sure we never saw him again. I'd write him out of this wedding and our lives.

But when I burst into the room, out of breath and on the verge of tears, Holly turned away from the mirror and looked at me expectantly.

"How was he doing?" she asked, her nerves apparent in her shaky voice. "Did he look good? Did he look ready?"

Holly could never know about this, I realized. I wouldn't be the person to ruin her perfect wedding, one of the best days of her entire life.

"He looked ready," I told her honestly, and I promised myself that I'd do whatever it took to make sure Max didn't mess anything up. I watched him during the ceremony, prepared to full-body tackle him if he tried to say anything, but he never did. He stood there, face impassive as a really grumpy statue, and didn't say a single word.

I got through the rest of the day with him—his refusal to be fun, his belief that he was too good to hit the dance floor, the fact that he clearly didn't think I was cool enough to hang out with—because it was for Holly, but as Holly and Darius drove off that evening, clanging cans trailing behind their Honda, I knew I'd never see Max Beckett again if I could help it.

"There's nothing you could tell me that would ever make up for what you said," I say now, and I mean it. What explanation could he possibly have? He started a new medication that had the unfortunate side effect of making him hate my sister? I walked into a one-act play about a wedding that he and Darius were rehearsing? Unlikely.

"I really think," he continues in his level, logical Max voice, "that if I could tell you why I said that, you'd understand."

"Understand?" I sit straight up in bed, like I'm a vampire hopping out of a coffin in a terrifying automated Halloween lawn decoration. "You think there's something you could say that would make me understand why you tried to get Darius to leave Holly at the altar?"

"Okay." He deflates. "Maybe not understand, but . . . forgive me."

He says the last part so quietly that I can barely hear him, especially because my own anger roars through my head. "I will never forgive you. You wanted my sister to live out the worst scene from any number of movies. You wanted her to be Adam Sandler in *The Wedding Singer*. Jilted. I don't care what your reasoning was. You wanted to ruin Holly's life, so, no, I won't ever forgive you."

Max doesn't say anything as I lie back down, turning

away from him to face the bedroom door. I pull out my Air-Pods and open the Calm app—if I'm going to get back to sleep tonight after that spike of adrenaline, I'm going to need the most soothing meditation the app offers.

"Unfortunately for you," I say as I scroll through the sleep stories, "Darius loves Holly way too much to listen to you."

I press Play and pinch my eyes closed, willing the words to lull me to sleep, or to any imaginary world where I can pretend I'm not right beside my nemesis.

"I know," Max says. "I know he loves Holly, and I'm glad he does. And Laurel . . . I can't tell you how sorry I am that I said that."

The regret in his voice snags my resolve to ignore him—but no, I remind myself. Just because we shared a couple of nice moments today doesn't mean he's suddenly completed his transformation from villain to hero. It isn't fair that he tried to ruin Holly's life and she doesn't even know it. I won't ever tell her, but that doesn't mean Max and I are going to become best buddies.

"I'm sorry," I say. "I'm trying to get some sleep because I have a big day of pretending to own a farm tomorrow, so if you don't mind, please keep your mouth shut. Harry Styles is reading me a bedtime story, and your voice is drowning out his dulcet tones."

Max doesn't say anything else, and eventually I realize that he's done. I hope he fell asleep because if he's waiting for me to clear his guilty conscience by forgiving him, he'll be waiting a long time.

Chapter Fourteen

I SMELL PINE, AND for a moment, I wonder if I'm waking up in a bowl full of holiday potpourri. I wouldn't put it past Holly to stick some in the guest room. She once told me "scent is an often overlooked facet of hospitality" as she lit a candle.

But this isn't potpourri. This is deodorant. Male deodorant.

I open my eyes and come face-to-face (face to . . . pit?) with Max's underarm. I am snuggled against him, like I'm a tiny baby koala hanging on to its mother. We're so close it's like we're one person, our chests rising and falling in unison as we breathe our sleepy breaths.

He puts his arm around me and tightens it, bringing me even closer, pulling me on top of him. I don't resist because I *can't* resist, don't want to resist. All of a sudden, I don't even care about the argument we had last night, or about what he said before the wedding. All those little things I've noticed about Max over the past day: His eyes that can only be described, regrettably, as soulful. His voice, thrumming deep like a bass guitar. The broadness of his shoulders, which I'm now getting an up-close-and-personal view of. They all come together to paint a picture called Uh-Oh, I am *into* Max. I'm inches from his face when he says, "I thought this would never happen."

It feels inevitable that our lips meet—I don't know who kisses whom, and given that I'm on top of him, it's probably me, but it doesn't matter. We both want this. I can feel that we both want this, in our frenzied panting and the way his hand grabs my thigh.

He lets out a guttural noise that is the sexiest thing I've ever heard in my life, and I shush him. "We're going to wake up the kids!" I whisper-hiss, and all of a sudden, things blur. Whose kids? Darius and Holly's kids? Or are they our kids? Is this real or pretend? Am I awake or dreaming or—

"I didn't say anything."

I bolt upright in bed. Max stands in the doorway of the en suite bathroom, a toothbrush in his mouth.

"What?" I croak.

He spits into the sink and rinses out his mouth. "You were muttering something about not waking the kids. Unless they have supersonic hearing that results in my toothbrushing waking them up, I think we're good."

I blink a few times. This is real life. That . . . that wasn't. I never kissed Max. I never straddled him as he palmed my thighs. I never woke up snuggled against him.

I had an almost sex dream about Max.

"Why are you looking at me like that?" he asks, and I shake my head.

"Sorry. I . . . uh . . ."

The door to our room opens and Holly sticks her head in. "Hey, lovebirds!"

"Please stop," I say, diving back into the bed and putting a pillow over my head. Maybe I can go back to sleep and have a less awkward dream to overwrite this one. You know, like the recurring one where I'm walking topless through the Short North and I only realize I'm not wearing a shirt when I run into my tenth-grade Algebra teacher outside Prologue Bookshop and she says, "Young lady, put some clothes on."

That would be a much less unsettling dream to have rattling around in my head all day.

Holly steps into the room and pulls the pillow off my head. "You can't go back to sleep."

"Don't you remember how every time I stay over, I use the mug that says 'I Don't Do Mornings'? I love it because it puts into words what I've always felt deeply but never had the courage to say."

"Don't *you* remember that the last time you stayed here you dropped that mug and broke it?" Holly asks.

"Was it in the morning?" I squint at her. "Because I told you, I don't do them. I don't have a strong grip until I'm caffeinated."

"Do you have one that says 'Don't Talk to Me Until I've Had My Coffee'?"

I'd forgotten Max was there, watching us, leaning against the doorframe.

"Someone at work has that one," he says. "And frankly, I think it's an unfriendly vibe to have at the office."

His hair is a little mussed, like he hasn't combed it, and I wonder if that's what it would look like if we actually woke up together after a night spent having not-almost not-dream sex.

I shake my head quickly. After the conversation Max and I had before I fell asleep, the last thing I need to be thinking about is my dirty dream.

"What's wrong?" Holly asks, studying my face. "You look like you saw a ghost."

If that ghost was the memory of a time when I had sex regularly, then sure. Because that's the only explanation for my subconscious whipping me into a horny frenzy over Max.

"Don't say that too loud," I remind her. "Gilbert might hear you."

"Oh, he's already downstairs and he's drinking out of the Mommy Fuel mug," Holly says.

"Is there a reason why you have so many mugs with inane sayings on them?" Max asks, crossing his arms.

"Because they're hilarious," Holly and I answer together.

"And because Laurel keeps buying them for me," Holly continues.

"What can I say. I see a mug with a picture of a llama that says 'Llamaste,' and I think . . . yes, that's my sister."

"Anyway," Holly says, switching into business mode. "You need to feed and milk the goats. Gilbert's under the impression that you do it every morning."

I groan. "Can't we skip it?"

Holly sighs and tilts her head to the side, like I'm one of the twins trying to get out of brushing my teeth before bed. "Goats have to be fed and milked twice a day. It's not optional. Darius snuck out there and took care of them last night while Gilbert was sleeping."

"And he wants to do it again, right?"

Holly eyes me with skepticism and what might be a little disappointment. "I thought you were really trying to sell this. Gilbert thinks you care for the goats—didn't you write that entire blog post about the rhythms of a day on the farm, and how you start every morning by rising early, enjoying the feeling of the crisp winter air on your face as the sun shines through the ice crystals on the trees?"

I frown. "Are you quoting me to me?"

She nods. "It was evocative."

"Damn," I mutter. "I made milking goats sound good, didn't I?"

Then I walk over to the window and peek through the blinds. "There's no sun shining on the unspoiled snow right now, though. It's barely starting to come up."

"The girls aren't going to be happy if you make them wait much longer," Holly says. "Listen, I can take care of breakfast this morning—I'll tell Gilbert that I'm helping you out because you're so busy with the goats."

"You're a lifesaver," I say, wrapping her in a hug. "I would much rather feed goats than people."

"Good, because the cinnamon rolls are already halfway through their second rise," she says, her voice muffled in my shoulder.

"How early do you wake up?" I ask, pulling back.

"Get some clothes on and get to milkin'!" she says, smacking me on the butt before she heads downstairs.

"Wait!" I call after her, and she pops her head back into the room.

"I just wondered . . . how do the goats get pregnant if they're all female?"

"Oh, that. We lease a buck when it's time to breed," she says dismissively over her shoulder as she leaves.

I gasp, even though she's not there to hear me. "Leasing? That's so tawdry."

I hear a snort behind me. Max is still leaning against the doorframe, watching me, arms crossed. "They're goats. I don't think there's a lot of romance in it."

"Right," I say, hurrying out of the room before any other animalistic thoughts can cross my mind.

Chapter Fifteen

FIVE MINUTES LATER, I'm making my way to the barn and thinking I really should've volunteered for breakfast duty. I may only know how to make cinnamon rolls from a can, but that would still be better than what I'm facing out here. The only saving grace is that Gilbert didn't follow me out to the barn, preferring to stay inside with his mug full of mommy fuel. As for me, I wish I could've taken another coffee mug's advice and Namaste-d in Bed. And as I'm trudging through knee-deep snow, I ask myself if this is really worth it.

Unfortunately, it is. I like my job, and the idea of not having it—of being unemployed once again—makes my skin itch. It's not only the lack of income and insurance but the idea that my own bad decisions could torpedo my life again. I've got to be over this. I've got to get it together. Yes, I lied to my boss about owning and operating a farm, and yes, that's caused things to spiral wildly out of control (see: me, boots filling with snow as I slowly make my way to care for a bunch of goats), but I can pull it together. I have to. Because if I can't prove to myself that I've changed, that I'm no longer Old Laurel, then I think that might actually break me.

The wind whips around me, blowing my hair in my face even though I've shoved it under a thick knit hat (hand-knit by Holly, naturally). The snow drifted against the barn door overnight, meaning I can't get it open. I can hear the goats' petulant *maaaas* on the other side as I tug at the door, and eventually, using my gloved hands, I scoop enough snow out of the way to open the door a crack and cram my body through. Somehow, I have a feeling Holly doesn't begin her mornings this way. For starters, she probably knows where she keeps a shovel, but I can't exactly go inside and ask about that in front of Gilbert. Maybe I should've asked Max to help me, the same way he's helped me with everything else, but I couldn't stand the thought. Especially after reliving the worst parts of Holly's wedding last night, I think the less time we spend together, the better.

"Hey, guys . . . I mean, ladies," I say shakily as the six of them rush toward me. They're eager for something—whether it's food or being milked—and I feel like I'm in the midst of a zombie apocalypse. Except that the zombies are goats and I have to milk them, so maybe that analogy doesn't really pan out.

All the goats need to eat, of course, but I only need to milk two of them. Holly explained their entire breeding and kidding schedule to me back when I wrote my column, but there's simply not enough room in my brain for an encyclopedic knowledge of Christmas films *and* information about goats. After all, I never assumed I'd be in this situation. And, like a complete idiot, I left my phone inside so I can't even look up the article I wrote to see if there's anything in there that could help me out right now. All I know is that I have to milk Barnaby and Sally.

"So." I direct my question toward Barnaby, the biggest goat with the floppiest brown ears. "Any notes on what I should do here?"

Seeing as she's the biggest, I assume she must be the HBIC of the goat world. The GOAT, if you will. I laugh at my own joke, then realize Barnaby is chewing lightly on my coat.

"Hey!" I shout. "Step off!"

But it's too late—she rips a goat-bite-size patch of fabric off the bottom of my bright green peacoat, and I groan. "Barnaby, babe," I say. "Do you think I have the money to buy a new coat? Help me out here. Quit eating my clothes."

Barnaby responds with a petulant, "Maaaa!"

"Why is your name Barnaby, anyway?" I mutter. "Pretty sure that's a male name. Also an unusual name for a goat, in general."

Barnaby doesn't take kindly to this and advances toward me again. The other goats (Dolly, Sally, Olympia, and the babies of the family, Sparklefoot and Peanut Butter, so named by the twins), follow along behind her menacingly.

"Okay, okay!" I say, backing up. "I'll milk you. Sheesh."

I've never been *that* into my own birthday—I mean, I don't start celebrating my birth month at 12:01 a.m. on December 1 or anything. I don't remind people it's my birthday. I don't even usually have any sort of party (which is easy, because I'm always with my entire family for Christmas, anyway). But I do try to spend at least a couple of moments leading up to my birthday doing something I enjoy, or reflecting on the past year, or envisioning the months ahead.

What I've never wanted to do the day before my birthday is hang out in a freezing-cold barn as a petulant goat eats my pocket. Alas, here we are.

With a pail in hand that Holly gave me, I find a stool inside a cubby. This must be the milking spot, and Barnaby follows me inside as Dolly mills around, making agitated noises that mean she's either (a) pissed that a stranger is here, (b) jealous that she's not getting milked, or (c) hungry. With my limited knowledge of goats, I can only assume the latter.

"Okay, here we go," I mutter, taking a seat on the stool in front of a raised wooden platform. Is Barnaby supposed to get up there? I look at the platform, then Barnaby, then the platform again. She's a big girl, and my YouTube fitness challenges haven't made me strong enough to think I could lift her up there. Do goats even like being lifted? Thanks to social media, I know they love yoga, specifically climbing on people during Cat-Cow pose, but I'm not sure if being picked up is really their jam.

As I'm contemplating this, Barnaby hops up on the platform herself.

"Well, then," I say. "I guess you're ready."

She stomps her little hooves impatiently, and I place the pail underneath her. She immediately kicks it with her back foot, and I groan as I pick it up.

"You've gotta help me out here, girlfriend," I say. "Let me milk you!"

I reach out to . . . well, there's really no delicate way to say this. I reach out and grab her teat, then pull. She shouts and steps backward, knocking over the pail again.

"Hold still!" I screech, but I can't really blame her. If someone was indelicately pulling on my nipple, I might make a few noises, too.

"Gentler this time," I murmur, setting the pail up again. "I hear you, loud and clear."

I try to remember something, anything, from the article I wrote about the goats, but I didn't really get into the details. The general public only wants to hear about the more romantic side of farming, not the down-and-dirty details like early-morning milkings. I squeeze the teat again, pulling down slightly, and the first stream of milk shoots out.

"Yes!" I yell, startling Barnaby.

"It's okay." I stroke her back. "I'll chill out. I'm excited, that's all."

I pull down once more, but this time, Barnaby steps to the side and my hand slips. Before I can readjust myself, I'm squirting a stream of goat milk directly onto my own coat.

"Oh, no," I say, standing up. "It's all over me."

There's maybe a fourth of a cup of milk in the pail, and I know that's not enough for my girl Barnaby. Not to mention I haven't even milked Dolly yet, and the rest of the goats look like they're about ready to eat the walls of the barn if I don't feed them soon.

"Okay," I huff, sitting back down. "Let's finish you up and then we'll break for food—"

But as I sit back down, Barnaby kicks her back leg again, sending the pail—and the milk—flying. Droplets of it land on my face, in my hair, and all over me. I am never, ever going to get the milk smell out of my coat.

"Fine," I say, defeated, as I stand up and Barnaby jumps off the platform. "Food first, then milk. Got it."

But as I spin slowly in the middle of the barn, I realize I have absolutely no idea how to feed the goats. I inspect my surroundings, looking for a clue as to what I'm supposed to do. The goat barn is as nice as everything at Holly's—in fact, I'd say it's nicer (and certainly bigger) than some apartments I've lived in, although my apartment floors were never coated in sawdust. The goats have a heated water tank to make sure their drinking water doesn't freeze in the winter, and they have plenty of space to move around in here. Of course, they're only confined to the barn during the worst of the winter weather—in the summer, they're free to graze, keeping the acres of land mowed with nothing more than their insatiable appetites and terrifyingly weird teeth.

"I am strong," I remind myself, reciting my mantra. "I am capable. I can totally find the goat food."

Olympia *maas* loudly at me. "I'm doing my best here!" I yell. "What do you guys eat? Is there some kind of goat kibble in here?"

"Hay."

I turn around to see Max squeezing his body through the gap in the barn door. "Hey yourself?" I say cautiously.

"No, *hay*. They eat hay in the winter," he says.

"What?"

"When they're not able to graze—such as now, when there's this much snow on the ground—the goats need to be fed something like hay. Goats will eat almost anything, so sometimes Holly gives them kitchen scraps, but she buys goat food down at the feed store, too."

I can't help my face from wrinkling up into a ball of confusion. "Since when did you become the human embodiment of a library book on goats?"

"Since I started regularly helping out with the goats," he says, hoisting hay out of a cubby I never even noticed and easily putting it into a contraption that I now clearly see is a goat feeder. The goats swarm around it as I wonder why seeing a man feeding goats feels surprisingly sexy. Nothing involving goats should be sexy.

"You don't seem like a goat guy," I say.

He turns to look at me, eyebrows raised. "And what does a goat guy look like?"

I shrug. "I'd know one if I saw one. And you're not one, which I can confidently say because I'm not a goat girl."

"Why not?" Max asks, and I don't even know where to begin with that question.

"Well, the teeth, for starters. And the fact that Barnaby ate part of my coat. They're kind of terrifying. And I don't like the idea of someone relying on me for food twice a day."

"They're not so bad, you know," Max says so quietly that I almost don't hear his voice over the sound of the goats gnawing on hay. I watch them for a moment before I sense the unmistakable feeling of a man's eyes on me. I slowly look up.

"What?" I ask, internally squirming at being the subject of Max's gaze. Despite his (many, many) downsides, the man sure can look at a woman. And the way he's looking at me right now is full of intent, full of—

My breath hitches as he steps closer to me, his boots thudding against the dirt floor. Even the sound of the goats' teeth gnashing fades away as he reaches a hand toward me, his fingers brushing my face.

My lips instinctively part as I suck in a breath. What is happening? Why is Max looking at me and touching me like that? What is he—

"It *is* goat milk," he says. "How did you get goat milk on your face?"

I step back, hastily wiping my face on my coat sleeve—after all, it's not like this coat can get more ruined.

"Milking mishap," I say. "Don't worry about it."

"Have they both been milked?" he asks.

I groan, remembering that I still have to do that. "No. I had some issues, clearly. Barnaby kept kicking the pail."

"Right." Max heads purposefully over to the milking cubby and glances in. "The first thing you'll want to do is fill the little feed bin with their goat snack mix. That helps them stay put."

"Goat snack mix?" I repeat.

He locates a container I've never seen full of what looks like pet food and pours some of it in the bowl as the goats come running.

"One at a time, ladies," he says, motioning Barnaby onto the platform. She hops up and starts chowing down immediately. "There's enough to go around."

"That the first time you've ever had to say that?" I ask, one eyebrow arched.

He turns to look at me and sighs with his entire body, his mouth in a flat line. "I'm not going to dignify that with a response. You're welcome for handling the goats, by the way."

"Thank you," I reluctantly mumble, watching as he makes quick work of milking both Barnaby and Dolly. I can't even come up with a sarcastic retort the entire time because I'm so amazed. Max is the goat whisperer.

"So why, exactly, do you know so much about the care and feeding of the goats?" I ask him.

"I told you," he says, brushing his hands on his jeans. "I'm here a lot, and Darius and Holly can use the help."

"You're giving me more questions than answers," I continue, trying to stay far away from Barnaby, lest she get confused and mistake my coat for hay. I really can't handle losing another pocket. "Why are you here so much?"

Max turns to look at me fully, his arms crossed across his chest. "Darius and I have been best friends since we were kids. Why is it so unbelievable to you that someone might like spending time with me? Or that I might like spending time with my friends? Believe it or not, a dislike of dancing and karaoke doesn't mean I have a black heart and hate everyone."

"Okay, well . . ." I stumble on my words, because I might have had that exact thought about Max at one point. "I didn't say you had a black heart."

"I don't know, I think you might've used those words," he mumbles, scratching Sally behind the ear as if she's a cat. Sally rubs up against his leg, hungry for more attention.

"You can't be mad at *me* about this. You don't even like Holly! Which, as we've established, I heard you say. I'm only trying to figure out what you're doing here."

Max rubs a hand over his face, and Sally headbutts his leg, eager for more attention. "Laurel, if you would let me explain what happened—"

I laugh so loudly that Sally looks at me, offended. "There is no explanation. You said those words, right? You told Darius that he shouldn't marry Holly, or are you trying to tell me I'm imagining it?"

He sighs. "You're not imagining it."

I throw my hands in the air. "Then there's nothing to explain."

"Why are you so infuriating?" he shouts, and even Sally steps away from him. "Why does everything, every holiday, every conversation, have to be on your terms?"

"I don't know, why are *you* such a buzzkill?" I ask. "Did you come out here to yell at me about how I'm doing everything wrong?"

"No, I came out here to help you, but I don't know why I bothered." Max runs a hand through his hair, leaving it sticking straight up. Even though I'm *so* angry right now, I still have to stick my hands in my pockets to stop myself from reaching out and smoothing it down.

"Well . . . thanks!" I shout. "It was actually very helpful, even though I'm mad at you!"

"What else is new." He leans in close to me. "A lot of things have changed since the wedding. *I've* changed. But if you won't even let me explain myself, then what's the point? Let's just get through the rest of this holiday, and then we can go back to Columbus and continue avoiding each other."

"Sounds like a plan," I spit out. "I'd say, 'Don't let the door hit you on the way out,' but the door is currently not operational."

And then he turns and leaves, his dramatic exit foiled when he has to squeeze out of the tiny opening in the barn door again. The goats mill around forlornly, their sense of purpose gone in his absence.

"He'd better watch himself," I mutter, absentmindedly giving Sally a scratch behind the ear.

"Maa!" Sally bleats angrily, attempting to bite my finger. I try not to be offended that the goats like Max more than me.

"Okay, geez, I'm going!" I say. It's fine that the goats hate me, because I have a bigger mission here. I have to get through the rest of this holiday with my job intact, even if it kills me.

Chapter Sixteen

I STOMP MY BOOTS on the entryway rug, then pry them off my feet. I'm shaking the snow out of my hair when Holly calls out, "Laurel? Is that you?"

"Nope. I'm a Christmas Eve robber, here to steal your sentimental ornaments," I say. I struggle to pull my stuck arm out of my coat sleeve until it miraculously slides off. I turn around to see Max standing there, helping me out of my coat.

I frown at him.

"What?" he asks, holding my coat.

"Gilbert's not even out here," I say. "You don't have to pretend right now."

Now it's his turn to frown. "I'm not pretending. I'm being nice."

"Well, *stop*."

"Hey!"

I turn and freeze when I see Holly standing in front of us, hands on her hips. She's wearing an apron that says "Kiss the

Cook but Don't Touch the Buns" that I bought for Darius last year, and she has a dish towel in her hand. She looks like she belongs here, at the farm, in the kitchen, because she does. She's not a hopeless pretender like me.

"Quit it with all the bickering." She waves the spatula at us. "You're almost as bad as the twins, and you don't want Gilbert to hear you."

I angle my body so I'm standing between her and Max. "How's breakfast going? Are you pretending to be incompetent?" I whisper.

She slumps over dramatically. "I burned half the bacon. It killed me to do it, but I did. I was like, 'Oh, no, I *wish* Laurel were in here to show me what to do. She's the *real* chef in the Grant family.'"

"Good girl." I pat her on the shoulder.

"You're both enjoying this, aren't you?" Max asks, crossing his arms.

"Oh, like you didn't enjoy telling Gilbert that story about how we met." I look over my shoulder at him and narrow my eyes. "We're not the only ones with a flair for the dramatic."

Max looks away, hand reaching for the back of his neck. "What can I say? I was in the holiday spirit."

"News flash!" I say. "The holiday spirit convinces surly businessmen to give gifts to struggling single moms in Hallmark Christmas movies. The holiday spirit doesn't have anything to do with telling my boss about the Suck for a Buck shirt."

Max tilts his head as if he's thinking. "I guess it expresses itself differently through me."

"Why are you allowing this disrespectful behavior from a guest?" I ask Holly.

She widens her eyes innocently. "This isn't my house. Hold on, I have to go get the half-burned bacon."

She heads back into the kitchen. I groan, hitting my head against the wall. "I need to shovel Gilbert's car out so we can end this ridiculous facade."

"Laurel."

I roll my forehead against the wall so I'm looking at Max with my right eye. "What?"

"Gilbert's not leaving today. None of us are."

"Just because you have a defeatist attitude—"

"No, I have a decently accurate weather app. I can't understand why you refuse to look at one."

"I don't trust weather forecasts," I say to the wall.

"Breakfast!" Holly calls, swinging through the door with a platter in her hands. She stops and looks at us with confusion on her face. "Why are you two still standing in the foyer? Why are you leaning against the wall like that?"

"Because I'm depressed," I say.

"Because Laurel doesn't believe in weather," Max says.

Holly rolls her eyes as our phones buzz. "Hold this," Holly says, shoving the platter into my hands. She pulls her phone out of her apron pocket and reads, "'Car got stuck in snowbank and I thought we were gonna die but some dude pulled us out! Might have to stay in hotel tonight but see you tomorrow!' Followed by a robot emoji."

I frown as Holly texts back, narrating her words out loud. "Stay there! Be safe!"

"Is he going to be okay?" Max asks, his voice sounding genuinely concerned. "I mean, he did barf on me—"

"We know," I say with a beleaguered sigh.

"But I don't want him to get stuck in a ditch."

Holly shakes her head. "This is what it's like being Doug's sister. No idea what he's doing, constantly worrying about him, always confused."

"Also getting picked up a lot," I add. "He's very proud of his gains at the gym, and he likes to show that by lifting his sisters."

Holly nods. "He says his next challenge is being able to pick both of us up at once."

"I'd complain, but we probably deserve worse for all the stuff we used to do to him when he was little. A lot of noogies, a lot of wedgies, a lot of freezing his jockstraps when he got older."

"Oh, and we used to put our dresses on him when he was little and try to convince people that he was our triplet named—"

"Dougina," we say at the same time, laughing.

I glance at Max as I crack up. His smile doesn't quite reach his eyes, and I can't figure out why—does he have a traumatic noogie experience and we're bringing up bad memories?

"Anyway," Holly says, snapping her dish towel at me before she takes the platter back. "It's time to eat, so go wash off the goat stink and get ready."

She goes back into the kitchen, and as the door swings open, I can see Gilbert on his hands and knees, one of the twins climbing onto his back like he's a horse. Okay, so this Christmas is different than most—my brother's snowed in somewhere between here and the ski lodge. My parents are on a beach, no snow in sight. I just milked a goat. But all things considered, maybe it's still turning out better than I feared.

I turn around to see what Max is doing, but he's gone. Great. I've finally scared him off.

"THIS IS THE best meal I've ever had in my life," Gilbert says, closing his eyes as he chews.

"Didn't you say that last night at dinner?" Holly asks with a smile.

"Every meal I've had here has been the best of my life." Gilbert takes another bite of his cinnamon roll. "I can't believe that this evening I'll have to go back to a life of frozen pizza."

"Was Charlene the cook in your family?" Holly asks, and I try to kick her foot to remind her not to bring up Gilbert's relationship trauma. I'm trying to keep him as emotionally stable as possible. But Holly's too far away, and instead I kick Max, who yells, "Ow!" I shoot him an unapologetic look. He deserves a light kick, as far as I'm concerned.

Holly looks questioningly at us as Gilbert says, "Oh! I didn't even think about that. It was always *her* job to bake the frozen pizzas. Without her around, I'm not sure . . ."

He trails off, his nose wiggling like a cartoon bunny. "I know you can follow the instructions on the box," I tell him.

"And if you have any problems, you can call me and I'll talk you through it."

He nods gratefully.

Darius chews and looks out the window thoughtfully. "I don't know, buddy. I don't think you'll be getting out of here today. We're still under a snow emergency, and more's coming soon."

Frank wanders in, sniffing around the table. Frank doesn't care to move unless there's a promise of meat falling on the floor.

"No way, Frank," Holly says without looking up from her plate. "You already had your breakfast."

"He's shameless," I say as Max discreetly slides a piece of bacon off the table and into Frank's open and willing mouth.

"Max!" I chide. "He shouldn't have table food!"

Max frowns. Again. His default expression is a frown. If he was a *Winnie the Pooh* character, he'd be Eeyore, grumping around the Hundred Acre Wood and complaining.

"Dogs love bacon," he says.

"Dogs love all kinds of things," I point out. "Fatty meats. Running into traffic. Pooping inside when it's raining instead of going in the yard. That doesn't mean we should let them do whatever they want."

"I'm not sure Frank's ever run into traffic," Max says, pointing at Frank, who already devoured the bacon and is patiently waiting for another piece. "Given that the driveway's about a mile long and he hasn't run anywhere in, what . . . five years?"

"Don't shame Frank because he's not out there running

marathons," I say. "The vet in Baileyville told us that he'll get pancreatitis if he eats too much table food, and now Frank's very worried about his health."

Max stares at Frank. Frank stares back, his drool beginning to pool on the hardwood floor.

"He doesn't look so worried to me."

"Well, he is," I say firmly. "That's what the pet psychic said, anyway."

Max spins his head away from Frank and toward me so fast that I'm surprised he doesn't get whiplash. "I'm sorry, did you say pet psychic?"

I press my lips into a thin line. "Honey. Sweetie. Darling. Don't you remember when Holly so kindly gave me that gift certificate for Christmas? A visit to the pet psychic?"

Max turns to look at Holly. "Did you, now?"

Holly nods slowly. "I sure did. And in case you forgot, she preferred to be called an animal communicator. Pet psychic is a little derogatory."

"You're right. Thank you. That was a very creative gift, if you ask me. In fact, I might say that Holly's the best gift giver I've ever met."

Okay, so this was actually a gift that I gave Holly, because once she said that she wished she knew what Frank was thinking. This is because Frank, not being the most active of dogs, spends most of his time asleep on the couch, asleep in front of the fireplace, asleep on his personalized blanket that covers his dog bed, or, to mix things up a little bit, asleep behind the couch.

"Oh, this is interesting," Gilbert says, leaning forward on the table, the sleeve of his shirt dipping into the cream cheese frosting on his cinnamon roll. "So, tell me, is the pet psychic—I'm sorry, *animal communicator*—a pet? Or a human?"

I pause for a moment before answering, picturing a black lab wearing glasses and holding a notepad. "She was a very nice woman," I tell him. "A human woman."

"A human woman with a unique sense of style," Holly adds. "So many bangles. So many scarves. Leopard-print boots."

"I'm sure that added to the atmosphere," Max muses. "Do you think she's ever read the mind of a leopard?"

"Anyway," I continue, "we learned a lot about what goes on inside Frank's brain that evening, didn't we?"

Holly nods, and Max asks, "Was it 'bacon bacon bacon bacon bacon'?"

"No," I say primly. "Frank is much more interesting than you give him credit for. In fact, I can't believe you don't remember this. We learned about his deepest fears, his greatest joys, his past lives—"

Max coughs, choking on a sip of coffee. "I'm sorry," he says through a cough. "Frank has a past life?"

"He sure does!" Holly says brightly. "We were really surprised, but then when we learned about it, it kind of made sense that he used to be a racing greyhound."

"Is that why he's so tired?" Max asks. "He spent so much time running in his last life that he has to spend the entirety of this life sleeping?"

"You know what?" I ask. Because Frank isn't the only one who's tired—I am, too. I'm tired of Max's crappy attitude. I'm tired of him laughing at me for enjoying the lighter side of life. I'm tired of him making fun of everything I think is interesting. Maybe animal communicators might seem silly, but Holly and I had fun that night with the be-bangled and be-scarved psychic. She may have had questionable taste in footwear, but she was funny and smart and Frank loved the attention. Who cares whether it was respectable or not . . . it was fun.

"No, but I'm sure you'll tell me," Max mutters, taking a sip of coffee.

"There's nothing wrong with seeing an animal communicator. I know you think it's some other silly, pointless thing like Mariah Carey or throw pillows or squeezing the last bit of juice out of life, but we had a good time."

"We had a *great* time," Holly says. "And so did Frank. The communicator gave him organic dog treats. He doesn't get those at home."

"What I don't understand," Max says, turning to face me, "is how you can be skeptical of the weather forecast but totally buy into whatever a pet psychic says. People go to school to learn about meteorology. No one goes to school to learn how to bilk people out of their hard-earned money so they can make up lies about their pets' past lives."

I gasp as Holly says, "To be fair, no one had to bilk us out of anything. We willingly handed over that money."

"There has to be a school for psychics," Gilbert says thoughtfully. "Where else would they learn how to see into the future?"

"I agree," Darius says. "Everyone has to start somewhere."

"Not you, too, Darius," Max says with a groan. "They're not *learning* anything. They're making it up. They're pulling these ridiculous stories out of their butts and preying on vulnerable people who—"

"We had a *great* time at the pet psychic who, once again, prefers to be known as an animal communicator. Maybe it wasn't real. Probably it wasn't necessary. But not everything in life has to be utilitarian and boring and useless. Maybe for once you can shut up and stop making fun of me."

The table is silent except for the sound of Frank, who has his front paws on the table and is licking my empty plate. I gently push him off the table.

"*Shut up* is a bad word," Noah says. "We're not allowed to say it."

I blink as I look around the table. Gilbert's eyes are wide. The kids both look like they're waiting for me to get in trouble. Darius looks uncomfortable enough that I'm surprised he hasn't left the table. Holly holds her breath, waiting to see how I dig myself out of this one.

And Max? Max won't look at me. He stands up, his chair scooting across the floor.

"Excuse me," he mutters, and I suppress a groan. Yelling at Max about pet psychics was the result of some intense built-up tension, but everyone at the table doesn't know that. To them, it looks like I yelled at my husband out of nowhere.

"I'm so sorry, everyone," I say as soon as he leaves the room. "That was uncalled for. Noah, Lexie, you're right. We don't say *shut up*, not to anyone but especially not to family. It's not kind."

"It certainly isn't," Holly says crisply.

"Honestly, this is refreshing," Gilbert says.

"In what way?" I ask, scratching Frank behind his ears. It's not his fault that his love of bacon started a fight.

"Even people who are truly in love have fights. Even when you're pound sign couple goals, you still have bad days."

I think about what he said for a moment. "Oh, you mean hashtag."

He waves me off. "Hashtag, pound sign. Potato, po-tah-to. All I'm saying is, you two give me hope that maybe Charlene and I can work things out."

Uh-oh. On the one hand, it's great that he thinks Max and I are simply having a lovers' (ugh) spat. On the other hand, I don't really want to encourage him to keep the light on for Charlene. He should be turning that light all the way off. Perhaps even removing the light bulb entirely. I might not know the whole story about why she left him, but I don't want hope to crush his heart.

"So!" Gilbert claps his palms together. "Who wants to help dig my car out?"

"Me!" the twins shout in unison. They love using shovels, even though they're too small to do any effective work and Holly always ends up taking the shovels away because they try to start sword fights with them.

Holly chuckles wryly. "Oh, Gilbert. You're not going anywhere today."

Gilbert looks out the window in concern. "Really? The snow stopped."

"Sure, but there's at least a foot of it. And more coming in about an hour."

I look at her, brows furrowed, and she says, "Do not get on my case about believing a weather app."

"They're always wrong on Christmas, that's all!" I throw my hands in the air. "Everyone's always white Christmas this, winter wonderland that, but it so rarely happens. I'm not going to jinx it by believing their promises of more snow."

But then I frown, remembering that, my love of a white Christmas aside, I would actually love for this snow to melt so that Gilbert can get the hell out of Dodge (Dodge being Holly's house and my Christmas morning). I pull my phone out of my pocket and look up the weather.

"Wow, another nine inches by nightfall?" I raise my eyebrows.

"Oh." Gilbert slumps over. "I'm intruding."

"You aren't at all," Holly assures him. "Right, sis?"

I shove my phone back in my pocket. I've effectively jinxed the snow, so now I'm sure it will all melt immediately. "Right. We have plenty of food, plenty of space, and you can stay as long as you want. Maybe the snow will keep on coming and you can stay all week!"

The look on Holly's face lets me know that I might be overdoing it.

"At least for one more night," I say.

Gilbert shakes his head. "I can't be here on Christmas. It's too much. Christmas should be spent with family." And then he looks down at his plate, his fork drawing circles in the pooled cinnamon-roll icing. "Of course, we usually spent Christmas with Charlene's family. We played Monopoly and Life for hours and ate fruitcake. But I can try to get back to the house and make Christmas the best it can be all by myself. Although I've never tried to play Monopoly alone."

Coming from anyone else, I would assume this was nothing

but a ploy to get an invite. But coming from Gilbert, I think it's serious. He really will go back to his lonely home and play solo Monopoly, which I don't even think is possible. And why does it make me feel so sad that Gilbert played the most boring board games and ate the most unappealing baked good every Christmas? He deserves more this year.

"Well, you're family now, Gilbert," I say, standing up so quickly that Frank grumbles in shock before he wanders off to find a chair to sleep on.

Gilbert drops his fork. "What?"

"Who says family has to be related by blood? You're here, it's Christmas, and you're not going anywhere."

"Not with that little thing out there," Holly mutters.

"You're a Grant now, and you're staying with us," I say.

Gilbert puts his hands on his heart. "Laurel, this is above and beyond. I can't think of a single other employee who would invite me into their home for Christmas."

I certainly can't think of one . . . mostly because I didn't technically invite Gilbert to my home.

"I was going to wait to tell you this until after the new year, but . . . what the heck! We're spreading holiday cheer! You're getting a raise next year. I'll give you the full details once we get back to the office, but it's a pretty hefty one."

Darius and Holly clap, and Darius puts his hands over his mouth and mimics the sound of a crowd cheering. The twins clap, too, although they can't possibly know what a raise is.

"Really?" I ask. It's ridiculous, but I almost feel like I might cry right here at the table. It's not the money—although, to be clear, I can really, really use the money. It's the idea that someone believes in me. Someone thinks I'm doing a good job. Someone wants to keep me around for reasons that have nothing to do with sex. Gilbert thinks I'm good at my job.

Gilbert nods. "I can't imagine what we'd do without you. You're reliable, you have great ideas, and your work is top-notch."

I beam like I'm a second grader being complimented on her artwork. Since I'm still standing while everyone else is sitting, it feels a little bit like an awards ceremony.

"In fact," he says, folding up his napkin and looking, for the first time since he got here, like an actual boss instead of a sad shell of his former self, "I know you've been wanting to write more instead of mostly doing social media. I'd like to explore that for you, maybe try out a few test articles that aren't about the farm."

My eyes widen. "I would love that."

"I think it's gonna go great. You have a unique point of view, Laurel, and that's what makes you such an important part of our team. You understand rural life because you're living it, and I love that you've shared your life with all of us. And I know I can trust you to keep producing quality work."

I sit down with a thump, as if I've been pulled into my seat by the cold, hard weight of reality. *I can trust you.* The words bounce around in my head like they're part of a 1990s screen-saver, neon pink and screaming at me. *I can trust you.*

Can he trust me? I've been lying to him since the second we met, and while it started out feeling so harmless, so inconsequential, now it's grown into something monstrous. I can't tell him now, not when so much is on the line. My job, my security, my insurance, my reputation, myself.

Not to mention that revealing the truth now, while he's so emotionally fragile, would crush him. Well, more than he's already crushed.

I give Holly a shaky smile, and she looks back at me with concern.

"Thanks, Gilbert," I say quietly. "You can trust me."

"I know," he says, and then he reaches over and pats my hand like he's an uncle or a father instead of what he really is—the boss I'm deceiving who's strangely becoming like an extra family member to me. "Now go talk to your husband. Fix things right away while you have the chance."

Chapter Seventeen

I CAN'T EXACTLY TELL Gilbert that I have no desire to fix things with Max because there's nothing to fix, so I give him a thin smile and wander off to find out where Max could possibly have gone. Holly's house is big, but it's not *that* big, and I don't know what dark and depressing activity he could be getting into right now. Staring at a wall? Watching Lars von Trier films on his phone? Eating a bowl of unsweetened oatmeal?

I'm laughing at my mental list when I open the door to the guest room and see him lying on the bed, a book in hand.

"Oh!" I don't know why I react as if I've walked in on him getting out of the shower, like this is one of those romantic movies where the leads somehow end up accidentally seeing each other naked. He's on the bed, fully clothed, holding a book. Something about it is oddly vulnerable, though, like I'm looking behind a curtain that Max always keeps up.

He puts the book down and sits up. "I'm sorry."

If my eyebrows went any higher, they'd merge with my hairline. "What?"

He marks his place in his book with a bookmark. Of course Max uses a bookmark—who knows what he would do if he found out I dog-ear pages like an agent of chaos. "I said I'm sorry."

"Oh, no, I heard you," I clarify, shaking my head. "I just didn't know you knew those words."

"Ah," he says, letting out a weary sigh. "You're making fun of me."

"I'm not! Or, okay, I am. A little. But not in a bad way."

He lifts his glasses up and rubs his eyes. "Is there a good way to make fun of someone, Laurel?"

"Yes! Yes, absolutely there is!" I sit down beside him on the bed, moving several decorative pillows out of the way. "Seriously, where does Holly store these when they're not in season?"

"I think the attic is primarily pillow storage," Max says.

"Seems like a fire hazard." I meet his eyes.

"Indeed." He raises his eyebrows, just a little, as if he's asking me to go on or at least explain why I came in here and interrupted his reading time.

"It's possible to make fun of people in a good way," I insist. "Holly and I do it all the time. I'm always like, 'I'm Holly, I can use power tools and provide for a family,' and she's like, 'I'm Laurel, and I don't understand how to make a meal or replace a button.'"

"That doesn't sound like making fun of someone so much as simply listing their characteristics."

"Well, it's better in the moment. The button thing is real,

though. She's always making fun of me because I can't sew on a button. But we make fun of Darius, too, for being so nice all the time. Sometimes you can make fun of someone because you like them."

Max pauses, flips his paperback over, and then looks at me. "Do you like me, Laurel? Is that what this is about?" he asks in a low voice.

Time freezes. The twins' voices carry up the stairs. The clock on the bedside table ticks, tocks, ticks, as those words enter my bloodstream and go straight to my heart.

"What are you sorry about?" I ask quickly.

"Being an asshole," he says, so simply and honestly that I laugh out loud.

"Oh, is that it?"

"I was a jerk about the pet psychic—"

"Animal communicator," I say.

He points at me. "See? I'm doing it again. I was a jerk about the animal-communicator thing for no real reason. I mean, there was a reason. I do think it's ridiculous. Why would anyone fork over their hard-earned money to learn that their cat *really* likes tuna?"

"Is this part of the apology?" I ask, gesturing toward him.

"No. Sorry. I'm making it worse."

I nod. "You are. Go on."

"It doesn't matter what I think about pet psy—animal communicators. You and Holly were talking about something that was fun for you, and I should've, as you so aptly put it, shut up. It's not all that different from LEGO, when you think about it."

I nod. "You're right. They're both fun, other people don't

understand them, they're a way to connect with the people . . . or animals . . . you love. I guess the only difference is that animal communicators don't have a community based on acronyms."

"That you know of."

"True." And then I cringe a little as I find myself doing something I never imagined I'd do . . . apologizing to Max Beckett. "Maybe I owe you an apology, too. I mean, I definitely do. I shouldn't have told you to shut up in front of my entire family."

Max shrugs. "I deserved it."

I pinch my fingers together. "A little bit."

He sighs. "I'm sorry. I wish I hadn't said that. Can I take it back?"

"You can," I say. "I'll pretend you didn't go on a rant worthy of an antiestablishment podcast host, and you can pretend I didn't tell you to shut up, which is, by the way, a bad word in this house."

He winces. "Please tell me you don't think of me as an antiestablishment podcast host."

I think about it for a moment. A couple of days ago, I might've said that I did. Yesterday, even, when he was complaining about the decorative throw pillows. But, strangely enough, I'm getting to see another side of Max now. One that doesn't drive me up the wall. One that can sometimes be a little bit funny, even if he does refuse to dance.

Also he's kind of right about the pillows. Holly has way too many of them.

"Maybe not anymore. It's not your fault you can't stop speaking truth to bullshit and/or seasonal décor."

"Sometimes it's hard to ignore all the bullshit," he admits.

"Okay, Holden Caulfield." I smirk. "But maybe sometimes it's okay to let things be bullshit. Maybe sometimes a little bit of bullshit is even good."

"Spoken like a true poet," Max says softly, and I smile.

"What are you reading?" I point to the paperback in his hand. "More Salinger? Commiserating about phonies?"

"Actually, no." Max flips it over. "Ann Patchett this time."

I look at the cover of *The Dutch House*. I don't know what I expected Max to read, but it wasn't a family saga from one of America's greatest living writers. "Oh, I listened to the audiobook of that one because it was read by Tom Hanks. Wait, don't tell me—you don't think audiobooks are real books, do you?"

Max smiles, a little bit sadly. "Wow, you really think I'm an asshole."

"I'll reserve judgment until you answer this question."

He laughs. "No, I think they're real books. Actually, we used to listen to Roald Dahl audiobooks in the car with Darius's family when we took trips to Cedar Point in the summer. I loved them."

"That sounds really nice," I say softly, although I note that I've heard Max mention Darius's parents several times, and his own parents not once.

"It was," he says. "And I think I might have to listen to the audiobook after I read this one. It's Tom Hanks, after all."

"An American treasure," we say at the same time, then laugh.

My phone buzzes, and I pull it out of my pocket. My mom.

We miss you kids! Hope you're having fun without us! But not too much fun! Did you know that your dad is afraid of scuba diving? I found out the hard way!

I frown at my phone, wondering why she didn't include more details.

"Text from a hot date?"

I look up, confused, to see Max staring at me. He nods at the phone.

"Ah. Yes. A hot date known as my mom." I waggle the phone in the air. "Apparently she and my dad are scuba diving. I'm glad they're having fun, but honestly, I don't get it. Why do they want to miss all this? I wouldn't want to be anywhere but here on Christmas."

"Me neither," Max says, and I'm sure I must have misheard him. After all, there's no way that Max—who made it very clear over the past two days how much he doesn't want to be here helping me—could possibly be enjoying himself. I think about what he told me when I asked him why he was here. *I have nowhere else to go.* Why doesn't he?

"Don't you miss being with your parents?" I ask.

"What do you know about my parents?" he asks sharply. When I flinch, he softens. "I'm sorry. But they're . . . not like your parents. The whole warm, fuzzy childhood you had? I didn't have one of those."

"Why not?" I ask. Something about being here, in the guest room alone with Max, makes it feel okay to ask this. Only snow and ice are visible through the window, making the house seem like a little cocoon. The light from the warm, soft lamp on his bedside table casts a cozy glow over everything.

"Because my parents . . . they weren't warm and fuzzy. *Aren't* warm and fuzzy. All the stuff you guys have . . . the big, happy family. The holiday traditions. Dressing up a little brother and renaming him Dougina."

I nod. "Yes. That's the Grant way."

"That wasn't the Beckett way. The Beckett way was around-the-clock fighting and shouting that only got worse on Christmas, because inevitably my dad would get mad that my mom did some imaginary thing wrong, and then my mom would get upset that my dad forgot about something that didn't even matter, and the next thing I knew, they were screaming at each other and forgetting I even existed. All of this stuff, all of these things you do . . . the albums you listen to every year and the cookie decorating contest . . . none of this is normal for me."

I feel a pang of sympathy for Max, as well as a pang of regret that I hated him for avoiding all of the holiday traditions that, for me, are pure joy. Of course those things felt weird for him—they were reminders of what he didn't have.

"I'm sorry," I say softly. My hand reaches out of its own accord and squeezes his. "So you don't ever see your parents at Christmas?"

He smiles sadly. "A lot of therapy has helped me figure out that it's actually best if I don't see them at all. I usually ride out the day by myself and wait for life to get back to normal. Darius and Holly always invite me over, but this is the first year I've accepted."

The thought of him spending a holiday all alone in an

apartment that probably doesn't have any tinsel, scented candles, or carefully wrapped gifts breaks my heart a little bit. Suddenly, I'm *glad* that Max Beckett is with us.

"Well, you're here now," I say, injecting my voice with more enthusiasm than I feel. "And since the twins call you Uncle Max, I guess you're part of the family."

"Me and Gilbert both," Max says.

"I'm not sure they'll ever start calling him *Uncle Gilbert*, but we'll have to wait and see."

I tilt my head, puzzled, as I study his face. He really isn't bad looking. In fact, that face and that hair and those broad shoulders might be quite appealing on an entirely different person—one who didn't have such a complicated history with my family.

Max looks back at me, and I feel it—a small moment of *something* passes between us, an electric charge that runs through my body. I'm not cold—it's impossible to be cold in Holly's home, since you're constantly surrounded by throw blankets and cozy crackling fires—but I shiver.

I can't be attracted to the man who didn't want Darius to marry my sister. The man who won't dance or pose for silly photo booth pictures; the one who hates all things frivolous and fun; the one who, up until recently, only laughed when he was laughing at me.

I can't deny, however, that there's part of me that wants to be the one who makes Max laugh. The one who convinces him to dance (like no one or everyone is watching). The one who cracks him open to see what's underneath that protective shell. I feel like this moment, this conversation, has shown me another side of Max. Maybe there's more to him than I thought.

I realize, with a start, that I'm still holding Max's hand, and we've been sitting here in silence for way too long. Yes, it's a comfortable silence, but it's a confusing silence, and I need to get back to the rest of my family. Back to things that make sense. I drop his hand and give myself a shake.

"Well, let's go downstairs and show Gilbert that we're still happily married. What do you say?"

Without waiting for a response from him, I stand up and walk toward the door. And I only roll my eyes a little bit when he quietly responds, "Sure thing . . . lover."

Chapter Eighteen

"You know what I'd love to do?" Gilbert asks, standing in the middle of the room, hands on his hips.

I'm afraid to know the answer to this question.

"What's that, bud?" Darius asks as he eats a cookie.

"Go ice-skating!" Gilbert claps his hands once, a show of excitement that somehow feels like a pronouncement.

"Ice-skating?" I ask cautiously. "Why?"

Gilbert tilts his head. "Well, you made it sound like so much fun."

I frown, trying to remember when Gilbert and I talked about ice-skating. Given that I haven't laced up a pair of skates since I was nine because I'm the least coordinated person on the planet, I can't imagine why the topic would've come up.

"In your post," Gilbert says, as if he's jogging my memory. He reaches into his pocket and pulls out his phone, taps away, and then holds it out to me.

It's a picture of the small pond behind Holly's house, the ice glimmering in the bright winter sunshine. He pulls the phone back and reads, "No better way to spend a winter afternoon than skating on the pond with the whole family. Thankful for these precious memories on the ice. Pound sign farm life, pound sign shop local."

"Ah, yes," I say, nodding, my mind whirring a million miles a minute as I try to figure out what to do here. "How could I forget writing that?"

"And, of course, you mentioned it in your farm-life column. What do you say?" Gilbert walks over to the window and peers out. "It doesn't look like it's snowing right now."

I glance at Holly, widening my eyes to ask: *What the hell am I supposed to do here*?

She looks back at me and shrugs.

"It's definitely been cold enough this week," Darius says. "The pond is frozen solid, so it's safe. And we have plenty of extra skates."

"Darius!" I hiss.

"Well, it is!" he says, not understanding that what I want is an excuse to get out of ice-skating, not assurance that it's safe.

"I know Laurel would love to show you her moves," Max says. "I can hardly keep up with her on the ice."

I turn to look at him slowly, my jaw clenched in frustration. "Max, sweetie, you must be blinded by your undying love for me. I'm not that good."

"Ice-skating prowess is in the eye of the beholder. Isn't that what they always say?" he asks, an innocent look on his face.

"Haven't heard that one before," I reply flatly.

"It would look great on a mug." He looks off into the distance thoughtfully as if picturing the mug.

"It really would," Gilbert agrees, turning away from the window.

"Let's go!" Darius shouts, literally running to the closet to grab the ice skates.

"Holly!" I mutter, turning away from Gilbert. "What is he doing?"

"I'm sorry!" Holly whispers helplessly. "Darius loves ice-skating. He probably forgot that you're terrible at it."

"Um, ouch," I say. "*Terrible* is an exaggeration."

But as I hobble onto the ice ten minutes later, legs buckling underneath me like I'm a baby deer taking its first wobbly steps, I realize that Holly wasn't exaggerating at all. I'm actually quite bad on skates. Egregiously bad. Depressingly bad. Laughably bad.

Because someone is laughing at me right now, covering his face with his hand so Gilbert won't see him.

"Wow," Max says, skating backward. "I thought you were being self-deprecating, but you weren't kidding. You're awful."

"If I could move right now," I say, attempting to slide across the ice and instead clumsily shuffling, "I would come over there and hurt you."

"I'm very scared." He nods.

"You should be. These skates are sharp. How do you even know how to skate so well?"

"Darius's mom used to take us," he says, easily skating past me on one foot as I inch forward.

I look at Gilbert, who's currently being pulled across the

ice by Darius, the two of them laughing like they're on a cute but awkward first date. Even Gilbert, who admittedly had never been skating, is doing better than me.

"At least he's smiling."

It takes me a moment to register what Max said. "Gilbert?"

"Yeah." Max watches them. "He seemed pretty broken up about the whole situation."

"Well, he did get his heart stomped on. But there's something about Holly's place that's healing. She should rent it out as a retreat for the recently brokenhearted," I say, trying to scoot across the ice. Instinctively, I know I should be using my legs, but I've created a move where I gently thrust my hips. It may resemble a vaguely suggestive dance move, but at least I'm in motion. "I know I feel much better when I come here."

"Are you recently brokenhearted?" Max asks, skating around me in a circle. I can't even be mad that he's totally showing off because I'm impressed.

"Semi-recently. Before I started working for Gilbert, I was an accidental other woman for my boss/roommate/boyfriend. I guess you could say I'm still working through it, but something about being here makes it all seem . . . unimportant. Like, who cares that John dumped and fired me and it was one of the most humiliating experiences of my life? I'm on a pristine frozen pond in the middle of nowhere, and after this, we're probably going to have homemade hot chocolate. Life is good."

Max laughs, shaking his head.

"What?" I ask, an edge to my voice. Maybe I shouldn't have trusted Max with one of my most embarrassing, unflattering stories.

"That guy must've been a total idiot," he says, not looking at me as he skates backward beside me. "To dump you."

My skate snags on a bump, and my arms flail as I try not to fall.

Without breaking his stride, Max reaches out and steadies me.

"Thanks," I mutter, my face growing warm, both from the unexpected contact and the compliment.

"Laurel," Gilbert says as he skates near us. "You were right! This is so much fun!"

He's skating on his own now, arms spread wide to help keep himself balanced as Darius and Holly effortlessly glide around the pond like they're competing in the winter Olympics.

Gilbert is so focused on staying upright that he hasn't seemed to notice how unsteady I am, thankfully. The twins, uninterested in the ice, are playing in the snow and complaining loudly about how they want to go drink hot chocolate.

I trip again and Max grabs my hand. "You're gonna faceplant, Grant," he says.

"I am not!" I say with a laugh. I notice Gilbert staring at us.

"You two," he says, eyes welling with tears. "The way he helps you out, the way you have someone to depend on. It's so sweet. It . . ."

He reaches up to wipe away a tear and stumbles. It all happens in slow motion. Gilbert starts to fall, and I don't even think, I just move across the ice, my skates clacking loudly as I reach for him.

But as I grab him, I realize that I should've thought about this a little more. I can't support Gilbert's weight when I, myself, am falling over. The two of us tumble to the ice as if we're the leads in a made-for-TV Christmas movie, except that instead of landing with our faces an inch away from each other and unbearable sexual tension between us, we land in an awkward heap, my ankle pinned under Gilbert's knee.

"Laurel!" Gilbert shouts, trying and failing to stand up. "You broke my fall with your body!"

"No problem," I say, my face contorted in pain. "But do you think you could, uh . . . stand up?"

Darius reaches for Gilbert's hand and pulls him off my leg. "Can you get up?" Darius asks.

"Yep," I say, but I wince as soon as I try to put weight on my ankle. "Uh-oh."

"Are you okay?" Holly shouts, skating gracefully across the ice even in her worry. The twins look up from their blob of a snowman, temporarily distracted by the high-pitched moaning noise.

Oh, that's me. *I'm* the one making that high-pitched moaning noise.

I clap my hand over my mouth. "I'm sorry. It . . . it hurts."

"Let me pick you up," Holly says, bending over, but I wave her off.

"We're the same size," I say. "Maybe ask your strapping husband to—"

But before I can finish my sentence, Max skates through everyone and kneels beside me. Without looking at my face, he pulls off my skate gently, hardly jostling my foot at all, and rolls down my sock.

"Does this hurt?" he asks as he presses on my ankle lightly, and I suck in a quick burst of air.

"That sounds like a yes," he mutters, looking at my foot

again, but I don't tell him that my reaction was more about him touching my bare foot. I make a note to thank Jamilah for taking me out for a pedicure as a pre-Christmas gift.

"It's not that bad," I finally say. "But it hurts when I try to stand up."

"It's not broken," Max pronounces. "You'll be fine if you ice and elevate it."

"Why are you, like, a foot expert?" I ask. "Why should I trust you? Frankly, I'm worried you're some kind of fetishist and—"

But I never get to finish my thought (which is just as well, because what was I implying? That Max has a fetish for injured ankles, specifically?) because the words dry up when Max quickly hoists me over his shoulder, picking me up like he's the lead in an out-of-date Western that current viewers would decry for its casual sexism.

"Help!" I shout, reaching toward the twins. "I'm being kidnapped by this strange man!"

"Don't joke, Laurel," Holly chastises me. "They're learning about stranger danger, and this is going to confuse them."

The twins aren't the least bit concerned. "I want a piggyback ride, too!" Noah screeches.

From my awkward vantage point (slung over Max's shoulder), I crane my neck up to watch Holly and Darius each hoist a kid onto their back.

"Stop moving around," Max says. "I'm going to drop you."

"You're not," I say. "If you dropped me, you'd only have to pick me up again, and then I'd probably be even more injured, but in new and exciting ways. You'd be creating a headache for yourself."

Max grunts, and then, quietly, says, "You yourself are a headache designed expressly for me."

This should probably hurt my feelings, but I feel pride blossom like a spring flower in my chest. "Thank you," I say with as much sophistication as I can muster. "I feel the same way about you, but perhaps more vehemently. You're a custom-made night terror."

Max lets out a laugh. "I'll put that on my business cards."

He takes the porch stairs gently, opening the front door with one hand while using the other to keep me upright. The blood is rushing to my head, but I find that I don't mind it so much. Being carried around by Max is quite comfortable, and knowing that I'm giving him a headache might actually make the experience better.

Max walks into the living room and deposits me on the couch with more gentleness than I would have thought possible from him. There's a moment, right when he's letting me go, when his hands are on my shoulders and his face is inches from mine, that one word flashes in my mind like a neon light in a bar window: *tender.* It's not a word I normally use to describe anything other than a steak, but that's how this feels: soft and sweet and like it might leave a little bit of a bruise if I'm not cautious. Max placing me here so carefully, his hands gripping me so securely yet so lightly, his presence in front of me so solid, and his eyes . . .

For a second, just for a second, I can't look away. His deep brown eyes transfix me, and it's like I'm frozen, a dog waiting for a Beggin' Strip. And that's how I feel, like Max is dangling a treat above me, teasing me, even though he isn't saying a word, even though he isn't doing anything but looking at me.

"Thank you for carrying me," I say softly.

"Right." He clears his throat and stands up, and the moment dissolves and floats off into space.

The rest of the family (including Gilbert, who, I guess, is part of the family now) tromps into the house, shouting "put me down!" and "pick me back up!" and "Laurel, are you okay?"

Holly sends the twins upstairs for some coveted iPad time, then runs to the couch and kneels down beside me. Gilbert heads to the bathroom, because a man who drinks that much hot chocolate needs a lot of pee breaks.

"I only hurt my foot," I say. "I don't think the damage is permanent."

"It's a sprain. We'll keep it iced and elevated," Max says. "No walking for the rest of the day."

I salute him. "Aye-aye, Captain."

He heads upstairs quickly, as if he has another patient to see. "Why does Max know so much about foot injuries? What, is he secretly a doctor?" I ask Holly.

"No, but he did go to part of medical school," Darius says casually from the fireplace, where he's hanging the twins' wet scarves up to dry.

"What?" I ask, sitting up straight. "How did I not know this?"

Holly snorts. "Maybe because you and Max haven't had any conversations that aren't solely comprised of you being upset with him?"

"That's hardly fair. Max and I have a *mutual* dislike of each other." I say it instinctively, even though I'm not sure *dislike* is the correct word to describe what I feel for Max anymore. I'm not sure there *is* a word to describe how I feel about Max now.

Holly nods. "True. You guys are like the couple in a Christmas rom-com, where the woman owns an adorable Christmas tree farm and the guy is a developer from the city, and he's like, 'I need to tear down your farm!' and she's like, 'Oh, no, you don't, mister!'"

"Is this the level of dialogue you expect from Christmas films?" I ask. "Because I've heard much better. Maybe we need to bust out some of the classics tonight."

"I don't know," Darius says thoughtfully. "I think *Fir Crazy* is a modern classic."

"Oh, I love that one," Gilbert agrees as he comes back into the room. He holds his hands in front of the fire as if we've been hiking for hours in the cold instead of ice-skating for a few minutes. "Definitely a classic for us. Well, for *me*."

"Hey!" Darius says as he notices that Gilbert's nose is doing the telltale twitch that precedes a Charlene-induced sob. Once again, I bless Darius for his emotional intelligence. "Gilbert, do you want to do a tour of the woodshop with me?"

"Do I ever!" Gilbert says, turning from the fire and heading to get his boots on. "Wait, don't we need Laurel to show us around?"

All of us realize Darius's mistake at the same time . . . Of course, that's supposed to be my woodshop, not Holly and Darius's.

"Nope!" Darius says, recovering quickly. "Laurel's actually been teaching me how to use the tools, so I know my way around pretty okay."

Gilbert accepts this easily, and when his back is turned, Darius gives me a thumbs-up that I return.

"Do not," I whisper to Darius as he passes the sofa, "under *any* circumstances allow that man to operate a power tool in his current depressed condition."

Darius gives me a dead serious look. "You can trust me."

The two of them head out, and since the twins are having their daily iPad time in their rooms and Max is . . . who knows where . . . the house is blessedly quiet for the first time since I got here. This seems like the perfect time to tell my sister a secret I've been keeping for years that might deeply upset her.

Well, when I put it like that, I'd much rather keep it to myself . . . but I don't think I have that option any longer. Things with Max are getting so convoluted and confusing that I finally need to talk to the person who knows me best.

Chapter Nineteen

HOLLY SINKS INTO the armchair, her entire body turning into jelly. She lets out a moan as if she's getting a particularly good massage.

"How do you handle it?" I ask. "The constant noise?"

She waves me off. "You get used to it. Eventually a constant background of screaming children is like a rain sounds app."

"I'll have to trust you on that one."

She closes her eyes, looking equal parts tired and peaceful. This gives me a moment to study her face, the one that looks so much like mine (even if, much like Mary-Kate and Ashley, we have subtle differences). Holly is an angel. A woodworking, pie-baking, goat-feeding angel, and right now, I'm feeling pretty dang terrible about the big secret I've been keeping from her. There was a time when we used to tell each other everything, but I haven't even told her that her husband's best friend—the one who is currently a guest in her home, the one who plays with her children, the one who she thinks of as her friend, too—tried to talk Darius out of marrying her.

"Holly," I say, apparently with too much force because her eyes fly open as she sits straight up.

"Is one of the kids bleeding?" she asks.

"No!" I say quickly, and she relaxes back into the chair, closing her eyes again.

"Sorry. I kind of dozed off there for a minute. I'm the queen of the three-minute nap. Honestly, you'd be surprised by how refreshed you can feel after sleeping for three minutes."

"I'm sure I would," I say, not believing her at all. I take a deep breath and say the words I've been holding in for years. "I have to tell you something about Max."

Holly doesn't even open her eyes. "Is it that you not-so-secretly have the hots for him?"

"What? I— No. No!" I sputter. "Why would I tell you *that*?"

She shrugs. "Fine. Don't tell me. What's up?"

"I don't have 'the hots,' as you so eloquently put it, for Max for a lot of reasons—like, everything about him. But the main reason is . . . well, I've been avoiding telling you this for years because I didn't want to upset you, but I think you have a right to know. I mean, Max is staying in your home, and this is important information to have . . ."

She still doesn't open her eyes. "Are you about to tell me that Max murdered someone? I need more details before I freak out. Did he have a sympathetic motive?"

"No! I . . . I hate being the one to tell you this, Holly, but right before your wedding, he told Darius that you two shouldn't get married."

She opens one eye and squints at me.

"I know," I say. "It's bad. And I know it's going to upset you, and I'm not trying to ruin your Christmas or our birthday, but—"

"How do you know about that?" she asks, sitting up straight (which is hard to do in that armchair . . . it's very cushy).

"Wait. What? You already *knew*?"

"Yeah, of course." Holly looks at me like she's waiting for me to catch up. "Darius and I tell each other everything. Like, *everything.* He knows even more about my digestive habits than you do."

I try not to be jealous about that, even as I realize it's totally weird to be jealous about that.

"He told me what Max said as soon as we got back from our honeymoon."

"And you . . . You're okay with it?" I shake my head.

"That was a long time ago," Holly says firmly. "And Max was dealing with a lot. He's changed since then, you know. He apologized for what he said—"

"He *apologized* to you?" I repeat.

"And he's done a lot of work on himself—actually, that's something you two have in common! Self-improvement! Maybe you've even read some of the same books."

"I highly doubt he has a Mind Oasis. If he does, it looks like the Unabomber's cabin," I say, but I don't really mean it. At this point, acting like Max is terrorizing me is more of a reflex than a real effort.

Holly points at me, wiggling her finger. "See, this? This isn't helping. You have a bad attitude when it comes to Max."

I cross my arms. "I thought you were always supposed to be on my side. You're my twin!"

Holly laughs. "Okay, now you're being ridiculous. I'm always on your side. If there was a Team Laurel, I'd be the captain. I'd have T-shirts made up. I'd bring snacks to every game. But this whole hating-Max thing . . . I thought you only did that because you were Team Holly. Didn't you hate him because of what he said about me?"

"Well . . . yes," I concede.

"And now you don't have to worry about that anymore!" She smiles brightly. "Problem solved! You can finally admit that Max is actually pretty nice and helpful, and, not for nothing, the man looks good when he's carrying heavy items around the farm."

I can't tell Holly, because I can barely admit it to myself, that I need to keep the flame of my hatred for Max burning because if I don't have that to hide behind, then my feelings are way too hard to explain. How can things change so much over the course of two days?

"I thought he was a jerk," I explain. "Mostly because of what he said about you, but also because of . . . well, everything else about him. He showed up acting like he couldn't believe he had to be fake married to me—"

"To be fair," Holly says, "we did kind of spring that on him."

"And he hated everything about all of our Christmas traditions," I continue.

Holly sighs, her eyes full of empathy. "Max didn't have the

childhood we did, Laurel. And he doesn't have the family we have."

"I know," I say. "But that doesn't explain why half the time he acts like a total jerk."

"Did you ever think," Holly says gently, "that maybe he's acting that way because half the time *you're* kind of a jerk to *him*?"

I gasp. "How dare you blame me for this dynamic!"

Holly shrugs. "I call 'em like I see 'em. I'm pretty sure Max likes you."

"He *likes* me? What are we, seven years old?" I ask, but I can feel my face growing hot.

"I've had a lot of time to observe you two over the past couple of days, and I can tell there's something there. He's not the person he used to be. Don't judge him for having one bad day."

"I'll agree to stop hating Max. But I don't think he likes me. I don't know why he would. Earlier today, he said I was a headache designed expressly for him."

"I don't think that's true, but even if it is . . . maybe he likes that you're different from him. Did you ever think about that?"

I nod as if I'm taking in her words, but I'm busy running through a mental list of the men who have loved and then left me. The ones who thought I was too messy. Too loud. Too irresponsible to work at Wendy's. Too *much*. Holly might think I'm great, but she's related to me, and she always says the right thing. Even if it's not really true.

My phone buzzes, and "Mom FaceTime" flashes on the screen.

"Aw, looks like Mom and Dad took a break from vacationing to remember their children in frigid Ohio," I say, answering the call.

Holly moves to sit beside me as my mom's ear fills the screen.

"Mom!" Holly shouts. "You're on a FaceTime call!"

"Oh!" There's a blurry jumble before my mom's face appears on-screen. "I didn't even know I did that!"

"So . . ." I try and fail to hold in my laughter. "How's island life?"

"Wonderful," my mom says, giving us a view of the inside of her nose. "Although yesterday your father thought he covered himself in spray-on sunscreen, but he actually used bug spray, so he's quite pink now."

"But no bug bites!" my dad says, appearing beside my mom.

"Ah!" Holly and I say in unison, leaning back from the screen. Our dad is the color of a ripe strawberry.

"Are you okay?" Holly asks, the tone of her voice making it clear that she does not, in fact, think Dad is okay.

"Oh, he's fine." My mom waves us off. "I want to hear about how you girls are. How was Christmas Eve Eve dinner? Are the kids excited for Christmas? Is Doug there yet?"

"No Doug yet," Holly says. "The kids are so excited, they've barely slept for a week. And dinner was great. Actually, Laurel made it!"

"Laurel?" Mom leans forward, the concerned wrinkles on her forehead taking up most of the screen. "But Laurel can't cook."

"It's kind of a long story—" I start, but the front door

opening interrupts me. The sound of boots on the floor and two extremely friendly men talking can only mean one thing: Darius and Gilbert are back inside, and Gilbert is seconds away from overhearing something that will destroy my entire charade.

Chapter Twenty

DINNER WAS GREAT!" I say as fast as I can. "And everything went perfectly, just like it always does!"

"I'm sure," Mom says slowly. "But what I want to know is why you were cooking when we all know about the Easy Mac."

I can hear Gilbert talking to Darius as he pulls off his boots in the foyer. My breath quickens.

"Enough about the Easy Mac," I whisper directly into the phone. "You're missing a lot of stuff by being in Hawaii right now, Mom. Things I don't even have time to explain."

"What?" my mom asks, her voice an octave higher. "What's going on there? Do we need to book a flight back?"

"No," Holly says reassuringly, placing a gentle hand on my arm that I think is an attempt to calm me down. But I can't stop glancing over my shoulder, waiting to see when Darius and Gilbert are going to walk in. "Everything's fine and I'll explain—"

"Laurel!" Gilbert shouts. "The woodshop was heavenly!

But Darius wouldn't let me use the band saw. Oh, well. Maybe next year."

"Who is that?" my mom asks.

I make a noise that's a combination of a grunt and a screech as I end the call, then throw the phone across the room, where it bounces off a pile of seasonal pillows and lands on another seasonal pillow. Thank God Holly's home is so well insulated.

"Why did you *throw* it?" Holly whispers, but Darius and Gilbert are behind us, so I turn and offer them a smile.

"Hi, guys!" I say cheerfully, a note of panic lacing my voice.

"Oh, man," Holly says to Darius. "I have a great story to tell you later."

I hit her with a pillow. "You do not."

"Oooh, I love stories!" Gilbert says, sitting down in the armchair Holly vacated.

I need a quick subject change. "Gilbert, do you want to watch a Christmas movie?"

"What movie? Oh, who am I kidding, I'll watch anything you pick out!" he says. I'm amazed that he's always game for anything.

I crack my knuckles. "You're in luck, because you're talking to a Christmas movie expert. Allow me to be your concierge."

"Lexie!" Noah shouts from upstairs with wild abandon. "We're watching a movie!"

"How did they hear that?" I ask, turning to Holly.

She glances at the faux-antique clock on the mantel. "Oh, the timer went off on their iPad, so they've probably been roaming around waiting for someone to give them more screen time."

"Screen time!" Lexie yells, running toward us with a half-eaten sugar cookie in each hand and the energy of someone who's ready to wreak havoc on purge night.

Holly raises her brows. "Are you sure you can handle this?"

"I'm their mom," I say generously, and Holly barely keeps herself from rolling her eyes—her body vibrates with the effort. "I think I can handle a little extra sugar and TV."

"Oooo-kay!" she says in a singsong voice.

I prepare a movie flight, if you will, for Gilbert that keeps things light, decidedly nonromantic, and family friendly because the kids are here. First up, *A Charlie Brown Christmas*, which wins points for having no romance at all, unless you count Snoopy kissing Lucy (which is more of a lick, really, given that he's a dog). Gilbert seems to enjoy it, although he cries very loudly when everyone decorates that little tree (who could blame him, though).

Next up is the twins' favorite: *Rudolph the Red-Nosed Reindeer.* They sing along loudly, and Gilbert clearly relates to the song about being a misfit. He cries at the end of this one, too, although I can't for the life of me figure out why. While there is a bit of romance in this movie, it's mostly an innocent crush between deer and unlikely to do any lasting harm to Gilbert's psyche.

But *Charlie Brown* and *Rudolph* were merely appetizers to the entrée of our Christmas movie night. After keeping my ankle elevated during both films, I'm in remarkably good spirits. Possibly because I can sit here without feeling the need to pretend I know how to cook or skate or care for goats.

Now, though, it's time for our main event. The pièce de résistance. We're watching one of the greatest Christmas movies known to humans of any age, one that appeals universally to kids from one to ninety-two: *Elf*.

"I haven't seen *Elf* in years," Gilbert says from his place on the love seat, where he's swaddled in a fleece blanket.

"It's very funny," I assure him. Yes, there is some romance between Buddy the Elf and Zooey Deschanel, but honestly it's one of those plotlines that's better when you don't think about it too much, so I'm hoping Gilbert will overlook it and focus on Buddy putting maple syrup on his spaghetti.

From the moment the opening credits begin, I couldn't feel more at home. I cuddle up with the twins on Holly's couch, their sticky hands leaving sugar all over my shirt. Holly brings in hot chocolate and cookies on a reindeer plate. Will Ferrell runs through a revolving door and pukes as "Pennies from Heaven" plays. At one point, Noah laughs so hard that he pees his pants and we have to pause the movie to get him new underwear. This, to me, is Christmas.

And by the end, as usual, I cry when Zooey Deschanel leads the crowd in an emotional sing-along of "Santa Claus Is Comin' to Town."

"Why are you crying?" Lexie asks, horrified. She doesn't bother to ask why Gilbert is crying—she's seen his tears frequently enough that she isn't fazed.

"She does that when she's happy sometimes," Noah answers, unaffected, chewing on a candy cane.

"I think it's beautiful, that's all," I say. "They all worked together and believed, and look what happened. They saved the day."

A loud gulp startles all of us, and I turn to look at Gilbert in the love seat. Tears cover his cheeks as he sobs, still watching the screen.

"Uh-oh," Noah says.

"Gilbert isn't crying because he's happy," Lexie points out, and she's not wrong. Gilbert looks more "miserably contemplating the state of his life" than "enjoying the cathartic emotional release of a family Christmas comedy."

"Why don't you guys go help out in the kitchen," I say, sitting up straight and gently pushing them off my lap. "Let me talk to Gilbert for a minute."

They run off, surely in search of more cookies, and I turn to Gilbert. "Hey."

He sniffles. "I'm sorry I ruined the movie with my loud crying."

I start to hand him a tissue, then change my mind and pass him the whole box. "That's okay."

"It's not the first time this has happened. Once I was asked to leave a showing of *Marley & Me* because several guests complained that my loud sobs were disrupting their viewing experience." He blows his nose.

"In my opinion, they shouldn't have gone to see *Marley & Me* if they didn't expect to encounter a man crying."

"Thanks, Laurel," Gilbert says, moving on to tissue number two. "Not everyone's comfortable with a grown man's tears."

I clap my hands on my knees. "Well, I'm plenty comfortable, so cry away. What's up?"

Gilbert sighs, looking at the TV, where the end credits are rolling. "Seeing a large elf fall in love with a cynical woman really made me think about how my marriage fell apart."

From anyone else, this sentence might seem ridiculous, but in this moment, from this person, I understand it deeply. "Does Jovie remind you of Charlene?"

He shakes his head quickly. "Oh, no. For starters, Charlene would never work at a department store. She's terrible at customer service."

That isn't really what I meant, but I nod, anyway.

"But it did make me remember how Charlene and I met. I was inside a polar bear costume at the Columbus Zoo. Before I found my calling in regional magazine editing, I primarily did mascot work. She was there with her friends. We locked eyes . . . Well, her eyes met my eyes, which were behind the mesh screen in the polar bear's mouth . . . and the rest was history. She'd always been scared of mascots before that—a bad experience when she was a kid with the Columbus Clippers' seal mascot—but she said that when she saw me dressed as a polar bear, she felt safe right away."

I almost ask what bad experience a child could possibly have with Lou Seal, the Columbus Clippers' mascot that dresses like a pirate, but I remember that isn't the point.

"And how did you feel with her?" I ask.

Gilbert gives me a defeated glance. "The same way. Safe. At home. I've never had a fear of mascots, thankfully, but there was something about Charlene that let me know that even if she was inside a giant mascot costume, I'd still see her. I'd still know her."

I frown. I'd expected, I don't know, a less serious answer from Gilbert. "Well, maybe safe isn't what you need. Maybe you need a little bit of excitement, a little bit of danger."

Gilbert shakes his head sadly. "Danger and excitement

aren't for me. I'm a rule follower, Laurel. I drive the speed limit. I never litter. I don't eat yogurt if it's even one day past the expiration date."

"But it's still totally fine to eat," I assure him.

His shoulders slump. "That's what they tell me, but I'm not willing to risk it. I don't want danger and excitement in my relationship. I want to know that someone will be there when I come home, that someone wants to work on puzzles while we watch *FBI*. And look where that got me. Charlene left me for an *accountant*. He probably hang glides and never does puzzles and eats expired yogurt all the time."

"I hope he gets food poisoning," I say with vigor.

Gilbert gives me a grateful smile. "Thanks, Laurel. I know you're my employee, but you're a good friend."

That admission, that I'm a good friend, should make me feel great about myself. But instead, it makes me a little sad. Shouldn't Gilbert have more people in his life? Shouldn't he have someone to talk to, someone to spend Christmas with, other than a mostly remote employee he sees once a month? Someone who isn't lying to him about her entire life?

"Gilbert," I say forcefully. "I didn't know that much about your relationship until recently. But believe me when I say this: you deserve better. You're caring, and you're friendly, and you're a hell of a boss. You didn't even make me feel bad that time I had to take two days off to get my tooth repaired because I chipped it when Noah slammed into me in the twins' birthday party bounce house."

Gilbert waves me off. "We've all been there."

"I've had a lot of bosses, and none of them have had as much kindness or as much warmth as you have in your pinky finger," I say, thinking for a moment about how my last boss was quite content to put me out on the street after essentially using me for sex and underpaid labor. "You're a good person, and you deserve whatever you want in a relationship. And if that's a person to do a puzzle with while you watch a CBS crime procedural, then so be it. There's no way Charlene's accountant is as good as you. It's her loss. Seriously."

Gilbert's face contorts into a grimace, and at first I'm afraid he's going to start crying again. Not that I can't handle the tears, but I've been trying to make him feel better.

But instead, he joins me on the couch and wraps me in a hug. "Wait, is it okay if I do this? Am I crossing a boss/employee boundary?"

I laugh. "I mean, you're already staying at my house for Christmas. I think we're past boundaries at this point. Hug away."

He sits back. "Technically I'm here for Christmas Eve. It's not Christmas yet."

The two of us turn our gazes toward the window, where the snow is once again coming down hard. It feels like we're the inhabitants of a tiny house in a snow globe.

"There's no way you're getting out of here tonight," I say. "Not in that sports car, and not even if Marge Jamison manages to get her plow out of the barn. I think you're going to get the full Grant-family-Christmas-morning experience."

Gilbert claps, then sobers up. "Wait. I'm intruding."

I shake my head. "We want you here."

And I realize as I say the words . . . I *do* want him here. Gilbert, my nerdy, risk-averse, encouraging boss is becoming an actual friend. He wears socks under his Birkenstocks into the office in the summer, and I don't even care. He's a good person, dad footwear be damned.

"Thanks," he says quietly. "Being around your family is the only thing making this holiday bearable."

I'm about to say something when the floor creaks behind us, and I whip my head around so fast I get hair in my mouth. Max stands at the foot of the stairs, watching us with an inscrutable look on his face. He's not looking at me the way he does when I'm singing Mariah Carey. He's not looking at me like he thinks I'm funny, which he's done way more than I ever expected over the past twenty-four hours. This is a new look, one I don't understand, but it brings back that feeling from when Max carried me inside and set me down on the couch, when our eyes met, and for a moment, I forgot who we were. I forgot I was Laurel, the woman who never met a good situation she couldn't screw up. And I forgot he was Max, the man who I hated for years without even knowing him.

And then I remember what Gilbert said about the moment he met Charlene, the moment her eyes found his through the mesh of the mascot mouth.

"Well, speak of the devil!" says Gilbert. "Although that's only a saying, of course, Max. You know I'd never imply you were Satan. I mean that I was telling Laurel how happy I am to be here with your family this Christmas. Seeing how much the two of you love each other . . . well, maybe it sounds silly, but it gives me hope."

I feel my eyes widen. The look on Max's face now is one I understand all too well, because I've seen it on him many times. Most times, actually. It's discomfort. I'm feeling it, too, given that I have all sorts of unwanted, mascot-eyes-feelings for Max. I need to do something to make this interminably awkward moment end.

"You missed *Elf*," I blurt.

"Oh, Max." Gilbert closes his eyes as if he's eaten a bite of decadent chocolate cake. "It was perfection."

"Transcendent," I say.

"Emotionally wrenching," Gilbert adds. He places his hands in his lap like an excited child waiting for Santa. "What's your favorite part of *Elf*? Because mine's when Buddy and Jovie sing 'Baby It's Cold Outside.'"

Max shakes his head. "I hate *Elf*."

Gilbert and I gasp, turning to look at each other, our eyes wide.

"Okay," Max says, casting his gaze toward the ceiling and letting out a rueful laugh. "Don't tell me you've never met anyone who hates that ridiculous movie."

"What can you hate about a joyful Christmas movie that's appropriate for all ages?"

Max sighs, then holds up a hand and starts counting on his fingers. "One, the elf costume is creepy. It makes me uncomfortable to see a grown man wear that for an entire film."

"Well, I think it's a nice look," Gilbert says quietly, and I nod my approval at him.

"Secondly, and most importantly, the romance is disturbing. You're telling me he's so childish that he eats cotton balls thinking they're candy, yet he impregnates Zooey Deschanel? That's gross."

I wrinkle my nose and turn to Gilbert, who's staring at Max with his mouth open. "It wasn't gross until you made it gross, perv," I say.

Max throws his hands in the air. "Oh, like you weren't all thinking it."

"I wasn't." I shake my head. "I wasn't thinking it."

"I wasn't thinking it, either," Gilbert says sadly. "Maybe this isn't the innocent, inspirational romance I thought it was."

"Look what you're doing," I say to Max as I point to Gilbert. "You're ruining the movie for him."

"The *movie*'s ruining the movie. All I did was point out a few questionable parts."

"Is Buddy creepy?" Gilbert asks, head in his hands. "Is it necessarily strange to meet your wife while in costume?"

"I mean, yeah, I'd say so," Max says.

"Gilbert and Charlene met while he was dressed in a polar bear costume at the zoo," I tell Max.

"And look how that turned out," Gilbert wails.

"Of course they did," Max mutters, but then he surprises me by sitting down on the other side of Gilbert. "Gilbert. Look at me."

Gilbert slowly lifts his head from his hands. I watch Max, arms crossed, with a "this better be good" expression on my face.

"I'm sorry for what I said about *Elf*." Max's expression is as serious as it always is. "I shouldn't have insulted something that means a lot to you, even if I think it's painfully unfunny and cringingly juvenile and—"

"Quit while you're ahead," I whisper, giving him a "wrap it up" gesture.

"Right. This is why Laurel and I work so well together. I'm the stick in the mud, and she's the kite tied to me, trying in vain to pull me out of the muck. She's the one who lets me know when I'm being a giant, contrarian asshole, when instead I could let people enjoy their interests without commenting."

I fall back onto the couch. This was all a lot easier when we were lightly bantering about the merits of a Will Ferrell movie. But when Max is being kind to Gilbert and saying nice things about me, I don't know what to think.

Gilbert sniffles. "You two seem perfect for each other."

"Exactly," I say, putting a hand on Gilbert's shoulder. "I'm the kite trying to fly away into the clouds, and Max is the stick that keeps me grounded by persistently pulling me back down into the dirt."

"I think there might be a more romantic way to put it," Max mutters.

"The dirt's not so bad if we're both there," I say, and while I say it as a joke, when I meet Max's eyes, it doesn't feel like one. It feels like we're a team.

"You deserve better, Gilbert," Max says. "I haven't known you long, but I can tell that you're kind and fun and an amazing boss to my wife. You'll find someone who can see how great you are."

"Thank you," Gilbert says, wiping away a tear. He sits up straight. "I think you're right."

"Dinner!" Holly calls, swinging through the kitchen door. While I was nursing an injured ankle, watching multiple movies, and being surprised that Max is so good at comforting my boss, she and Darius were the ones keeping this house running and making yet another meal.

"Wow." Gilbert shakes his head in wonder. "It's amazing

that both of you are such great cooks. Are your parents good at cooking, too?"

I nod and attempt to stand up before remembering why I've been watching movies all afternoon—my ankle. Before I can so much as wince, Max grabs my shoulder and puts his arm around me, holding me steady.

There's that word again, the one I can't stop using for him this weekend. Steady. Sure, he might be a stick in the mud, but a lot of other things are steady, too. A lot of things you can count on.

"Our parents are both amazing when it comes to food," I say as Max helps me into the dining room. We all take our seats as Holly and Darius bring out bowls and plates. The twins sit in their places, two crustless peanut butter sandwiches, one with jelly and one without, sitting in front of them.

Max gently places me in my seat, and I pat his arm as a thank-you, because that's what you would do for a real husband, right? "My mom loves making elaborate holiday dinners, and my dad's thing is breakfast."

"You should taste his cinnamon rolls," Holly says, sitting down. "We'll invite you over some weekend when they're back."

"I'd love that." Gilbert beams, placing his napkin on his lap as if he's somewhere far fancier than Holly's dining room.

And so we eat, all of us together like some weird thrown-together family. It's one of the best Christmas Eve dinners I've had, and not only because of the food—although Holly and Darius made a lasagna that is, as Gilbert put it, "better than Olive Garden, and I didn't think that was possible."

No, this is nice because of the company. Nice because Gilbert is here beaming like he didn't even get his heart stomped all over; nice because my sister is right across from me, smiling at me in our secret sister language when Gilbert makes that Olive Garden comment, because we're *definitely* going to discuss it later; nice because I know she's sitting beside the love of her life; nice because the twins launch a coordinated attack and throw peas at me. (Okay, so that last part isn't nice, but it does add a certain lively energy to the dinner.)

It's also nice that Max is beside me, not saying much but interjecting occasionally. Maybe, I've realized over the past couple of days, Max is less a grumpy asshole and more a man of few words. Maybe he stays quiet unless he has something to say. That's a way of life that I, personally, don't understand, being the girl who had her seat moved three separate times on the first day of second grade because I wouldn't stop talking to whomever sat next to me until the teacher eventually had to sit me next to the class pet, an iguana who could *not* hold up his end of the conversation. But maybe—you know, if I really thought about it—that could be a quality I appreciate in a person.

I try to avoid looking at Max, focusing on the food or the twins, but when I can't stop myself from glancing at him, I catch him looking right at me. And when he gives me a smile—one of the big ones, one of the smiles I never thought would be directed toward me—I can't help smiling back.

Chapter Twenty-One

After dinner, Holly volunteers to give the kids a bath and put them to bed.

"Thank you so much for taking care of them," I say from my post on the couch, where my ankle is propped up on a pillow. "You're a lifesaver. What would I, a busy mom, ever do without you?"

She narrows her eyes at me, but she smiles. "Right. Well, what are aunts for, you know?"

And then one of them yells, and she runs upstairs to prevent any more destruction, Darius right behind her. "You take it easy, Mama!" he calls to me. "We got this!" He also gives me an exaggerated thumbs-up, as if to say, *Are you amazed by how well I'm selling this?*

Gilbert stands in front of the Christmas tree, inspecting the salt dough ornaments the kids made last year, as I get myself situated on the couch.

Every Christmas Eve, I do the same thing: I watch *It's a*

Wonderful Life. As a kid, I used to watch it with Grandma Pat, who passed down her crush on Jimmy Stewart. Is it weird to have the same crush as your grandma? I'd prefer not to think about it too much. But she was the first one to show me the movie, and even though I found it boring as a small child, I sat through it because I could fall asleep on her shoulder, her heavy rose-scented lotion perfuming my dreams.

I wasn't wrong to be bored—it's not really a movie for small children. It's long, and there are no talking animals or fart jokes, which were all I cared about back then. But it's also painfully adult—not in the sense that it features anything sexual or inappropriate for a tiny kid, but because it's about adult concerns that a child couldn't possibly understand. What could a kid know about the idea of feeling like you wasted your life, your potential? About the idea of feeling like you're stuck? About the idea of feeling like you made all the wrong decisions and now it's too late, much too late, to change them?

Let's just say that when I was eight years old, those weren't the most pressing topics on my mind. I spent more time thinking about Christmas morning breakfast (cinnamon rolls) and what presents I hoped Santa would bring (one of those dolls that peed) than I did about adult regret.

As I got older, however, I appreciated some aspects of the film. Namely, I appreciated the fact that Jimmy Stewart was a huge babe. Tall, gangly, talked like no one I'd ever heard. But most importantly, the character he played, George Bailey, was solid. Upstanding. Always doing the right thing that helped other people—his brother, his father, his children, the town—even when it didn't help him. Even when it hurt him.

And he suffered. Oh, how he suffered. There's even a

scene—the crux of the movie, really, the part that brings on the angel and sets the whole moral of the story into motion—where he thinks about ending his life.

But what he learns—and we learn along with him—is that life is worth living, not for what we can get out of it, but for what we can give. Life isn't about your business succeeding or driving a flashy car. It's about all those little moments, the ones that seem so mundane at the time but end up being completely magical when you think about losing them. When the angel tells George Bailey that having friends means he isn't a failure, I lose it. It's physically impossible for me to make it through the entire movie without sobbing, and frankly, I don't want to know anyone who isn't emotionally affected by it.

I mean, Max could probably watch it with a stone face, but I like to think he'd be crying on the inside.

I don't expect anyone to watch it with me—Holly likes it fine, but last year she told me she has it memorized after a million viewings and has no desire to watch it again, which . . . okay, fair. I don't understand it, but I do respect it.

But Gilbert sits down on the love seat as if he can't imagine doing anything I'm not a part of. "What are we watching?" he asks.

I raise my eyebrows. "You're absolutely welcome to hang out with me, but you don't have to. If you want to go to bed, I'd understand."

Gilbert waves me off. "I don't want to go to bed yet. I feel like the *Stranger Things* LEGO is watching me."

I frown. "I thought Holly moved that."

Gilbert gives me a conspiratorial look. "She did, but don't you feel like it can see through walls?"

At this point, I think it might be best to start the movie. "Okay, so I'm watching *It's a Wonderful Life*, which is what I do every Christmas Eve. Have you seen it?"

Gilbert shakes his head.

"In that case, you're in for a treat," I say, cuing up the movie. I'm ready for two of my favorite hours of the whole year, when Max walks in, holding an ice bag.

"Your husband would never leave you alone on Christmas Eve, right?" he asks without looking at me. He gently lifts my leg, slides under it so it's on his lap, and then props it up on a pillow and places the ice bag on it.

"Um, thanks," I say. There may be a pillow and a bag of ice encasing my foot, but Max and I are doing a lot of touching.

Gilbert slaps his knees and stands up. "Well, that's my cue to turn in."

"What?" I ask, panic seeping into my voice as I realize Gilbert is about to leave me alone with Max. "But you wanted to watch *It's a Wonderful Life*! I thought you were scared of the *Stranger Things* LEGO!"

Gilbert shakes his head. "I'd rather move the *Stranger Things* LEGO into the hallway than be the third wheel on your Christmas Eve date night."

"This isn't a date night," I say quickly. Gilbert can't leave me here alone with Max, the two of us on the couch with my only slightly operational leg on his lap. I cannot be forced to deal with the complicated feelings I have for him, because

I've been trying to avoid thinking about what Holly said all day. Going from hating him for years to thinking he was kind of cute but still an enemy of my family to realizing that he might like me (and that Holly has totally forgiven him) is a confusing cocktail of emotions, and I'm not in the mood to face it.

But it's too late . . . Gilbert is already walking up the stairs. "Enjoy the movie," he says, giving us a bittersweet look over his shoulder. I can tell he's about to say something about how seeing us together makes him think of some random Charlene memory, but he shakes his head and keeps walking as if he thinks better of it.

"Wow," Max says. "He didn't mention the crushing weight of his broken heart once. I think that's progress."

"Yeah, but that might be because he was so focused on the scary LEGO." I glance at the stairs to make sure he's not coming back down. "Okay, you don't have to keep my leg on your lap anymore."

I start to slide it away, but Max carefully slides it back. "You can leave it. I don't mind."

I grab the remote. The sooner I start the movie, the sooner I can be sucked into the world of Bedford Falls, where I won't have to think about what it means that Max actually wants any part of my body on his lap.

I press Play and lean back against a throw pillow that says "Sleigh Queen Sleigh." Max doesn't offer up any complaints, and whenever I sneak glances at him during the film, he actually seems focused on the screen. He's not sighing or sleeping or checking his phone. He might even be . . . enjoying himself?

By the time we reach the last scene, I'm crying (as usual). I try to rein myself in—Max will make fun of me, probably, or I'll be subject to a litany of reasons why this movie is, the horror, even *worse* than *Elf*!

I turn to Max, about to tell him to keep his anti-Christmas-movie feelings to himself. But as the final scene ends, a tear rolls down his cheek . . . a single, perfect tear, as if his body is simply leaking feelings.

He wipes it away quickly with his sleeve, then cuts me a surreptitious glance. His shoulders slump when he sees me watching him.

"You had an emotion," I say softly.

He shakes his head. "Didn't."

"Did."

"Someone must've been cutting onions."

"At ten p.m.?"

"It's possible," Max says gruffly, not looking at me. "Holly's done weirder things than chop produce at ten p.m."

I can't argue with that. The DVD menu screen plays, and there's only so long we can stare at it before someone (okay, me) gets tired of the awkward silence and starts a conversation. The only sound is Frank snoring in the corner. I'm about ready to break the silence by telling him a knock-knock joke I googled last night to impress the twins when he asks, "So why do you like Christmas so much?"

He moves his eyes from the menu screen to me, and I feel it again: that full-body melt when his attention is on me. How does he do that? Related: Why doesn't he do it more often?

"You make it sound like you're asking me why I like

stepping on rusted nails. It's a pretty popular holiday. Some TV channels have built an entire business around it."

"Sure," he says. "But your love of it is particularly intense. Why?"

Talking about why I love Christmas is the easiest thing in the world, easier than explaining why I like cheeseburgers with chocolate milkshakes or seventy-degree days in the park, so I explain.

"Because Christmas is me. Me and Holly, I mean. Our family. We were born on Christmas, in case you hadn't heard. Hence the names."

Max smiles. My foot is still in his lap, and his hand rests lightly against my non-injured ankle. He must not notice that it's still there. "Ah, yes, the themed names. Your parents have a great sense of humor."

"Or they predicted how much we'd love Christmas. These names would've been extremely unfortunate if we hated the holiday. Can you imagine if *you* had a Christmas-themed name?"

Max furrows his brow. "What would that even be?"

"Rudolph," I say immediately, and he laughs. He actually laughs, and the sound of it is even better than the way his eyes make me feel. His laugh is warm and deep and, frankly, a little bit erotic. I blush, feeling my face becoming as red as Rudolph's nose.

"Nick, as in Saint," he says.

"Angel."

"Christian."

"Oh, good one," I say. "Krampus."

He laughs again, this time louder, and I shush him. "Don't

wake the twins. They're snug in their beds, dreaming about sugarplums."

"No one would ever name their child Krampus," he says in a low voice. "Not even my parents. So you like it because it's your birthday?"

I shake my head. "It's actually extremely inconvenient to have a birthday on the biggest holiday of the year. No one can come to your party because they're with their family or on a trip. And it's like, what do you do for your party?"

"Sledding," we say at the same time, and I laugh.

"Right. We had so many sledding parties that were held in January. I don't even like sledding that much. I hate getting snow in my boots. Honestly, I'd much rather have a pool party like all the summer babies, but it's, like, sledding, ice-skating, or skiing. Those are the options.

"I love Christmas on its own," I say as the fire crackles. I'm almost *too* warm here, with my feet on Max's lap and the blanket on me, but the last thing I want to do is move. "It's the most special day in our family, the most special time of year. All of our family traditions revolve around these holidays. My parents always did everything they could to make it over the top and magical—and I don't mean gifts. Honestly, we didn't have a ton of money when I was little, so it was never about flashy presents. It was about being together. That's what all of this is about. The cookies. The movies. Every time I do those things, I think about all the other times I've done them. I love the music because listening to it makes me think of all the other times I've listened to it. Like, I heard these same songs when I was decorating cookies made from this same recipe with my grandma when I was ten years old.

And now I'm an adult and I'm doing the same thing with Holly's kids. Of course, this Christmas is a little different from the others . . ."

Max raises a hand. "Because I'm here?"

"Well, yeah. That. And the Gilbert of it all. And the, uh . . ."

"Deception," Max supplies.

"One might call it that."

"If one was being accurate."

"I'd kick you right now if my foot wasn't broken."

"Your foot isn't broken," he says, and what I might've read as condescension earlier now seems like reassurance. "Injured, yes. But not broken."

"Why did you go to medical school if you're not a doctor?" I ask, and he frowns.

"A lot of questions tonight."

"Well, Holly pointed out that I know almost nothing about you, and I realized she's right."

He looks at me skeptically. "You've been hating me based on zero knowledge?"

"I never said I hated you."

"Not in those exact words, but you've come close."

"You hated me first," I say.

He turns those deep brown eyes on me, their spotlight shining directly inside me, and says, "I didn't hate you. I was occasionally frustrated with you. I wondered why you were so mean to me, and sometimes, I'm ashamed to admit, I was mean back. But I never hated you."

I'm momentarily too stunned to speak, the air pushed out of me like all those times I flew off my sled during sledding birthday parties and landed hard on the ground. "You did, though."

"Didn't," he says, an echo of our earlier conversation.

I shake my head. "But you were such a jerk to me at the wedding. You acted like dancing with me was a punishment."

"Because you were a jerk to me!" he says, so exasperated he barks out a laugh. "You were scowling at me the entire length of the song. And now you know how I feel about dancing."

"Well, I didn't know that then," I say. "You could've warned me."

"What was I supposed to say? Should I have emailed you and said, 'Nice to meet you, I'm Max and I hate dancing, karaoke, and the general concept of fun'?"

"Yeah, maybe," I say with a laugh. "That would've been a nice heads-up. But that doesn't explain why you were so pissed to see me when you walked in Holly's front door on Christmas Eve Eve."

"Because you were pissed at me and I didn't even know why. How was I supposed to react?"

"I don't really think that's my fault. You *did* insult my favorite person in the world, and if you hated Holly, you might as well hate me. We have the same birthday and the same face."

"You don't have the same face," he says brusquely. "Your eyes are bluer. Your hair is lighter. Your lips are fuller."

He's been thinking about my lips? And my hair and my eyes and . . . me?

"I know you think there's no possible way I could have an excuse for what I said about Holly at the wedding, and I'm not saying this makes it okay, but now that we're talking, and now that we don't hate each other . . . can I explain myself?"

He looks at me so earnestly, those brown eyes pleading, but he doesn't even have to ask. I don't have it in me to push him away anymore—if Holly's forgiven him, so have I.

"Go ahead."

"What you overheard before the ceremony was . . . correct. I'm not going to pretend I didn't say that, and I'm not going to pretend it wasn't shitty. But I didn't say it because I hated Holly. I said it because . . . well . . . remember how I told you that my family isn't like yours?"

I nod.

He gently moves my foot as he shifts on the sofa to face me. "Darius's family is a lot like yours, though. Big and loud and fun."

"Oh, yeah." I smile, remembering what they were like at the wedding. Much like Darius, they're full of enthusiasm, and they were all too happy to hit the dance floor and take advantage of the photo booth.

"I spent a lot of time at their house when I was a kid. His parents were nice and normal. They only yelled at us when we deserved it, they didn't drink at all, they rarely fought, and when they did, it never ended with one of them storming out of the house. It was the complete opposite of my house, where I never knew how drunk my parents would be, how mad they would get, or which one of them would slam the front door and end up wrapping their car around a tree. Darius's house was where I learned what a family was supposed to be, what it could be if you actually cared about each other. And then . . . we found LEGO."

"And LEGOs changed your life?"

Max sighs. "I hate to be like this, but . . . it's LEGO. Not plural. You can say LEGO bricks, but never LEGOs."

"Oh my God," I breathe. "You're a nerd."

Max looks at me, his mouth in a straight line.

I widen my eyes. "Are you gonna report me to the AFOL boards?"

"I regret ever telling you this."

"I'm kidding! I think it's great. Hobbies are nice, and trust me, no one understands the need to connect to your inner child more than me. Most of the time, I'm living as my inner child, but unfortunately, she's chaotic and could never sit still long enough to build LEGOs. I'm sorry, *LEGO*."

Max studies me, and I freeze as I feel his eyes over my face, as tangible as if his fingers were there. "I don't know," he finally says. "I bet you could do the sets that are designed for ages four and up."

"But not the big-kid sets," I say with mock seriousness.

"Definitely not the eighteen-plussers," he agrees. "Not without help, anyway."

"Fortunately, I happen to know a LEGO master or two. But stop trying to change the subject."

"Right. So Darius's family had this finished basement where we could watch cartoons and build. It was this completely safe, secret world where my parents didn't exist, where I was a normal kid. His parents would bring us snacks instead of forgetting about us and making us scavenge for our own dinner. Sometimes his sisters would come downstairs and we'd pretend we wanted them to leave, but I loved it. Just having someone else around, someone who paid attention to me. It was great."

"It *sounds* great," I say, and he nods.

"Those were my only good childhood memories," he said. "And when Darius said he was getting married, I couldn't understand it. Because I knew what marriage was—or I thought I did—and it sucked. I knew happy marriages existed—I mean, I saw Darius's parents—but it seemed like too big a risk to take. I didn't know why he'd want to put himself in that situation, one where he and Holly could grow to hate each other and maybe even terrorize a child. And a part of me . . . it's embarrassing to admit it, but a part of me was jealous. He was my best friend—my *only* friend—and he had someone else who was way more important to him than me. I thought maybe we'd grow apart and I'd be . . . alone."

He sighs, rubbing his hands over his face. "It feels so stupid to admit that. I'm an adult, and I was worried about being left out."

"I don't think it's stupid," I say. I imagine Max as a little boy, hiding away so he wouldn't get shouted at, spending all his time with Darius. Being alone. Being lonely.

Max looks up at the ceiling, like he's ashamed to look me in the eye. "So I said what I said to Darius. On his wedding day. Like the world's biggest asshole."

"There are probably bigger assholes," I say.

He looks at me, finally. "Oh, yeah? Up until two days ago, who would you say was Asshole Number One?"

Deep brown eyes. I can't lie. "Well, okay. You."

"That's what I thought."

"But in my defense, I didn't know anything about you! I didn't know any of this."

"Most people don't know my entire personal history, but I

still don't want them to think I'm an asshole. Anyway, eventually Darius told me that if I wanted to be part of his life, I couldn't treat Holly like she was some expendable interloper. He told me I was a brother to him, but that Holly always came first. And it made me realize two things—one, I was being a massive asshole. And two, that maybe I would've seen marriage as something different if that's what I grew up with. You know, if my dad had looked at my mom the way Darius looks at Holly."

I smile softly. "They really are in love, aren't they?"

"Sickeningly so."

"They make me want to vomit sometimes," I agree.

"The matching coffee mugs," we say at the same time, and then laugh.

I can't believe Max shared all this with me. I can't believe I never knew all of this. I can't believe the raw seasonal power of *It's a Wonderful Life* made this happen.

"Thanks for telling me," I say quietly. "And I'm sorry I didn't let you explain yourself earlier."

"It's okay," Max says. "I'm still pretty ashamed that I ever said that. But what I'm really sorry about is that it kept me from getting to know you. I think if we could've talked, like we are right now . . . two people on a couch, who are actually listening to each other? Maybe we would've gotten along this entire time. Maybe we would've been friends."

Or more than friends, says the voice in my head, and I can't tell if it's Old Laurel or New Laurel. All I know is that I want to listen to her.

"Hey," I say, nudging Max with my good foot. "Want to see my favorite Christmas tradition?"

He points over his shoulder at the TV. "I thought this was it."

"Close. But this one's my very favorite. Come on." I hoist myself up and hobble over to the tree, Max right behind me. I carefully lower myself onto the ground. "Down here."

"On the floor?"

"Yep. Right under the tree. Scoot on over here." I push a few gifts out of the way until my head is right by the tree collar.

"Under the tree?" Max's voice floats down to me.

"Please don't leave me all alone under the tree," I say. "Get down here."

He sighs heavily, and then I feel him scooting in beside me. His right shoulder bumps into my left one, but I don't move. I let the heat from his body transfer into mine. "Now what?" he says, his voice close and slightly muffled by the pine needles.

"Now look up," I say, and I keep my eyes trained straight ahead. The branches, the lights. Green and brown and Technicolor glowing.

"This was my favorite thing to do when I was little," I say quietly, feeling like I should keep my voice reverently low. "It felt like my own little world, like some sort of enchanted holiday forest. Sometimes, when things are stressful and it's, like, August, I'll close my eyes and pretend I'm here under the tree, looking up at the branches and anticipating Christmas. It's better than a Mind Oasis."

"What's a Mind Oasis?"

"Don't worry about it," I say quickly.

"And does that make you feel better?" Max asks. I can tell by the puff of breath on the side of my face that he's looking at me, not up at the tree.

"It actually does," I say. "But you need to look up. It's a beautiful view you'll want to remember."

There's a slight pause, and then Max says, "I'm already looking at something I want to remember, and trust me, I can't think of a more beautiful view."

We're close, so close, that it's like our fingers intertwine of their own accord. My hand grasps his, our faces inches from each other and inches from the branches, and I hold my breath. Bite my lip. What is happening?

"Hey, Laurel," Max says, his low, rumbly voice so quiet that I barely hear him.

"Yeah?" I say on a shaky exhale.

"Happy birthday," he says as the grandfather clock strikes midnight.

I let out a little laugh. "Oh. Wow. I'm thirty-four."

"How does it feel?" he asks.

Magical. Enchanting. Surprising. Completely different than I expected. I squeeze his hand and say, "Pretty damn good, actually."

I finally turn my head to see his face, which I've been too afraid to do because I didn't know what would happen, didn't know if I'd be able to stop myself from pressing my lips to his right here under Holly's Christmas tree, right here under the twins' ornaments and the fuzzy silver-and-gold garland. The twinkling lights reflect in his glasses, a blue-and-red-and-green Christmas wonderland sparkling back at me on Max's face. I am, I realize, perfectly happy in this moment. Perfectly comfortable. Perfectly myself.

"I have to tell you something," Max says, and there's no part of me that has any idea what he's about to say. It seems like I've learned so much about him over the course of a couple of days—his LEGO fanaticism, his terrible parents, his hatred of Christmas, and his loneliness. Twenty-four hours ago, I would've thought it was fine—deserved, even—that someone like Max was painfully lonely. But now it seems like a crime, like a grave injustice that Max Beckett doesn't have more people in his life.

"What?" I ask, and although I'm going for sultry, my voice comes out in a squeak.

"Remember how I told Gilbert the story about how we met?"

I nod, the tree branches brushing against my cheeks. Everything around me smells like pine and Max.

"It was all true," he says, and my heart thumps loudly, the clip-clopping horse hooves at the beginning of "Sleigh Ride." "That party was a nightmare, but then I saw you. And you were so comfortable, so fun, so . . . you. I've never been that *myself* around people, and you did it so easily. I admired you."

"Then why . . ." I swallow. "Then why did you act like you hated me?"

Max shakes his head. "I was so miserable and I was taking it out on everyone. And when you made it clear you weren't exactly fond of me—"

"Sorry." I wince.

"Well, you were an easy target. You wouldn't care if I didn't want to hang out with you, because you didn't want to hang out with me, either. Everything else I told Gilbert—that I was going through a breakup, that I was switching jobs—it was all true. I hated medical school and I dropped out. I was surrounded by people who knew that their purpose in life was to become a doctor, and I didn't know that at all. In fact, with every day that went by, I was pretty sure I didn't want to be a doctor. Getting a front-row seat to so many of the worst parts of people's lives reminded me that I was wasting my one life going after something I didn't even want. So I quit. When the wedding rolled around, I was figuring out what I wanted to do, but I wasn't there yet, so I felt like a failure."

"But you weren't a failure," I say.

"You, however," he continues, ignoring me, "you didn't look like a failure at all. I looked at you and thought . . . that woman is the opposite of miserable. That woman knows what she wants."

I wrinkle my nose. "At the time, if I recall correctly, I was working as the photo assistant for a photographer I was dating, which meant I was the person who had to hold the little squeaky toys to make the babies look at the camera. It wasn't a glamorous life. Also." I lean forward to whisper conspiratorially to him, which only has the effect of bringing us even closer together, "he dumped me after he hooked up with a model he was taking pictures of."

Max doesn't even laugh at this. "But you knew what you wanted out of life."

I let out a little laugh. "I was a mess. I *am* a mess."

"Is that how you see yourself?" Max asks, brow crinkled in concern.

I nod, as easily as I can nod when I'm lying on my back

under a Christmas tree. "Hot Mess Express, coming through. Get off the tracks, because this train will *not* stop until it's messed up every situation possible."

Max keeps staring at me, so I add a sad "choo choo."

"No, I got the train metaphor without sound effects," he says. "I'm wondering how you can possibly think of yourself that way. You're the one who pulled this off, Laurel. The one who made Gilbert feel better. The one who . . . the one who showed me how to have fun."

I can't stop myself from beaming, because inside I feel like I'm glowing, like I'm the star on the top of a Christmas tree. "Really?" I ask. "I showed you how to have fun?"

"As much as anyone can," he says with a solemn nod. "I have it on good authority that I can't relax."

"Ouch. You heard me say that?" I ask, wincing.

"I heard a few of the million times you said it, yes. But . . . it's deserved. I rarely relax. But sometimes I can have fun. Like, for example, when I'm with you."

"Well," I say, and I don't know what makes me feel so bold. Maybe it's that we're in the safest, coziest space possible. Maybe it's my inner Christmas-tree-star feeling. Maybe it's everything Max confided to me just now. Maybe it's the power of Christmas, Mariah Carey, and Hallmark movies all mixed together, but I say, "I think I can make you like Christmas."

"Oh," Max says, and the look on his face just about kills me. "I'm liking it plenty right now."

I watch him for a moment, the Christmas tree lights casting a red-and-green-and-blue glow on his cheeks. Even in the semidarkness here under the tree, his eyes are burning.

I move my head toward his and feel his coming toward me. We're so close. I'm about to kiss Max Beckett, archenemy, nemesis, the man who I thought hated my family up until very recently. I can't believe this is—

"Laurel!" Gilbert shouts.

Chapter Twenty-Two

I SIT UPRIGHT, MY head crashing into the lowest tree branches. Gilbert stands on the stairs, his hair sticking straight up and his eyes wild.

"Laurel, where are you?" Gilbert yells—no, *screams*—as the tree crashes to the ground in slow motion, like a lumberjack cut it down. But it's no lumberjack—just me, struggling to stand up and remembering too late not to put weight on my ankle.

"What's wrong?" I ask breathlessly as I wobble to the side. Max grabs my elbow, preventing me from slowly tilting over like the tree.

"I got up to get a glass of water, and I stepped on the *Stranger Things* LEGO in the hallway!" Gilbert says. "I think a brick may be embedded in my big toe. Also I'm feeling an intense urge to text Charlene right now. I'm not used to sleeping alone, and I can't stop thinking about the Upside Down."

Apparently he doesn't notice or care that the tree fell over, and you know what? That's fair. He's a man in crisis.

"It's okay," I say, exhaling as I realize this isn't a real emergency. "I'm sure you don't actually have any LEGOs—"

"LEGO bricks," Max mutters.

"—stuck in your foot," I finish. "It just feels like that because those tiny pieces hurt like a mother when you step on them. I've been there. And we're not gonna text Charlene, okay? A late-night text will only make things worse. Trust me."

Gilbert nods, looking at his phone with an expression of confusion. "You're probably right. What's that smell, by the way?"

The three of us stop and sniff the air, and then Max yells, "The tree!"

Smoke billows out of the fireplace, where the tip of the tree has knocked over the fireplace screen and caught on fire.

As I open my mouth to ask what we're supposed to do in this situation, the smoke alarm blares through the house.

"Aaaah!" Gilbert shouts, running down the final few stairs. He grabs a half-full hot chocolate mug on the coffee table and tosses it into the flame. The fire remains unappeased.

"What is happening?" Holly stumbles down the stairs in a red plaid robe, the kids bleary-eyed behind her.

"Laurel's house is burning down and I destroyed a LEGO set!" Gilbert shouts.

"We need to calm down," Max says in an authoritative voice that is, despite (or because of) the danger, kind of sexy. "What we need is the—"

"Fire extinguisher!" Darius shouts, running into the room and vaulting over the couch. He aims the fire extinguisher toward the fireplace and wields it like he's the star in an action movie, vanquishing some sort of evil beast.

The fire sizzles out, smoke curling through the room in resignation.

"You tried to defeat us," Darius says, pointing to the tree. "But we're stronger than you."

I cross my arms. "Have you been waiting for a moment to do something like this?"

He nods, breathless. "Yes."

Holly crosses the room and puts her arms around him. She kisses his cheek, and I notice that they're wearing matching robes. "Great job, babe. You saved the house."

"You saved us all!" Gilbert says, wrapping his arms around Darius from the other side.

Holly and I raise our eyebrows at each other, and then her gaze shifts to the left of me, where Max stands, his hand still on my elbow. I shake my head, a quick "don't ask" gesture.

"Hey."

On my right, Noah stares up at me.

"Hey, bud," I say. "You can go back to sleep. Everything's okay."

"You almost burned our house down," he says.

"I wouldn't go that far," I say. "I started a fire by knocking the tree into the fireplace, but at no point was the fire in danger of taking over."

He looks at me skeptically. "Has Santa been here yet? Did you burn up our presents?"

"Oh, no," Lexie says with a low moan. "This is the worst Christmas ever."

"Santa hasn't been here yet, which means it's time for everyone to go to sleep," I say.

"Don't we have a bit of a mess to clean up?" Holly asks, tilting her head at me. "This rug—your rug, I might add, one that you really love because you found it at an estate sale and technically it can't be replaced—looks like it's covered in ashes and fire extinguisher foam."

"Hmm. So it does," I say, staring at the rug. "It's unfortunate."

"It is." She nods slowly. "One might ask what you were doing that caused you to knock over the Christmas tree, nearly destroying your own home and some of its priceless décor."

"One might, or one could keep one's mouth shut," I say with a smile.

"Why do I understand your words, but I have no idea what you're saying?" Gilbert asks, looking between both of us.

"Welcome to my world, dude," Darius says, clapping him on the back. "Max, you wanna help me hoist this tree back up?"

Fifteen minutes later (after Frank stands up and stretches, having slept through the entire crisis), you'd never even know there was a fire emergency here. Well, except for the burned treetop, and the fact that Holly rolled up the rug, lips pursed, and promised she'd take it to a dry cleaner "for me" as soon as the holiday is over.

"Seriously," she hisses to me as I help her carry the rug into the garage. "What the hell is happening? Why are you and Max standing so close together? He was touching you.

And what were you doing that knocked the tree over?" She wiggles her eyebrows.

"I'm sorry, what are you insinuating?" I grunt as we try to fit the rug through the door. "That we were having sex under the tree? Against the tree? *In* the tree? What sort of sexy action do you think results in a tree falling into the fire? Also why am I the one helping you move this when I'm injured? I can barely walk."

She shakes her head. "Because I wanted to talk to you alone. Listen, I'm your sister. I can tell when you're lying and sexually frustrated, and both of those vibes are pulsing off of you right now."

"Don't say *pulsing*," I mutter. "You're not helping with the sexually frustrated part."

"Throbbing," she says as we prop the rug up against the wall and head back into the house. "Pounding. Aching."

"Holly, stop it!" I smack her on the arm. "What are you, twelve?"

"Vibrating. Quivering. Erect."

"Uh."

We stop so quickly that Holly almost slides out of her slippers. Max stands right in front of us, arms crossed.

"Hey," I say quickly, going for a "wow, I'm so casual and we definitely didn't almost kiss under the tree before I set it on fire" vibe.

"Hey," he says back. "What's going on?"

"Vocab lesson," Holly says with a wink, and I shoot her a look of complete disgust. "Bedtime, you two. I'll put the kids back to sleep."

Bedtime. Right. The bed we're sharing tonight.

"Happy birthday, by the way," she says, leaning forward to give me a hug. Holly is, bar none, the best hugger I've ever met in my life. She has a firm squeeze and she doesn't let go too early—leave it to Holly to master the art of hugging.

"You, too," I say. "Can you believe I almost forgot about it?"

"Oh, I can believe it," she says, stepping back and giving me a pat on the arm. "There's a lot going on."

"Right," I say as she walks away, leaving me alone in the hallway with Max.

I clear my throat and scoot past him. "I'll head up first, then, and get ready while you—"

"Laurel," he says, and his voice stops me in my tracks. It reminds me of a yoga challenge I did on YouTube when I was unemployed, and how the teacher talked about sitting up straight and pretending that a beam of light was traveling up and down your spine. That's what it feels like, like Max's voice is in my body, caressing my nerve endings.

"Yeah?" I ask, my voice barely audible. I can hear the twins running around upstairs, but back in this hallway between the garage and the pantry, we're hidden away from everyone, half shrouded in darkness.

"We got interrupted earlier—"

"By the tree on fire," I say.

"Right," Max says, one side of his mouth quirking up. "But there's something I didn't get a chance to tell you."

"What?" I ask, but the word's not even out before he kisses me, closing the space between us. I'm already pressed against the wall, but we're not close enough, so I grab his shoulders and pull him into me, hard. How did I not know Max would kiss like this, like he's thirsty and I'm the only source of water for miles? How did I ever look at him and think he was annoying, instead of wondering what his hands would feel like on my arms, on my neck, on my cheeks?

I want this kiss to last for minutes, for hours, forever, but he pulls away. "All right," he says.

"All . . . right?" I'm panting, as if I ran a marathon, or at least what I imagine it might be like to run a marathon.

"Good night, Laurel," he says, a smile on his face that promises so much yet raises so many questions.

"Max, I—" I start, but he walks away, leaving me alone in the hallway, wondering what the hell just happened.

EVERYONE ELSE IS already in their rooms when I emerge from the back hallway, the smell of burnt tree lingering in the air. I eye the stairs apprehensively—maybe I should sleep on the couch? It might be safer. Because I'm not sure totally jumping Max's bones in my sister's guest room where anyone could hear us is a super smart idea.

Although I guess if Gilbert overheard us, it would add a certain verisimilitude to our plan. Not that I'm eager for my boss to overhear me having sex—that feels like Old Laurel behavior. New Laurel only has sex at appropriate times and places, not Christmas Eve (now Christmas Day) at her sister's house with a man she only recently realized wasn't her enemy.

I take a deep breath and walk up the stairs. I can do this. I'll simply tell Max that, flattered as I am by the kiss and the conversation and all that, we need to take things slowly. We simply cannot hook up tonight. We *cannot.*

But when I open the guest room door and see Max coming

out of the bathroom, a gray T-shirt clinging to his body and those too-long pajama pants slung low on his hips as he dries his face with a towel, all that comes out of my mouth is a guttural moan that resembles one of the goats in the barn.

"What was that?" he asks, dropping the towel into the hamper.

I resolve right then to let Max have his way with me. Who cares that I'm at my sister's house? Who cares that my boss is down the hall? Screw waiting. Screw responsibility. Screw New Laurel. Old Laurel was fun, and she may not have had regular employment, but she sure knew how to have a good time.

But he doesn't grab me by the shoulders and finish what we started in the hallway downstairs. He grabs his pillow and tosses it to the floor.

I do not say, "I'd like to be grabbed."

I do not say, "I'd like to be tossed."

Even though I want to.

No, I simply ask, "What are you doing?" like a normal, well-adjusted woman who isn't going through what could charitably be described as a sexual, romantic, and even emotional drought of epic proportions.

"Sleeping on the floor," he says, picking up the folded blanket at the end of the bed. That's the thing about Holly being your hostess—you're always gonna have extra folded blankets in your room.

"Why?" I attempt to be smooth, but it comes out strangled. What I mean is, "Could we not simply spend the night with our bodies tangled together, coming up for air only when and if necessary?"

He finally meets my eyes. "I think you know why, Laurel."

I flush. What's he trying to say? Has my kissing game gotten thrown off that much in these months without physical contact? Should I have been practicing on stuffed animals like I did when I was thirteen? Did I drool on him? Did I bite him?

"Did I bite you?" I ask with more urgency than is strictly required.

He pulls back a bit, startled. "No. Why, do you *think* you bit me? Are you in the habit of biting men you kiss?"

I shake my head. "Not without explicit verbal consent."

He smirks, looking down. "Verbal consent."

"Or written." I shrug. "I'm flexible."

"You're funny, Laurel," he says, and he looks at me with a pained expression (apparently not because I bit him). "And you're . . . a lot of other things, too."

Now *there's* something I've been told over and over in my life, by teachers and frenemies and coworkers and boyfriends. I'm too spontaneous, impulsive, loud, hyperactive. Too this, too that, too so many things that all add up to *too much*. And, of course, I'd be too much for Max, a man who's always perfectly in control. The words I've heard a million times in my life come back to me. *Can't you be a little more normal? Can't you be like everyone else? Can't you be less . . .* you*?*

"I know," I say. "General consensus seems to be that I am . . . a lot."

"Laurel," Max says, his voice as firm as if his hands were on my shoulders, and my head snaps up to look at him. "Do you think I mean that in a bad way?"

I nod slowly. "Well . . . yeah. Everyone else does."

"Everyone else," Max says slowly, each word precise and clear, "is an absolute idiot. Do you hear me?"

"I do," I say, and that's the truth, but while I may hear him, I don't really understand him.

"I've never met anyone like you, and I mean that in the best possible way. And that's why I'm sleeping on the floor tonight." He points toward the rug-covered hardwood.

"Because you . . . think I'm so special that you can't stand to be near me?" I ask helplessly. *Make it make sense.*

"No," he says, a gruff laugh escaping his throat. "Because I don't want this to happen at your sister's house. Or when I smell like a burnt pine tree. Or when we have to wake up in a few hours to watch two kids tear open their presents. I don't want this to happen at a place or a time when we have to keep our voices down, or when we only have a few hours. And honestly, I don't trust myself when you're next to me. I stayed awake all last night, and I don't think I can do that again."

I feel my jaw drop open, and I stand there staring at him like a largemouth bass wall hanging. He stretches his arms above his head, revealing a tantalizing sliver of lower abdomen, before saying, "Well, good night," and clicking off his bedside lamp.

He disappears below the bed to the floor, and I crawl into bed and pull the quilt over myself. I switch off my lamp and stare into the darkness, eyes wide and images of our bodies pressed together flashing in my mind as vividly as if I was watching a movie. My entire body is on fire—I'm a sentient ball of flame here in this bed, and I don't know how I'll ever fall asleep.

Chapter Twenty-Three

LAUREL. LAUREL. LAUREL!"

I open my eyes to see Noah and Lexie, their tiny round faces taking up my entire field of vision.

"It's Christmas," Lexie pants, her spittle flying into my forehead.

I wipe off my face and gently push the kids aside as I sit up. "It's still dark. Are you sure it's not yesterday?"

"It can't ever be yesterday," Lexie says, exasperation lacing her voice. "That doesn't even make sense."

"Okay, okay," I say, swinging my legs to the side. The last thing I want to do is deprive two children of their Christmas-morning happiness, one of the purest and most uncomplicated joys they'll ever have.

"But Mom says you need to wear these," Noah says, pointing to folded pajamas at the foot of the bed. "She said she forgot to pass them out last night."

"Oh!" I'm not typically one to forget a tradition, but with

all the excitement (fire, kissing, etc.) of last night, our matching family pajama tradition completely slipped my mind. This year, Holly picked out a pattern with tiny Santa-hat-wearing sloths hanging off of Christmas light strands. The twins are already wearing theirs.

"Let me go put these on and then we can—" I start, but I trail off when Max comes out of the bathroom wearing his own set of sloth pajamas.

I can't help the laugh that escapes from my throat.

"Please don't make fun of how silly I look," he says, and I'll never tell him that I didn't laugh because he looks silly. I laughed because he, somehow and against all reason, looks downright gorgeous even in button-down sloth pajamas. His hair is slightly mussed, the beginnings of stubble are growing on his chin, he's covered in holiday sloths, and I would love to ravage him right here on this bed if given the chance.

But that, of course, is not a possibility for me right now. Instead of satisfying my animalistic lust, I take my turn in the bathroom and put on my own sloth pajamas. My ankle feels much better—whether it's from elevating it or from the healing properties of Max's lap, who can say.

Before we head downstairs, I check my phone—what are birthdays for, after all, if not the cheap validation of everyone you know saying that they're glad you exist? I have an emoji-laden text from my parents and HAPPY BIRTHDAY! Let's celebrate when you get back!!! Hope you're currently in bed with Sexy Max! from Jamilah, who's spending Christmas in Cincinnati with her family. I frown at her text, given that we've never called him Sexy Max before.

"That hot date texting you again?" he asks. I'd forgotten he was right behind me.

"Again, my mom." I quickly shove the phone in my breast pocket before he sees that Jamilah called him sexy.

"Right." He walks past me, his shoulder brushing mine. "Those look good on you, by the way."

"Right back at you," I offer up weakly before pulling my phone out again.

DO NOT call him Sexy Max although, yes, accurate. We kissed. Also started a small fire, I text Jamilah.

She texts back within seconds. !!!!! Literal or metaphorical?

I frown and tap out another text. Literal, sadly. Hopefully metaphorical fires will happen soon. More later. Merry Christmas!

She texts several kissy-face emojis, and I slide the phone back into my pocket. Nothing from Doug, which I hope means he's still asleep instead of stuck in another ditch somewhere.

By the time I get downstairs, Gilbert is already there, mug in hand and wearing the same pajamas as the rest of us.

"How did you . . ." I whisper to Holly.

"I went out and got an extra pair the second you told me he was coming over for Christmas Eve Eve," she whispers, holding her coffee mug up to her mouth. "Don't you remember I asked what size you thought he wore?"

"I thought you were making really weird, specific conversation," I say. "But wait. You didn't know he'd be here on Christmas."

"A good hostess is prepared for anything."

I raise my eyebrows. "Including a freak blizzard that traps everyone in your home for days?"

"Especially that," she says. "That's why I stockpile canned goods in the basement."

"And because you're a doomsday prepper who thinks we're going to need thirty jars of mayonnaise."

She sighs heavily. "If doomsday preppers understand the importance of keeping a large amount of condiments on hand, then fine. Guilty as charged."

"I'm not complaining," I tell her, nodding my thanks to Darius as he hands me a cup of much-needed coffee. "I'm totally hiding out here in the event of a mayonnaise-less apocalypse."

"You guys talking about all the mayo in the basement?" Darius asks cheerfully. "Because I've gotta say, I don't understand it. We barely even eat mayonnaise!"

"If you guys would like to stock the basement shelves, then by all means, have at it and see if you can do a better job," Holly says. "All I'm saying is that if we ever have a mayonnaise shortage and you or our neighbors are looking for some, you're gonna be glad I prepared."

"If there's a mayonnaise shortage, it will be because you bought it all and kept it in your basement," I mutter, and Holly shoots daggers at me with her eyes while Darius laughs.

Even though I'm trying to play it cool, I can't help my eyes from drifting over to Max. He shakes a wrapped gift, and upon hearing the telltale rattle of a LEGO set, firmly says, "It's socks. Definitely a box full of socks."

Lexie and Noah squeal in disgust. I bite my lip, wondering how I could've gotten Max so, so wrong all these years.

"So is it time for presents?" Darius asks. "Because it looks like someone's about ready to rip open the wrapping paper."

"Oh, I don't mind waiting," Gilbert says, and I stifle a laugh.

"I meant the twins," Darius says affably, "but I'm glad you're so excited."

This is perfect. All of us here. Everyone's happy. Even Gilbert is doing better. I have my family, I have Christmas, and I have the promise of whatever's to come with Max. It's warm, it's cozy, we're wearing matching pajamas, and—

I don't get to finish my thought because the front door swings open, banging against the wall. All of us whip our heads around to look, and at first all I see is snow blowing in, wild and swirling. But then a man stomps inside, caked in snow up to his waist, his face shrouded by a ski mask.

"We made it!" says the man, voice muffled.

"It's a monster!" Noah shouts.

"It's two monsters!" Lexie shouts as another man steps in behind him.

It's two robbers who announced themselves upon entering, I think.

"It's Doug!" Darius says happily. "Hey, man, we didn't think you'd make it!"

Doug rips the ski mask off his face, breathing heavily. "Dude. Do you have any idea how long your driveway is? Our car got stuck, like, a mile down the road because apparently no one here believes in plows, but I was like, hell no, I'm not missing Christmas with my family."

The man beside him pulls off his ski mask, sending snow chunks flying. "Hey, Holly."

"Shivan!" she says, greeting Doug's best friend.

"Hope it's okay that I'm here," he says, as out of breath as Doug.

"Of course. You're always welcome."

"Chloe and Nick stayed at the ski lodge because I guess they thought it was, like, hella romantic to be stuck in a snowstorm," Doug continues, referring to his other best friends, "and Shivan's flight back to his parents' got canceled, so I was like . . . dude, come to Holly's. It's a winter wonderland here."

Come to Holly's. The words remind me that none of us have briefed Doug on what's happening, given that we all assumed he wouldn't make it. He has no idea that I'm Holly, and Holly's me, and my boss is here, and everything's a lie.

"Doug!" I say, my face frozen in a smile. "Would you come to the kitchen with me? I need your help with something."

"Maybe also let's close the door," Holly says, stepping around them to push the door shut against the howling wind.

"Who's this?" Doug asks, kicking off his boots and spraying snow everywhere with typical little-brother energy. He walks across the living room and toward Gilbert. "I'm Doug, Holly and Laurel's brother."

"Gilbert," Gilbert says, standing up and shaking Doug's hand. "Laurel was kind enough to invite me to spend the holiday here because my wife left me for my accountant."

Doug nods. "Wow. All right. Well, I'm glad you're here, man."

He turns to me and stops in his tracks. "Uh, what's going on?"

"Doug," I say, pleading with my eyes. "Kitchen. Please."

He points between me and Max. "What's happening with this? Are you hooking up with Can't Relax Max? I thought you hated him."

I realize, blood draining from my face, that Max's arm has been around me this entire time. "I—"

"Because I'll be real with you, I totally thought he had a thing for you at Holly's wedding, and I'm *pretty* good at noticing when people are into each other. He stared at you a lot. Like, *a lot*."

I hazard a quick glance at Gilbert, who looks like that meme of the blond woman attempting to solve a math equation.

"At . . . Holly's wedding?" he asks slowly.

"Speaking of weird stuff, why are you wearing an apron?" Doug asks, wrinkling his nose. "You don't know how to cook. Dude." He turns to Gilbert, laughing. "It's, like, Grant family legend that Laurel once burned Easy Mac in the microwave."

"Laurel?" Gilbert asks. "No, Laurel's an amazing cook. She made Christmas Eve Eve dinner for us here at her home. And . . ."

"No." Doug shakes his head and speaks slowly to Gilbert like he's explaining subtraction to a first grader. "That's *Holly*. I know it's confusing because they're twins and they look a lot alike. I'm related to them, and sometimes even I'm like, 'Wait, which one is this.' But Holly's the one who owns the farm and knows how to do stuff. Laurel's the other one."

The other one. Of course Doug thinks about me like this. Doug likes me, perhaps even loves me in his own Doug way, and he still thinks of me as the other one. I snag on this and almost don't notice what he just revealed.

"Laurel?" Gilbert asks, a heartbreaking crack in his voice. "Is this true?"

I freeze, looking toward Holly and Darius and Max in quick succession, but all of them wait for me to take the lead on this one. As they should. I'm the one who created this problem, the one who cast them as players in my elaborate deception.

"I can explain what happened . . ." I start, but Gilbert shakes his head in disbelief and keeps asking questions.

"So this isn't your house? Did you . . . did you lie to me? Are you and Max even married?"

"Whoa." Doug holds up his hands. "Max and Laurel? Married? Seriously, what's happened since I've been gone?"

"Doug," Shivan says. "I think you need to stop talking."

I'm grateful to Shivan for, unlike Doug, understanding the value of shutting your damn mouth for a moment.

"I need an explanation here," Gilbert says, sounding for the first time like my actual boss.

"I swear, there's a completely reasonable explanation," I start, then falter when I look at Holly and see the sympathy on her face. There isn't a completely reasonable explanation. This is the opposite of a reasonable explanation. This is an "I'm a liar and I ruined everything" explanation.

"Fine," I say, deflating like an overused beach ball. I take a step away from Max and look at Gilbert, facing my own dishonesty head-on. "I don't actually live here on the farm. I live in a two-bedroom apartment with no outdoor space in Columbus. I don't know how to make beef Wellington, I can't take care of the animals, one of the goats ate part of my jacket, I can't ice-skate, I'm a terrible baker, and these aren't my children. They're Holly and Darius's, because this is their farm, their home, their job, and their life."

I take a glance back at Max. "I'm not married, either. Not to Max, not to anyone."

"Why . . ." Gilbert trails off.

"Because you were so impressed when you thought I was a farmer. Remember how you said the team needed someone with my point of view, someone who didn't live in the city? And yes, I could've explained to you right then and there that I was only running Holly's social media and that I didn't actually know anything about farming, but I needed the job. And I wanted . . . I wanted you to like me."

I take a deep breath. "So I lied. It wasn't on purpose, but I lied. I could have corrected you when you assumed I was some sort of Ohio Martha Stewart, but then you offered me my own column. I wanted to write so badly that I decided to carry on this ridiculous, over-the-top deception, and I really, really wish I didn't. Because now I've gotten to know you, Gilbert, and you're a good person. You don't deserve this."

I realize I'm echoing my speech to him last night about Charlene. I may not have cheated on Gilbert with his accountant, but maybe I'm just as bad.

Gilbert shakes his head, his lips pursed in an expression of not only sadness but disappointment, too. I've let down yet another person, yet another boss. Of course I have. Because Holly's the one who knows how to do things, the one who can create her own job out of thin air. And I'm the one who screws up every job I've ever had.

I'm the other one.

"I thought we were friends, Laurel," he says, avoiding my eyes. "I think I need a moment alone."

He walks past us and to the stairs as all of us watch him silently. Doug catches my eye and mouths, *Sorry?* with a confused shrug. I shake my head. I can't even be mad at him—I'm the one who made the big mistakes here.

But before Gilbert makes it to the second stair, the door blows open once again, more drifting snow whooshing through the entryway.

"Does anyone know how to knock?" Holly asks, picking up her broom.

"Gilbert!" shouts a woman who appears to be blond underneath her scarf and her knit cap and her oversized peacoat. She begins pulling everything off, and I realize who it is the second Gilbert does.

"Charlene!" he gasps.

"Charlene?" I ask.

"Wait, *the* Charlene?" Darius asks, eyes wide.

"Who the hell is Charlene?" Doug asks.

"I was wrong!" Charlene pants, ignoring all of us and looking only at Gilbert, who's still on the first step. "Gil, I thought I wanted excitement. I thought I wanted adventure. I thought I wanted our accountant, Stu."

"Typically the first place you go when you want excitement," Holly mutters. "An accountant named Stu."

"But I don't want any of that. I want you. I want Saturday nights doing puzzles and watching *FBI*. I want stability. I want reliability. I want . . . I want someone I can trust. I'm so, so sorry, and I hope you can take me back."

"How did you find Gilbert?" Darius asks, caught up in the excitement of the moment.

Gilbert looks at us with guilt in his eyes. "Well, I *did* text Charlene last night. I couldn't sleep after the tree caught on fire—"

"Okay," Doug says, turning to inspect the burnt top of the tree. "What did I miss?"

"And I couldn't help myself, I told her I was staying here." He walks down the steps, eyes on Charlene. "Are you really sorry?"

She nods, tears on her face. I hear a sniffle and turn to see Darius is crying.

"What?" He gestures toward them. "This is all so romantic."

"One condition," Gilbert says, and we all hold our breaths as we wait to hear what he has to say.

"Anything," Charlene says.

"We need to get a new accountant," Gilbert says firmly.

"Oh, yes, of course, Gil!" Charlene cries, then throws her arms around his neck. And then Gilbert surprises us all by hoisting Charlene into his arms and carrying her upstairs.

"Whoo!" Doug yells, cupping his hands around his mouth.

"I don't know either of you, but congrats!" Shivan yells.

"You'd be surprised how many romantic moments the two of us have witnessed," Doug says, pointing to Shivan.

"I probably would," Max says.

"Okay, so . . . who are those people, exactly?" Doug asks. "And can anyone explain to me what's going on?"

"When are we opening presents?" Noah wails.

"Do we have to wait for Gilbert?" Lexie asks.

"I *can't* wait!" Noah shouts.

"Okay, everyone, calm down!" Darius holds his hands up.

Holly crosses her arms. "What are they doing up there in the LEGO room, anyway? Do I even want to know?"

"I feel like I walked into chaos," Doug says.

This is my nightmare. This entire frenzied moment, with the crying and the yelling and the snow all over the floor, is my fault. The Christmas tree is half burnt and the rug is ruined. I probably don't even have a job anymore, and that's what I deserve. I wasn't a good employee or a good friend to Gilbert. And Max . . . he must think I'm a mess, and he's right. There's no such person as New Laurel; I'm just Laurel, the one who screws up everything she tries, the one who has the opposite of a golden touch. My touch ruins everything good in my life.

Before the tears can spill out of my eyes, I pull my coat off the coatrack, sling it on over my pajamas, and shove my feet into boots.

"Laurel?" Holly calls. "Where are you going?"

I ignore her and slam the door behind me. I limp my way through the snow, which is still deep, but at least it's no longer falling. The wind bites my skin through the thin fabric of my pajama pants, and my coat whips open in the breeze. Maybe I'll be able to get out of here soon and head back to my normal life where I have no job, no love life, and no future prospects.

There aren't exactly a lot of places to go out here, so I pull the barn door open enough to squeeze myself through.

"Hey, guys," I say to the goats. For once, they don't make angry noises at me—maybe even the goats are too pissed to talk to me now.

"It's fine," I say. "We don't need to talk. We can hang out in comfortable silence."

Barnaby advances toward me, her bottom teeth jutting out menacingly.

"Or not, it's fine!" I say, backing up.

"Hey."

For a second, I think the goats have gained the power of speech, but then I sense a human presence behind me and turn to find Max.

"Is this another *hay/hey* joke?" I ask. "Because I don't have it in me right now."

"This was a normal *hey*," he says. "I fed them this morning while you were sleeping."

I wince. This is my problem—not only did I forget to feed the goats, but I didn't even *know* I'd forgotten. I can't be trusted with anything—not goats, not jobs, not Christmas trees. I'm hopeless. I can read all the self-help books in the world, but it doesn't matter. Books alone can't turn me into a take-no-prisoners badass bitch who's in control of her life. I'm screwing everything up.

I don't realize I said that last part out loud until Max asks, "What are you screwing up?"

He's standing there in his sloth pajamas, looking at me with such concern that I want to (a) cry because he's so cute and (b) marvel at the fact that this is happening. A few days ago, I wouldn't have imagined I'd ever see Max Beckett in sloth pajamas, and I wouldn't have imagined that I'd care what he thought of me. Because a few days ago, I had no idea that Max Beckett was actually an incredibly kind, vulnerable person, one who was hiding who he was behind a protective grumpy shell. And I want him to like me—I want him to like me more than I've ever wanted anything, except possibly employment.

"Everything," I finally tell him, crossing my arms so my hands aren't anywhere near Barnaby's mouth. "Like, I literally set a tree on fire, Max."

One corner of Max's mouth quirks up. "I think both of us are guilty of that one."

I shake my head, my eyes on my boots. "It's not just that. It's . . . all of it. I ruined Christmas. The kids are probably in there screaming right now because they can't open their presents yet. I made Holly spend her entire holiday pretending she doesn't live here. There's no way Gilbert will want me to keep working for him after I lied to him for so long. I thought I could do it, but I can't. I screwed this up exactly like I screwed up my last job, and the one before that. At some point, when you mess up enough times, you have to realize that it's not everyone else's problem. It's yours. The only common denominator in all these situations is *me*. I've been reading all these books that are supposed to help me, and they're *not* helping me. I'm immune to help. There's no mantra in the world that's strong enough to counteract the force of nature that is Laurel Grant."

I wipe the snot off my nose with the back of my sleeve, finally glancing up at Max.

"Is that really how you see yourself?" he asks softly.

I let out one bitter, snot-filled laugh. "That's how I am, yes."

He takes a step closer to me. "Can I tell you what I see?"

I can feel my heart thumping through my pajamas and my coat as he gets closer. "I guess I can't stop you."

"I see someone who keeps on trying, even when things don't work out the first time. I see someone who loves her family more than anything in the world. I see someone who talked her boss through a breakup, and someone who is willing to forgive people who make complete asses of themselves."

"Who would that last one be?" I mutter, wiping my eyes.

"When I look at you, I don't see a screwup. I see someone who tries and cares. You really do dance like no one's watching, Laurel."

"Okay, you're going full-on Maxxinista."

He reaches out and places his hands on my shoulders. "The first time I saw you, I thought, *I wish I was more like her.* And then I realized I didn't want to be like you. I wanted to know you. You were something I never thought I could be . . . free and fun. But being with you makes me feel like maybe I could try."

I swallow. "You really, really seemed like you hated me at the wedding."

Max lets out a low chuckle. "I hated myself. We've established that, right? It took a lot of hours of therapy for me to, as my therapist Louis would say, unpack that."

"Louis sounds like a smart man," I say quietly.

"I'm not interested in talking about Louis right now," Max says, ducking a bit so that I have to look in his eyes. "I'm interested in talking about you. Because you're amazing, Laurel. You don't need any of those stupid books. You're always repeating those ridiculous lines . . ."

"You heard my mantras?" I ask, betrayed. "I whispered them to myself."

"You don't really have an inside voice. But that's not the point. The point is that I don't ever want you to change, because you're perfect the way you are."

He leans down slowly, too slowly, so I throw my arms around his shoulders and pull him toward me. I can feel his lips form a smile as I kiss him, and then I fully make out with Max Beckett, former nemesis, former family enemy, current best guy I know, right here in the barn with an audience of two uninterested goats.

I have never, not once in my life, felt the way that I do in this moment. I've never felt this held, this cherished, this understood. The worst parts of me have been on display this weekend as I've messed up everything I've touched. Max saw it all, and he only saw the good in me. He saw the real me.

"Maybe," I say, pulling back from him, "I should learn how to microwave mac and cheese, though."

"Small changes, then," Max says. "But nothing big."

"Are you sure about this?" I ask. "Are you sure you can see past the mayhem and the mess and everything else? Are you sure you're not going to get tired of me?"

"Never." Max's thumb strokes my cheek and he leans forward to whisper, right in my ear, words that I want to remember forever, ones that I'll tattoo on my heart: "I see you, Laurel. Just you."

I feel a gentle tugging at the hem of my coat, and I pull away from Max. I look down to see Barnaby gnawing on the thick wool.

"Not the other pocket!" I yell.

"Barnaby," Max says sternly. "You're really killing the mood here."

Barnaby lets out a loud *maaaa* in response.

"I think she's jealous," I say as I tilt my head, watching her.

"You know what I think?" Max asks. "I think I'm standing in a barn in my pajamas. What do you say we go back inside?"

I wince, thinking of the mess I'll be walking into. "You sure we can't stay out here?"

Max nods. "Yes, I'm sure we can't spend the rest of Christmas in the goat barn."

"Frankly, I don't see why not. It's cozy, there's hay . . ."

Barnaby lets out another loud noise and advances toward me.

"Okay, great point," I say. "Let's go inside."

And even though I don't know what's waiting for me in there—aside from at least one person to whom I owe an apology—when Max takes my hand and squeezes it tightly, I feel like I can handle it.

Chapter Twenty-Four

I DON'T KNOW WHAT I expect to find inside . . . chaos. Anger. A room full of people with arms crossed, all waiting for me to explain myself.

But when we walk in, everyone's so busy that they don't even hear us open the door. The twins are barely visible through the flurry of ripped wrapping paper flying through the air, Doug's wearing a Santa hat and passing out presents, Holly and Shivan are earnestly discussing the Christmas ornaments, and Darius is talking to Gilbert and Charlene. Frankly, everyone looks like they're having the time of their lives.

"Uh, hello?" I ask, yanking off my boots.

"Oh, you're back!" Holly says, walking toward us. "I hope you don't mind that we started the presents without you."

"Noah and Lexie were about to have a meltdown," Darius says from his perch on the arm of the couch.

Holly laughs. "Some might say they were already having

meltdowns. But what's Christmas morning without a temper tantrum or two?"

I narrow my eyes as I slip out of my now-tattered coat, taking in the scene. "So you're . . . not mad at me?"

Holly puts her hands on her hips, looking genuinely confused. "Why would I be mad at you?"

"Because I ruined Christmas!" I say, throwing my hands in the air.

"Sweetie." Holly puts a hand on my shoulder. "Haven't you learned anything from all those Christmas movies we watch? You can't ruin Christmas. It's unruinable."

"I don't think that's a word," I mutter.

"So," she says, drawing the word out like it has five syllables and looking pointedly at Max's and my entwined fingers. "What happened out there in the barn?"

"None of your business," I say quickly at the same time that Max says, "We kissed."

"Yes!" Holly says, high-fiving his free hand.

I'm having a hard time focusing on Holly treating my personal life like a football game, because Gilbert is watching me from the sofa. He offers me a tiny smile, and I wave.

"Hi, Laurel," he says as he walks over to me. "I think we need to talk."

It feels like a golf ball, softball, or possibly even a basketball is stuck in my throat. "Sure," I say. He nods toward the kitchen. Max gives my hand a reassuring squeeze before I follow Gilbert through the door.

As soon as the door swings shut behind us, I say, "I'm sorry."

Gilbert leans against the counter. "You lied to me."

"I know." I swallow hard.

"It really hurt my feelings," Gilbert says plainly.

"I never meant to hurt you," I tell him. "You've been so kind to me, and you're a great boss. The best boss I've ever had, not that there's much competition."

"I feel like a gullible fool," Gilbert says, looking around the kitchen as if he's seeing it for the first time. "Your children—I mean, your niece and nephew—look so much like your brother-in-law. And you're a *terrible* ice-skater. But you and Max seemed so happy together, and I was grateful to be here. I guess I was willing to overlook a lot of things if it meant I didn't have to spend Christmas alone."

I nod. My guilt is so overwhelming that I want to crawl under the kitchen table and not come back out until Christmas is over.

"Why did you do it, Laurel?" Gilbert asks, confusion in his eyes.

I take a deep breath. "I needed this job, but more than that, I *wanted* this job. You talked to me like I was a competent professional, like I could actually be an important part of your team, and I've never had that before. And when you told me you liked that I had a farm . . . well, it made me feel special. I thought I'd tell you eventually, but then you gave me a chance to write, and I . . . I should have told you. But it was too hard, and I was too scared. I was a coward."

Gilbert looks at me, sympathy in his eyes. "You're a lot of things, but you're not a coward."

"Thanks," I say softly. "So I guess this is it, right?"

He frowns. "What do you mean?"

"I mean . . . this is the end of the road for me at *Buckeye*

State of Mind. I understand that you don't want me to work for you anymore after all this, and—"

"Laurel." Gilbert crosses his arms. "You know the sign I have in my office that says 'Nobody's Perfect: That's Why Pencils Have Erasers'?"

I nod. "Of course. One of your best signs."

"Thank you. Well, I don't put a sign on my wall unless I believe in it. What you did was wrong, and it hurt me, but that doesn't mean I won't forgive you."

"I . . . Really?" It's hard for me to talk, what with my jaw dropping.

He nods. "Charlene showed up and apologized, and even though she did something wrong, I forgive her. And I forgive you, too. I know you won't do anything like that again."

I shake my head quickly. "I absolutely won't."

"So . . . let's agree to let the past be the past. We can look toward the future, okay?" He holds out his hand, and I shake it.

"Deal," I say. "Although if you want to take back that raise, I understand."

Gilbert shakes his head. "Nope. I meant it when I said you earned it."

The two of us rejoin the group in the living room. Max raises his eyebrows toward me, and I give him a thumbs-up. It feels good—so good—to communicate wordlessly with him like this, after not understanding him at all for far too long.

A loud buzz rips through the room, and all of us turn to see Doug standing by the tree, holding a kazoo to his lips.

"Now, where did he get a kazoo?" Holly mutters.

"Hear ye, hear ye!" Doug shouts, and I laugh into my hand.

"I didn't know this was a speech situation," Max whispers into my ear.

"Turns out there've been a lot of speech situations this weekend," I say.

"You two! In the back! Quiet!" Doug yells, pointing at us.

I pantomime zipping my lips.

"I think we can all agree that this has been one of the stranger Grant family Christmases," Doug says. "Like, my car is currently stuck a mile down the road. Mom and Dad decided they'd rather hang out on a beach. Shivan is here . . . Shout-out, Shivan!"

Shivan waves. "Sup."

"Laurel, like, made up an entire story about owning Holly and Darius's farm and then hooked up with Max."

I raise my hand. "Guilty."

"And I just met Gilbert, who I guess is Laurel's boss but is also a dope guy. You've gotta come bowling with us when we get back to Columbus."

"Oh, absolutely," Gilbert says, his arm around Charlene. "Although, fair warning, I *will* dominate. I get very aggressive when I put on those bowling shoes."

"Don't doubt it, bro," Doug says with a nod.

"How did Doug and Gilbert become best friends while we were out in the barn?" I whisper to Max.

"But most importantly," Doug says a little louder. "We're all here, together. It might look a little different than usual. There was, like, a lot of drama I don't fully understand. I think there might've been a small fire where I'm standing."

Holly nods. "Correct."

"But none of that matters. All that matters is that it's

Christmas, and we're family. This might be a weird Christmas, but that's okay, because Christmas is unruinable."

I gasp and look at Holly. "It's a word!" she says, triumph in her voice.

"Let's cheers to Christmas!" Doug yells, and he and Shivan raise beer cans in the air. We all cheer and clap, and Doug takes a swig and pumps a fist.

"Why do they have beer this early in the morning?" I ask.

Holly shrugs. "I figured . . . What the hell. Today can't get any stranger."

"Good point," I say as Max squeezes my hand.

Someone puts Christmas music on, and "Christmas Time Is Here" from *A Charlie Brown Christmas* plays as Noah and Lexie check out their new toys.

Max nudges my shoulder. "Don't you have any presents you want to open?"

"Nah," I say. "The greatest present I could ever receive is that you aren't complaining about the music."

"I'm keeping my complaints in my head," he says with a smile.

"That's good enough for me." I lean my head on his shoulder and look around.

This might be the weirdest birthday of my life, and it sure isn't the picture-perfect Christmas of a Hallmark movie—after all, the living room still kind of smells like burnt tree, and I'm pretty sure I owe Holly a new rug. And, self-help books be damned, I didn't transform into an entirely different person, one who always says the right thing and never makes mistakes. In fact, it's starting to seem like Old Laurel and New Laurel were never real people all along . . . maybe I'm just Laurel, just one lady who's trying her best, messing up a lot, and making it better.

I meet Gilbert's eye, and he gives me a wink as he squeezes Charlene closer. The song ends, and those first quiet notes of "All I Want for Christmas Is You" play. I gasp as Holly and I spin toward each other.

"Oh, no." Max groans.

"No complaining! It's our birthday!" I shout as the music grows faster. Holly grabs my hands and pulls me into the center of the living room, where the twins, toys forgotten, spin in circles around us. Doug jumps up and down while drinking his beer, his Santa hat bobbing. Gilbert wraps his arms around Charlene, and the two of them sway gently, as if this is a slow jam—but you know what? Perhaps the true power of Mariah is that this song can be all things to all people.

Speaking of which . . . after Darius cuts in and steals Holly, I spin around to see Max standing in front of me.

"Are you going to dance?" I ask, eyes wide.

"I thought I'd read a book," he deadpans.

I grab his hands and wave them as the music plays. "Dance with me, Max!"

He laughs. "Only for you. Not for anyone else but you, Laurel."

He moves a little, but more importantly, he laughs. I wanted to be the person to make this man laugh, and now I am. I'm the reason he's showing that glorious smile, the one that feels like lying under the Christmas tree, like all my best Christmas memories, like waking up on Christmas morning and realizing you got exactly what you wanted.

I take it all in as Mariah sings. My heart is full—I have a family who loves me no matter what, a boss who has become a friend, this cozy house that isn't mine but feels like home, and most importantly, Max. I know it isn't perfect, but right at this moment, it feels like a Christmas miracle.

Epilogue

Next Christmas Eve Eve

WHEN I PULL into Holly's driveway, there's a conspicuous lack of snow on the ground. In fact, there's no snow at all in the forecast.

I sigh as I get out of the car. "Looks like it's not going to be a white Christmas."

"Do you really want a repeat of last year?" Max asks, shutting his door.

"Well, some parts I wouldn't mind repeating." I smile, lacing my fingers through his as we walk up the stairs.

Holly yanks open the door before my hand is even on the doorknob. "Thank God you're here," she whispers. "Gilbert is telling us all about a personal wellness seminar he's been taking. He's talking a lot about *stepping into his power.*"

"Oooh!" I widen my eyes. "One of my favorite subjects!"

"How, exactly, does one step into one's power? Is there special footwear required? Hiking boots, maybe?" Max asks.

"Not now, Max," Holly mutters, pulling us both inside.

". . . I'm trying to connect to the goddess within," Gilbert is saying as we walk into the living room.

Darius nods intently. "Okay."

Gilbert pauses. "The course is typically for women who are going through crushing heartbreak, but the instructor let me in because she said I had a nurturing energy. I was the only man there, but it was a welcoming crowd."

"Aw," I say, taking the seat next to him. "You *do* have a nurturing energy."

Gilbert places a hand on his heart. "Thank you, Laurel. That means a lot coming from you."

Over the past year, things have changed for Gilbert. After talking things over extensively with Doug, he decided not to get back together with Charlene. If I was surprised that Gilbert joined Doug's Tuesday-night bowling league, then I was shocked that Doug proved to be exactly the friend Gilbert needed.

"Doug said that I need to choose myself," Gilbert told me one day over a working lunch. (Now that he knows I actually live in the city, I go into the office more often.) "I'm Team Gilbert."

Doug had "Team Gilbert" T-shirts made up for the entire bowling team. Later, when I asked him about his new friendship with Gilbert, Doug said, "I'm thinking about pivoting into life coaching," and—I can't believe I'm saying this—I think it might be a good direction for him.

Gilbert really did choose himself, throwing himself into a recreational pickleball league, joining a local AFOL group, putting himself on the dating apps, and even resurrecting his dormant Instagram account to document his adventures.

"I went for the handle FiftyNiftyandThriving," he told me and then, with concern, asked, "But what am I going to do when I turn fifty-one?" We decided on the handle FiftyOne-andStillHavingFun, when the time comes.

I wondered if things would be weird between us when we got back to work. I mean, we'd been through a lot in just one Christmas. But Gilbert made good on his promise to let me work on more stories, and I had an idea that changed the direction of the company. We're still doing the magazine and the website, but now we have a new component: a podcast.

It seems like every publication has a podcast these days, so why not us? Each week, Gilbert and I interview an Ohio business owner, activist, or general interesting person. I research guests and topics, and Gilbert is my cohost because he's great at asking questions. At the end of every episode, we answer questions from listeners. Not to brag, but Gilbert and I are great advice-givers. Between my self-help books and his love of inspirational office signs, we have a lot to offer our listeners.

"I would never have thought of this myself!" Gilbert told me one day as we finished recording. "I don't know what *Buckeye State of Mind* would do without you."

It might sound silly, but I don't think I've ever felt prouder of myself. I've finally found a job where I can be myself, where my natural curiosity and love of talking to strangers can actually help me thrive.

There was no way we were going to have a family Christmas without inviting Gilbert, and despite his busy social calendar, he said he wouldn't miss it for the world.

"I'm glad Christmas is back to normal," Doug says,

coming in from the kitchen with a tray of cookies in his hands. "I mean, except for Mom and Dad being gone again."

"Should we be offended that they decided to spend Christmas in Key West?" Holly asks thoughtfully. "Do they not want to spend time with us?"

"I am a little offended," I admit. "But this is pretty nice, too."

A couple of years ago, this would've seemed like a decidedly not normal Christmas Eve Eve. After all, Gilbert is here. Also, most importantly, I'm now dating Max Beckett, the man I formerly believed to be my mortal enemy.

As previously noted by philosophers like Ferris Bueller, life really *can* move pretty fast. Max and I were inseparable from the moment Marge Jamison plowed Holly's driveway last Christmas, and we moved in together a few months later. (Jamilah pretended to be sad I was leaving, but I think she was mostly happy to have her guest room back.) We've spent most of our time catching up on all the emotional movies Max has missed in his life—and, to my delight, he sometimes even ends up crying.

So being back here, to have Christmas Eve Eve at Holly's, feels like coming full circle. Except that, this time, I get to enjoy the holiday instead of pretending that I'm in charge.

A timer beeps and Holly stands up. "That means the beef is done resting! Almost time to eat."

"Thank goodness," Gilbert says. "I've been thinking about that beef Wellington all year."

"Me, too," Max says. "I've been trying to get Laurel to make one with me."

"And I never will," I say, because after last year, I decided never to make beef Wellington ever again. Max does most of the cooking in our home, although I have learned how to make a few basics (or, more accurately, I've learned not to burn so many things).

I'm done thinking that I'm the other twin. Sure, Holly knows how to do a lot of things I don't—operate power tools, raise animals, bake pies, and can grape jelly.

But now I know that there are things I'm good at, too. Like being a good friend, helping where I'm needed, making interviewees feel interesting, and lifting people up when they're at their lowest.

And at least I don't have a basement full of mayonnaise. We all have our strengths and weaknesses.

"Oh!" Gilbert stands and runs upstairs. "I need to feed Adele!"

There's a moment of confusion when I wonder why pop star Adele would be upstairs and, most importantly, why she would rely on Gilbert to feed her, but then I remember—Gilbert, free to make his own decisions, decided to finally get that bearded dragon. He named her after, as he put it, "the woman whose angelic voice got me through some of my darkest times."

"No reptiles at the table!" Holly calls after him as he runs upstairs.

He shouts down, "I wouldn't dream of it! You're not serving grasshoppers, anyway!"

Holly wrinkles her nose as she walks into the dining room. "He didn't want to leave Adele at home in case he got stuck here in another blizzard, so I told him he could keep her in the LEGO room while he's here."

"Wow, and you let him keep a bearded dragon in your LEGO lair?" I ask Darius as we all stand up and head to the kitchen.

Darius waves me off. "I'm not worried. After Gilbert became an AFOL, I have complete faith that he respects the bricks."

I look at Max with my eyebrows raised, and he elbows me. "That's enough out of you."

"Are you insinuating that I *don't* respect the bricks?" I ask.

"Not nearly enough," Max says, but I know he's kidding. Our coffee table is perpetually covered in whatever LEGO set he's currently working on, and I'm fine with it. It makes me happy to see Max do something that lights him up, even if I usually read a book or watch a movie while he's working because those complex instructions still might as well be written in another language.

Darius, Max, and I help Holly carry everything else from the kitchen and put it on the table.

"Doug!" I shout. "What are you doing? It's time to eat!"

He shakes his head as he flips through the Christmas CDs in the living room. "I'm trying to pick the perfect album. We need the right vibes."

"He's got a point," Holly says.

"What's a Christmas Eve Eve dinner without the right vibes?" Darius asks.

Gilbert comes back downstairs, Adele apparently satisfied with her meal of grasshoppers, as Michael Bublé's "Santa Baby" starts playing.

"*Doug!*" we all shout at the same time, except for Gilbert.

"Oooh, is this a new version of 'Santa Baby'?" he asks, as

if he's been waiting his whole life for an inventive gender-swapped take on the classic.

"Unfortunately, yes, and Doug loves to torture us with it," I say.

"Wait," Max says, scooping salad onto his plate. "I thought you liked all Christmas music."

I scowl at him. "We might have to break up because you clearly don't know the true me at all. I don't like all Christmas music. I like good Christmas music."

"Not a thing," Max says.

I ignore him. "But I do not like this song."

"I don't know, I still think it's kind of fun. He calls Santa 'dude,'" Doug says, walking into the room with a smile on his face. I'm not sure if Doug actually likes this song or if our dislike of it is enough to keep him going.

"This is what happens when you have a little brother," I say, leaning over to Max.

"You deserve worse," Doug says.

"Be quiet, Dougina," Holly says, and I almost choke on my potatoes.

Gilbert smiles and lets out a happy sigh. "I'm so glad I'm here. I know it was a bit of a winding road for us all to become friends. And I had to, well, sort of blow up my own life to get here . . . but I'm so glad things turned out the way they did."

"Oh!" Darius says, his eyes lighting up. "Let's go around the table and say one thing we're grateful for."

"Isn't that a Thanksgiving thing?" Holly asks.

"Gratitude isn't seasonal," I say, and she rolls her eyes at me.

"So true," Gilbert murmurs, taking another bite.

"I'm grateful we get presents soon!" Noah shouts.

"Me, too!" Lexie agrees.

Holly frowns. "I think I'm a bad parent."

"I'm grateful for Adele's presence in my life," Gilbert says, and while I'm not sure if he's referring to the bearded dragon or the singer, it's a nice sentiment either way.

"I'm grateful for my beautiful and talented wife," Darius says, wiggling his eyebrows at Holly.

"And I'm grateful for my extremely sexy husband," Holly says.

"Gross." I throw a napkin at her.

"Don't throw things at the table! You're setting a bad example!" Holly looks around, then says, "Oh, shoot. I forgot the rolls in the kitchen."

"I'll get them," I volunteer.

"I'll help," Max says, and even though I don't really need help grabbing one basket of dinner rolls, I'm not about to turn down the chance to spend a little solo time with him.

As the doors swing shut behind us, I hear Doug say, "I'm grateful that my boy Gilbert joined our bowling team this year."

"I keep forgetting that Gilbert and Doug hang out," I say. "It's weird, but it kind of makes sense—"

I don't get a chance to finish my sentence because Max kisses me, pushing me up against the counter. I grab his back and pull him closer.

"Well, hello," I say when I come up for air. "Why do I have the distinct feeling that you didn't come in here to help me carry the roll basket?"

"Because I didn't," Max says. "I wanted to be alone with you for a minute."

I give him a look of faux outrage. "I'm sorry, are you saying that you don't like being around my family?"

"Very funny," Max says. "I think we've established that I actually love being around your family."

"I guess you're right," I say, wrapping my arms around his neck. It's hard to believe that there was a time—a long time, actually—when I assumed that Max held antiGrant beliefs. Nothing could be further from the truth. He wasn't ever really a fun-hating, joy-hating, Grant-hating grump. Well, he might be a little grumpy about some things. But all along, he was only looking for a place to belong and a little push to see the bright side.

"Is it strange that it's kind of a turn-on to find out that you dislike a Christmas song?" Max asks, his mouth on my neck.

"Well, the song itself is, like, the opposite of a turn-on. It's honestly impressive how he takes an inherently sexy song and makes it gross. He uses the word *hotties* instead of *fellas*, and I find that offensive," I say. "Nothing against Michael Bublé. He's doing some great work on behalf of Christmas."

"Okay, now it's a turnoff that we're still talking about Michael Bublé," Max says, standing up straight.

I have the same involuntary response that I do whenever I get a chance to look at him—I smile. I swear, it's like when a doctor hits your knee with that little hammer thing and your leg kicks. That's the response I have when I see Max. A little thump-kick, right in my heart.

He smiles back at me, and I swear I could melt into a

puddle right there on the kitchen floor. To think that I spent so much time with him not seeing that smile, when now it's something I get to bask in every single day.

Like Gilbert said at the table, it was a winding road to get here. I tried to transform my whole life via questionable self-help books. I lied to my very nice boss for way too long. I faked an entire lifestyle and roped my whole family into the lie. It was, to put it mildly, a lot.

But Max was there for all of it. Helping me, even when it was ridiculous. Supporting me, even when I, frankly, probably shouldn't have had support. Making fun of me, sure, but only in the ultimately loving way that I make fun of him. And, most important, seeing me for who I really am. Not a mess. Not Old Laurel. Not New Laurel. Just Laurel, just a woman trying her best and getting it right at least half the time.

It was an unexpected start to a relationship, but if that's what it took to end up with Max, then I'd do it all over again and again, a million times.

"What are you thinking about?" Max asks, resting his forehead against mine. "You're muttering to yourself again."

"All I'm thinking is that we really need to get these rolls to the table, or Holly's going to come in here looking for them," I say. "Why, what are you thinking about?"

"Well." He looks at me, and I realize, for the millionth time, that Max can do a very good smolder. "I'm thinking about how much I'm looking forward to tonight, when we're alone in the guest room."

I gasp. "Max Beckett! Are you suggesting that you plan to besmirch the sanctity of my sister's guest room?"

"Stop it," he says, smiling as he kisses me. "You know I find it way too hot when you talk like you're in an old movie."

This Christmas is already shaping up to be better than last year's—I haven't started a single fire, a goat didn't eat one of my pockets, my ankle isn't sprained, and best of all, I'm not lying to anyone. I'm being myself, finally, and it feels good.

"Let's say one thing we're grateful for," I say, wrapping my arms more tightly around Max. "You first."

"Easy," Max says, and I smile in anticipation. "I'm grateful that Doug can be my life coach soon."

I lightly punch him in the arm.

"Okay, okay, kidding." He leans down and kisses my forehead. "I'm grateful for you, Laurel. Just you."

"Good answer," I say with a smile. "I'm grateful you were my fake husband last year so you can be my real boyfriend this year."

"Good answer," he echoes, grabbing the basket of rolls. "We'd better get back in there."

I hold his hand as we push through the swinging door, the dining room full of light and laughter and the people who mean the most to me. Doug is, for reasons unknown, wearing a cloth napkin as a headscarf and making the twins (and Gilbert) laugh so hard that I'm afraid someone is going to pee their pants again.

"What were you guys doing in there?" Holly asks me when she sees Max holding the rolls, then shoots me a suspicious look when Max blushes.

Darius grabs a roll before the basket is even on the table. "Leave them alone. They're young and in love."

Holly gives him a look. "We're the same age."

"Oh," Darius says, chewing. "Yeah."

As Max and I sit down beside the twins, who are still laughing and not eating their crustless sandwiches, a swell of happiness fills my whole body. I'm grateful for this moment and the imperfect perfection of it, grateful for every moment that led us here, and grateful that all the time we spent creating a fake Christmas led to one more genuine and amazing than I ever could have imagined.

But even more than that, I'm grateful for all the Christmases yet to come, for all the very real moments I get to experience with Max by my side.

Acknowledgments

Writing a book about Christmas, one of my favorite holidays, was a complete joy. It was a strange experience to write the majority of *Faking Christmas* in the middle of summer, blasting Christmas music under the blazing sun, but I learned that the spirit of Christmas can last all year if you really want it to. My Christmas playlist and an extensive collection of seasonal candles kept me going, but I also have to thank the following people who helped me make this book the best it could be.

First and foremost, thank you to my agent Stephen Barbara for believing in *Faking Christmas* from the very beginning. You really went above and beyond for this book, and I'm eternally grateful. Thank you to everyone at Inkwell, including Sidney Boker, Maria Whelan, and Jessie Thorsted.

Thank you to my team of super-editors, Cindy Hwang and Angela Kim. Cindy, you have always championed my books and there aren't enough words to express how grateful I am. Angela, your thoughtful and thorough edits shaped this book into what it is, and I don't know what I would have done without you! Thank you to the entire team at Berkley, including Tina Joell and Elisha Katz, for being such a warm and supportive publishing home.

Thank you to Catherine Stoner for (yet again!) answering all my animal questions, for letting me steal the name of Holly's farm from your family, and for introducing me to the concept of animal communicators. All goat errors are my own!

Thank you to my most trusted early reader, Lauren Dlugosz Rochford. Also thank you to Emily Adrian and Alicia Thompson for reading early drafts and offering encouragement.

I'm grateful for the authors who so kindly read an early copy and offered up blurbs: Sarah Hogle, Martha Waters, Lynn Painter, Sarah Adams, and Sarah Adler.

Many thanks to Mariah Carey, the elusive chanteuse herself. Thank you to Wham! for recording the perfect song "Last Christmas," which I kept on repeat while writing this book.

Thank you to all the booksellers who recommend my books to customers, post about them online, or let me do events at your stores. You're one of the greatest and most fun parts of publishing, and I'm so grateful to always feel at home in a bookstore. Special thanks, as always, to my local Columbus bookstores: Cover to Cover, Prologue, Gramercy, The Book Loft, and the Lennox Town Barnes and Noble.

Thank you to my parents for watching my kid so I could write. Sorry your home is now covered in Nerf darts.

Thank you to Hollis for being my romance novel hero and for not getting annoyed at the constant Christmas music or the fact that we left the Christmas tree up until February. Thank you also for checking all my LEGO references. I'm lucky to have a LEGO master in my house. Thank you to Harry, my little book lover, for inspiring me with your own prolific novel writing career.

While I was writing this book, a very important teacher in my life, Rick Jacox, passed away. I thanked him in the acknowledgments of my first book, but I wanted to be sure to thank him one more time because his encouragement and support meant the world. He was truly one of a kind.

Lastly, thank you to the readers. I genuinely couldn't do this without you. I spent years dreaming of other people reading my books, and sometimes I have to pinch myself when I remember that my dream came true. Your enthusiasm, your social media posts, your messages, and your emails mean the world to me. Seeing you at events is one of the highlights of this job, and I never take any of it for granted.

KERRY WINFREY

READERS GUIDE

Questions for Discussion

1. Max's hatred of Christmas is one of the reasons Laurel initially dislikes him. Are you more of a Max or a Laurel when it comes to holiday celebrations?

2. Even though Laurel loves Holly, she still sometimes feels jealous of her twin's accomplishments and doesn't feel secure about her role in their family. If you have siblings, do you ever feel conflicted about your role in your family, the way Laurel does?

3. Laurel tells a little white lie to Gilbert that spins out of control and leads to him inviting himself to her farm. You've probably never been in such a dramatic situation, but have you ever lied to a boss? What were the consequences?

4. Do you think it's unforgiveable that Laurel lied to Gilbert about owning a farm? Do you think she had understandable reasons for doing so? What would you have done in that situation?

5. *Faking Christmas* is loosely based on the 1945 film *Christmas in Connecticut*. If you've seen the movie, what parts of the plot are similar? What are the differences?

6. If you were going to write your own version of a classic Christmas movie, which movie would you choose?

7. Laurel watches *It's a Wonderful Life* every Christmas because it reminds her of all the times she watched it with her grandmother. Do you have any movies you watch every holiday season? What makes them special to you?

8. The Grant family has a lot of Christmas traditions, including cookie decorating. What holiday traditions are important to your family?

9. What do you think the future holds for Laurel and Max? What holiday traditions will they start for their own family?

10. Laurel tries to transform herself with self-help books because she doesn't want to be Old Laurel anymore. But eventually she realizes, "It's starting to seem like Old Laurel and New Laurel were never real people all along . . . maybe I'm just Laurel, just one lady who's

trying her best, messing up a lot, and making it better." What do you think she learned about herself, and the people who love her, over the course of the book? Do you think she'll continue to be so focused on self-improvement?

Photo by Alex Winfrey

Kerry Winfrey is the author of the romantic comedies *Waiting for Tom Hanks*, *Not Like the Movies*, *Very Sincerely Yours*, *Just Another Love Song*, and *Faking Christmas*. She is also the author of two young adult novels. She lives with her family in the middle of Ohio.

VISIT KERRY WINFREY ONLINE

KerryAnn

KerryWinfrey

KerryWinfrey.substack.com